THE BIG BOOK
OF KINK

THE BIG BOOK OF KINK

SEXY STORIES

Edited by
Alison Tyler

Foreword by
Dante Davidson

CLEiS
PRESS

Published in the United States by Cleis Press, an imprint of Start Midnight, LLC, 101 Hudson Street, 37th Floor, Suite 3705, Jersey City, NJ 07302.

Printed in the United States.
Cover design: Scott Idleman/Blink
Cover photograph: iStockphoto
Text design: Frank Wiedemann

First Edition.
10 9 8 7 6 5 4 3 2 1

Trade paper ISBN: 978-1-62778-155-8
E-book ISBN: 978-1-62778-157-2

"Appraising Love" by Dante Davidson originally appeared in *Naughty Stories from A to Z*, published by Pretty Things Press. "Blue Denim Pussy" by Clarice Alexander previously appeared in *Naughty Stories from A to Z* (Pretty Things Press) and was excerpted in *Never Say Never* (Cleis Press) both edited by Alison Tyler. "Clothes Make the Man" by Emilie Paris originally appeared in *Coupling*, edited by Sommer Marsden, published by Excessica. "Farm Fresh" by Dante Davidson previously appeared in *Juicy Erotica*, edited by Alison Tyler (Pretty Things Press). "Focus of Attention" by Shane Fowler was originally published by Pretty Things Press. "The Game" originally appeared *in Blue Sky Sideways*, published by Masquerade Books. "In Progress" originally appeared in *Blue Sky Sideways*, published by Masquerade. "Killing the Marabou Slippers" by Molly Laster previously appeared in *D Is for Dress-Up* and *Never Have the Same Sex Twice*, both edited by Alison Tyler, from Cleis Press. "Naked New Year" by Dante Davidson originally appeared on www.tinynibbles.com. "One Hot Slut" by N. T. Morley previously appeared in *Playing with Fire*, edited by Alison Tyler (Cleis Press). "Pink Elephants" by Eric Williams originally appeared in *Three-Way*, published by Cleis Press. "Quiet, Quiet," by Lucia Dixon originally appeared in *Naughty Spanking Stories from A to Z*, edited by Rachel Kramer Bussel, published by Pretty Things Press. "Roger's Fault" by Eric Williams originally appeared in *Sweet Life*, edited by Violet Blue, published by Cleis Press. "The Sex Test" was originally published in *Up All Night*, edited by Rachel Kramer Bussel. "Spring Cleaning" by Samantha Mallery originally appeared on www.goodvibes.com. "To Lola, With Love" by Alison Tyler previously appeared in *Sex Toy Tales*, edited by Anne Semans and Cathy Winks (Down There Press). "Underwater" by Emilie Paris originally appeared on www.goodvibes.com. "War Movies" originally appeared in *Naughty Stories from A to Z, Volume 1*, published by Pretty Things Press.

To SAM.
Always.

Contents

FOREWORD

Dante Davidson

I've known Alison Tyler for too many years to politely count. Suffice it to say, her hair was black when we met, and now the woman's a silver fox. We team write often, and we've reached a point in which we can finish each other's sentences—on the page and off.

But when she asked me to define *kink*, I drew a blank. What's kinky to me, or what's kinky to everyone? It's an impossible task. So instead, I said, "Let me paint you a picture." And I wrote:

You're in my bed. Your arms are cuffed over your head. The softest, lightest sheet is draped over your naked body. I sit at the foot of the bed and I watch you. I wait for you to move. You know that as soon as you do, as soon as you part your lips to beg, I will pounce.

It's a waiting game. And we're both Masters. Neither one of us wants to go first.

What's kinky to me?

The sheet rising slow and steady with your heartbeat. The

way you lick your lips in anticipation of what's to come. The fact that we have the whole night ahead of us to do every dirty thing we can imagine.

And guess what, lucky reader?

That's what you have. A whole book of stories destined to put you in that mindspace, where anything can happen if you make the first move.

INTRODUCTION: WHAT'S KINKY TO YOU?

W hat's your kink? Come on. We're all friends here. Oh, are you shy? Then pen me a naughty laundry list. Go on. Write down all of those filthy little fantasies that make your nighttimes naughty, that wake your mornings with wishful thinking, that fill your daydreams with delight.

If you're anything like me, your list will look something like this:

Exhibitionism
Sex with strangers
Dominant women
Blow jobs
Sex in public
Spanking
Bondage
Sex toys
Girl-Girl
Girl-Girl exhibitionism with sex toys...

Trust me. This is a kink-packed volume. So no matter what pushes your little buttons, I've curated a collection of stories that are destined to fill your erotic needs in the most varied and enlightening ways. In fact, you might find boxes to check that you didn't even know about.

Scroll down the table of contents to peruse the masters and mistresses of erotic literature. These writers know how to weave a tale, and how to do so in a way that will make your heart beat faster, your cock get harder, your panties get wetter.

You know what makes my editor's heart go pitter-patter?

Sultry short stories
A cornucopia of kink
Extremely exquisite X-rated writing
All throbbing together in one big, hard book.

See? I told you I'd fill every erotic need—including mine!

XXX,
Alison Tyler

APPRAISING LOVE

Dante Davidson

I have to admit it—and I hope this doesn't make me sound like a cad—those legs were what caught my attention first. In all my years of searching, I'd never seen perfection like that. Delicately curved, almost achingly arched, they surpassed my wildest fantasies. I could imagine running my fingers up and around their smooth, supple surface for hours, getting down on my hands and knees to worship them. I've always been something of a leg man.

Slowly, I moved closer, feigning interest in the stature of several other, less lovely creations nearby. With extra effort, I maneuvered myself through the crowd, and when I was close enough, I reached out my hand, wanting just one touch...

"Hey!" a female voice said, sounding surprised. "What are you doing?"

"It's a—," I lowered my voice as I named the maker. "Isn't it?"

The owner raised her painted-on eyebrows, giving me a quizzical stare that I processed before returning my gaze to my newfound love. "How could you know that without checking the label?" she asked.

I didn't look at her while I answered. My eyes were still captivated by her table, those flawless legs, that haughty, aristocratic stance. The color was a rich, unmarred caramel that had obviously been untouched since it left the original creator's hands. Often, at such appraisal road shows, we see once-beautiful objects, now destroyed by an owner's idiotic—if well-intentioned—attempts at refinishing. *Never* mess with perfection.

To be entirely sure that the treasure was indeed as priceless as I thought, I got on my knees and crawled under the table. My heart pounded even faster as I read that golden label beneath the rim. There, in unblemished perfection, were the artisan's engraved initials. I smiled broadly when I saw them.

"Are you okay?" the owner asked. I had forgotten all about her until she bent down to peer at me under the table. Thinking back, I must have looked fairly ridiculous, dressed impeccably in my gray suit and navy-blue tie, lying on the ground grinning up at the wood. The workmanship was remarkable, and I couldn't help but stroke the firm underside with the palms of my hands. If furniture could make a noise, this table would have purred.

"I'm fine," I said weakly, breaking free of my daze and looking at the owner's face. For the first time, I really noticed her. I took in her bright blue eyes and even brighter blue eye shadow. I told her my name and who I worked for.

Her attitude changed instantly, from "hands off" to "help yourself."

"You work here," she said, indicating the breadth of the show with a sweeping glance. As I climbed out from under the table, I continued my brief observation of her face. She had two perfectly round circles of rouge on her cheeks making her appear as if she'd been playing dress up with her mother's cosmetics. Her lips sported an orange-coral shade not often found in nature. Once an appraiser, always an appraiser. It can be difficult to turn off the critical voice in my head.

"My name's Lucy," she said, offering me a hand, the nails of which were long and polished a vibrant, glistening green, like the underbelly scales of a tropical snake. When I let go of her hand, she ran it through her platinum teased hair, raising the height another inch or so with the gesture. What a woman like her was doing with a table like this, I could not imagine. But it's my job to judge furniture, not people, and I plastered a false smile on my face and turned on my professional charm.

"Will you go on air with it?" I asked.

Lucy gave an excited, high-pitched squeal, like a contestant on a game show. The noise was loud enough for our producer to hear, and when Corrine met my eyes from across the room, I nodded to indicate I had a winner. Oh, did I have a winner. Corrine rushed over and I whispered into her ear what I'd found.

"Are you sure, Jonathan?" Corrine asked incredulously, inspecting Lucy's attire, which did not exactly fit the normal type of clothes we see. Most people arrive in jeans and T-shirts, shorts if it's a hot day. The table's owner was wearing a revealing pink floral sundress loosely laced up the front. Part of my brain quickly categorized it as "cheap," and possibly "slutty." But another part of my brain—the one attached to a lower segment of my anatomy—understood how someone might find a dress like that appealing. The laces had come slightly undone in the front, and for some reason I envisioned myself taking a step closer and tying the bow for Lucy, my fingers brushing the skin of her supple breasts, touching her just as gently as only moments before I'd stroked the leg of her table.

At that thought, I found myself looking down at Lucy's own legs. Clad in white fishnet stockings, they were a work of art unto themselves. What would *they* feel like beneath the palm of my hand, I wondered. And what kind of noise would Lucy make if my fingertips grazed her skin? The same shocked "Hey!" that she'd shrieked when I touched her table? Somehow, from the looks she was giving me in return, I didn't think so.

My producer nudged me and I shook my head, embarrassed, not having heard a word Corrine had said. But Lucy, standing a few feet away, shot me another interested smile, as if she understood exactly what my appraising glances meant.

It all happened quickly after that. Our producer whisked Lucy away to sign some papers and I consulted several other appraisers to get their opinion of the piece's value. My mind instantly and easily refocused on my work. A table in less quality condition had recently sold for a quarter of a million dollars at auction. I could barely contain myself imagining what this item might bring.

When we found ourselves seated in front of the camera, I turned my eyes from the table to Lucy, preparing to launch into the background history of the furniture maker. I am quite adept at my job, my mind filled with little-known facts, but when I looked at Lucy again, I forgot everything that I'd planned on saying. The makeup crew, in their haste, had removed her garish eye shadow and electrifying lipstick, but had not bothered to replace either. I was staring at a restored canvas, the beauty of her face shining clear now that it was free from the previous hideous coat of shellacking.

"Your beautiful—" I stammered, and then stopped. I'd been about to say, "Your beautiful table," but suddenly that wasn't what I meant at all. Change the "your" to "you're," is what I wanted to tell Lucy. "You're beautiful—" I said again, referring to her this time.

"My table," she said, prompting me when she realized I was tongue-tied. She gave me that same quizzical glance she had earlier, her eyes a softer blue now that they didn't have to compete with the seventies-style shadow. Her cheeks had a natural flush to them, and I wondered what hue they would turn in the throes of passion. If I picked her up and set her down on the table, slid that flimsy dress up her thighs and bent to kiss in a line down her throat to those loose laces, would her cheeks turn a dark, scarlet blush? Or was she the type whose skin would take on a petal-pink glow? I longed to find out, but I could suddenly feel my producer's eyes on me.

"My table" Lucy repeated, waiting.

"Yes," I said, nodding. "Your table is a masterpiece." I put my hand on the top of the surface for reassurance, and the wash of joy swept over me again. I found my words, launching into a history of this fantastic piece of furniture. I told of the maker's background, then described how each table was made by hand, focusing on the length of time it took to create a solitary leg.

"One of the most interesting aspects of this table," I said, near the end of my spiel, "is that although it appears quite delicate, it is remarkably sturdy."

"Really?" Lucy asked, shooting me a look that sent my mind spinning off into fantasyland all over again. "Sometimes delicate items can fool you."

At that comment, I tried desperately to reboard my train of thought, but failed. *She* looked delicate, yet I had the feeling that she would last through hours of raucous lovemaking. Was that the hidden message she was trying to tell me? Suddenly, I felt something brush softly against my own leg. It took only a second for me to process that Lucy had slipped out of one high-heeled sandal and was running her stockinged toes up my calf.

I managed to complete my talk, to give her an estimate of the table's worth, but somehow those numbers didn't interest me anymore. The director yelled "Cut," and the crew quickly moved across the room to film a segment on windup toys. Lucy and I were alone, between the makeshift curtained barriers, still sitting at the table looking at each other.

"You mentioned that it was surprisingly sturdy," Lucy said in a low voice. I watched as she ran her tongue along her top lip, as if tasting something sweet. The gesture tugged at me, and I wanted to lean forward and do the same thing to her, run my own tongue along both of her lips before taking her in my arms and kissing her. I inhaled deeply, trying to analyze what she had said.

"Yes," I nodded, "these tables have undergone stress tests. While some pieces are more for show than actual use, your table could easily support five hundred pounds."

"Wow," Lucy said, her mouth, pure and naked of lipstick, curving into a smile. "That's a lot of weight—three or four adults—when all it has to support is two."

This was all the encouragement I needed. Quickly, I motioned to a crew member and asked him to help me put the table into one of our back storage rooms. "I need a little more time to appraise it," I said, using my most businesslike tone. The man didn't concern himself with the explanation. Without hesitating, he and I hoisted the table together and brought it to one of the private rooms. Lucy followed, staring at me with what I can only describe as lustfully energetic looks.

When we were finally alone, I shut the door and lifted Lucy into my arms. I nuzzled into her neck as I carried her over to the table. She smelled delicious, spicy and exotic, and I sat her down on the edge of the table and began to kiss her skin. Lucy sighed, then leaned back fully onto the table, spreading her thighs and raising her arms over her head.

I didn't know where to start first. I wanted to keep kissing her, but I also wanted to peel off her dress and simply look at her body. As when I'm appraising a piece of furniture, I needed to know what I was working with. Lucy took control for me, slipping the dress over her head and then sprawling out in her white satin bra and panties, white fishnets, garter belt and sandals.

The room we were in contained several other pieces of furniture, including a full-length, gilt-edged mirror. I hurried to position it against the wall next to the table, and then grabbed Lucy around the waist and slid her toward me. I kissed her in a line down her body, starting with her lips and then moving to the hollow of her neck, her delicate collarbones, down to her breasts—where I lingered until she arched her back and moaned. Slowly, I kissed my way toward her satin-clad pussy, and when I reached it, I could smell the scent of her arousal.

I licked her through her panties first, teasing her with my tongue pressed hard against that shiny material. Then I helped her out of the undergarment and began to French-kiss her pussy, using my fingers to hold open her lips while my tongue made soft and slow circles around her clit.

After a moment, I looked into the mirror to see Lucy's face. Her head was turned to the side, mouth open and eyes shut. Her hair had come free from the ponytail and it fell loose to her shoulders. Now, brushed flat instead of teased, it perfectly framed her beautiful face. A face that I suddenly recognized—

"Oh god," I said.

"Yes," Lucy sighed, "Oh god, it's great."

"No," I stood looking down at her. "I know you."

She opened her eyes and locked on to my gaze. "Yes," she said, "I'm Lucy. We met out there." Her cheeks were flushed with pleasure, a soft pink as I'd imagined they would be, but her face was composed. She looked a lot more at ease than I felt, my cock throbbing beneath my slacks, desperate for contact with the warm, wet mouth of her sex. Still, I had to get something clear.

"You're not some—" I wanted to say "hick," but changed my mind quickly, "some innocent who just brought a table to be appraised," I said, watching as she pushed herself into a semi-upright position on the table, leaning up on one elbow. With her free hand, she began to stroke her naked pussy, slowly and sensuously teasing herself while I watched. She seemed to be waiting to see when I'd get it, and finally, when she tilted her head back as the sensations washed over her, I knew precisely who she was. I'd seen the look on her face before, at a recent auction in New York. Upon winning the piece she was after, she leaned her head back and sighed, the same look of ultimate pleasure on her face.

"Your name's Lucinda," I said, undoing my slacks now, unable to wait any longer. She worked for a competing firm!

She nodded, her hands helping to guide me between her

parted thighs. The contact of my cock with the dreamy wetness of her sex made me momentarily lose track of my thoughts. I plunged inside her and she let out that same, pleasurable sigh again, her hand going up to her throat, fingers beating there as if attempting to still her pounding pulse.

I stopped trying to figure it all out at that point, driving even deeper inside her. The table supported our weight, but I needed to feel her in my grip. Grabbing her around the waist, I lifted her into my arms and then pulled her down on me. Inspired, I took her over to the wall and pressed her against that antique mirror. I couldn't get deep enough inside her, slamming into her willing cunt and then pulling out to the tip, then slamming in again to make her sigh like that. She dragged her fingernails down my back and I had the vision of what they looked like, that obscene emerald green raking against my skin, leaving marks I'd have to remember this by. Suddenly, those nails didn't seem so offensive. There was something sexy in the whole slutty attire—fishnets still in place, sandal-clad feet hooked around my thighs.

"God, Jonathan, I'm going to come," Lucy said softly, and I took her to that fantasy place with me, fucking her harder and faster until she leaned down and bit my shoulder as the climax flew through her. I came a second after, pumping my cock inside her as those wavelike contractions washed over us.

There were several moments when I simply held her in my arms, leaning against the mirror, my eyes closed, breathing deeply. Then I carried her back to the wonderful table and set her down. She looked at me with a coy expression I hadn't seen before.

"It worked, you know," she said softly.

"I don't understand," I told her, watching sadly as she pulled her dress back over her head, that magnificent body disappearing from view.

"You love the creator's work, and I'm sort of partial to yours," she explained. "But I've never been able to catch your attention at the auctions. You always have your eyes on some piece of furniture or another, never seem aware of the piece of ass that wants you."

"So you came here—" I prompted.

"Somehow, I thought that you might find my getup exciting." When she said it, I realized she was right. I'd seen her often at the auctions, always dressed in some subdued black suit, elegant pearls around her neck, that white-blonde hair pulled back severely, tiny glasses perched on the end of her perfect nose. I never would have guessed she would doll herself up like this, and I couldn't have suspected that I would like the transformation.

"You knew what the table was worth, though," I said, telling her the one thing that nagged at my pride. "You wanted to fool me."

She made it all better with her answer.

"I wanted to *fuck* you," she said, leaning forward to whisper the words, her mouth against my ear, hot breath against my skin. "You were always so busy appraising everything, you never had eyes for me."

That made me stop thinking about my job and start thinking about what it would be like to make love to Lucy again, maybe on the four-poster bed I had seen in one of the other storage rooms...

"But you have eyes for me now," she continued, spreading her arms wide and taking the stance of a centerfold model. "So..." her voice was rich with humor. "What do you think I'd fetch?" A pause, and another one of those fantastic, cock-teasing lip licks, "I mean, if you were to put me up on auction."

Now, I took a step back, looking her over, taking a second before giving her my estimate. "You know how it is with a rare treasure," I said, pulling her toward me once again. "You can never put a label on something priceless."

MY PERFECT BOY

Sophia Valenti

When I entered the room, I found Cal positioned exactly as I had requested: in the center of the mattress, with his head down and ass up. His muscles were tense with expectation, and the sight of him warmed my heart—and soaked my pussy.

It never gets old: a big, strong man submitting to my will and sexually surrendering to me. Nothing else gets me off quite the same way.

I stood at the foot of the bed, stroking the thick, black phallus that jutted from the harness fitted around my hips. The gesture wasn't meant to be menacing; after all, he couldn't even see me with his face buried in the sheets. I felt as if that cock was an extension of me. I was already anticipating the perverse pleasure I would experience when my toy sank into his snug back door.

Cal's ass still bore the pink stripes that my belt had delivered earlier in the evening, and when I reached out and stroked his cheeks, I felt the residual heat radiating from his punished flesh. Unable to resist, I dragged my nails along those rosy marks, and his body trembled visibly. I had to bite back the moan that threatened to escape my lips. This was the absolute embodiment of all of my most treasured fantasies.

"Present, boy," I barked, trying to keep the quiver of excitement out of my voice. "Show your Mistress where you want her big, beautiful cock."

"Yes, Ma'am," came his muffled reply, and Cal immediately reached back and parted his cheeks. He balanced his weight carefully on one of his shoulders, his fingers tightly clutching each globe of his ass as he revealed his tender little asshole to me. I know it shamed him to be so exposed, which is exactly why I liked to make him do it.

Glancing around the mussed sheets, I spotted the bottle of lube and snatched it up. Slickening up a fingertip, I then circled his back hole teasingly, tracing the edges but not penetrating him—at least, not until he begged.

"Please, Ma'am, please," he beseeched, those whispered words lighting me up inside.

"Please what, boy?" I responded, continuing to make lazy circles around his opening. I was struggling to continue being playful; my resolve had nearly melted away.

"Please fuck me!" was his pained response. "Take my ass— it's yours to use."

I dipped my lubed fingers into his hole, eliciting a sexy sigh from him.

"You're right, baby. Your ass is mine," I answered, shoving my fingers in deeper to stretch and ready him for my cock. I could tell he was trying to remain still when I knew he wanted to rear back and impale himself. His hunger inspired my own, and I pulled back to slicken my shaft.

When the toy was glossy wet, I nudged his asshole with the dildo's tip.

"Don't make me do all the work, boy. If you want my cock, you take it."

Cal groaned helplessly, now that I'd given him permission to fully indulge his lust. I kept my eyes locked on the shiny

black toy as he leaned backward, taking in the dildo's length
with maddening slowness. I enjoyed watching each inch disap-
pear into his ass; the sight was a real treat for me because I had
no such patience. But he did. He really was everything I'd ever
craved in a sub.

"Oh, yes," I whispered, once I was buried balls-deep. "What
a good boy, taking all of your Mistress's cock. But now it's my
turn."

Unable to wait another second, I grabbed Cal's hips and
started to fuck him roughly, shoving my cock deep on each
inward stroke. His moans were making my cunt drip, and each
time I pounded him, the base of the toy would kiss my clit in the
most delicious way. I rode his ass hard, working myself closer
to what I knew would be a deeply satisfying climax. But I didn't
want Cal to be left behind.

"Grab your cock, baby. Stroke it—come for me," I ordered
breathlessly.

Cal was beyond words. I felt him reach beneath himself to
tug on his shaft as I continued to pound his back door. He could
read me as well as I do him, knowing by the sounds of my cries
when I had gotten myself off. Only then did he shudder through
his own release—my perfect boy, right to the end.

REALLY, MISTRESS

Thomas S. Roche

Rhonda comes home from a hard day at the office, and I can already tell she's going to take it out on me if I don't play my cards right. I'm not proud of the fact that it makes me kind of hot. But I guess I *am* proud of how I handle it.

While she stands sullenly at the table sorting the mail—all bills, from the looks of it—I put down the casserole and say, "You look like you could use a foot massage."

She cocks her head at me, ready to spit back a sharp stream of venom. I see her stop herself. She cocks her head even farther, her lips pursed and twisted in what could quickly become a frown.

"Really?" she asks. "Before dinner?"

"Really," I say. "Before dinner. The casserole needs to set up for twenty, anyway."

Her pursed-lip almost-pout becomes a frown for a split second. Pointing at the casserole, she barks: "Make sure the cat doesn't get into it!"

I say, "She won't, Mistress. She's asleep in the bedroom."

"Ugh," says Rhonda, making a beeline out of the stifling

kitchen. "I wish I was! With the air conditioner on!" She stops at the doorway and cocks her head back at me disapprovingly. "Really? 'Mistress'? That's how we're going to play it?"

"Yes, Mistress. That's how we're going to play it."

She sighs, the long-suffering spouse. "Fine," she says. "Suit yourself. Have it your way. Whatever." She heads for the living room, clawing at buttons, her high heels clicking succinctly on the hallway's wood floors.

"Wine, Ma'am?"

"Whiskey," she says. "Maybe wine later. *Maybe.*"

I see her shrug off her blouse just before she turns the corner. She leaves it on the hardwood, a whispering ghost, while her high-heeled click-clacks go muted on the living room carpet.

Two minutes later, I'm closing in with a MacTavish 12 blended, on the rocks. I even bring the bottle. I stoop down and pick up her blouse as I go. I pick up her bra and her skirt and her panties in a path from the living room doorway to the sofa. She's wearing her stockings and garter belt, still, nude beige and deep tan, respectively. Her open-toed pumps are navy to match her skirt, which is already gone. She's bare-breasted, her torso crisscrossed with faint pink lines from the hot commute in her bra and her blouse.

I give her the tumbler. She takes a sip. She says, "This is scotch."

"You said whiskey, Mistress," I say.

"I guess I should have said bourbon," she sighs. She cocks her head again. "Really? 'Mistress'?"

"Really," I tell her. "Mistress. I'm sorry, Ma'am, I thought you preferred scotch."

"Ma'am sounds like a schoolteacher."

"I'll stick to Mistress, then."

"Whatever."

I fold her blouse, skirt and bra reverently, her panties slightly less so. There's just no way to fold panties reverently when they aren't yours. Especially if they're moist and still slightly warm from her body.

"Fine," she says, sipping her scotch.

"Mistress is fine?"

"Scotch is fine," she says, finishing it. I guess she didn't see that I brought the bottle. When I drop to my knees and lean in to pour her another, she looks shocked and impressed.

"That's blended, I hope," she snaps bitterly.

I smile. "On the rocks? I should think so."

"So you're British tonight?" she asks sarcastically.

"Did I sound British?" I didn't speak with an accent, but maybe I'm channeling generations of long-suffering twats on BBC America.

"Just your choice of words," she says. "Whatever."

She sticks her right foot in my face and says, "Somebody promised a foot massage?"

"Of course, Mistress," I say. I take her foot in my hands and kiss her ankle. I unbuckle and take off her shoe. I kiss it and set it aside. She sticks her stocking-clad foot in my face. I kiss it as I reach up to her garters and start to unfasten them.

As I pull down her stockings, I let my tongue snake out. Even through the stocking, it's too much for her. She giggles.

"That tickles," she snaps. "Don't make me giggle. Bitches don't giggle!"

"Sorry, Mistress," I say. "You don't have to be a bitch if you don't want to."

"In that case, keep going." I slide off her stocking and start to caress her arch with my tongue while I fumble a little with her left pump. I get it off and caress her left thigh slightly as I undo her garters. I don't know if she squeals at the touch of my fingers on her thigh or at the strokes of my tongue on her foot. Rhonda is very ticklish. She keeps giggling.

"I don't have to be a bitch?" she says sharply, breathing hard from laughing. "What have you done with my husband?"

"You can be one if you want to," I say, breathing a little hard myself.

"We'll see," she says provocatively, and sticks her foot more aggressively in my face. I kiss it while she lifts her ass off the couch and lets me reach under to undo her garter belt. I take it away and place it on top of the neat pile I've formed beside us: Shoe, shoe, stocking, garter belt.

I go back to kissing her bare right foot. She rubs it in my face while I take down her left stocking and place it atop her shoes. Then her right foot is joined by her left, and I start to kiss them both. The smell's more intense now, a soft, leathery musk. I make love to her feet, licking each of her arches delicately. It takes a complete circuit of both of her arches before she stops laughing.

A few moments later, she's put down her tumbler and starts to claw at the sofa, gasping slightly.

I say, "Too much, Mist—"

"No! But...massage, much?"

"Of course, Ma'am," I say.

"No more 'Ma'am,'" she says.

"Of course...*Mistress*."

I start to massage her left arch with both thumbs. I do it gently at first, then more firmly as her eyes roll back. Her red mouth drops open. Her tongue lolls around a bit, almost like it's on a spring.

After a minute of that, I move on to her right foot. I give it the same treatment, working the muscles loose slowly.

Another minute, and I feel her left foot on my crotch. She leans into it slightly.

"Pervert," she says. I'm rock hard.

I feel myself blush. "What can I say?"

She pushes down with her right foot. I release it. She lowers her right foot to join her left on my swelling crotch.

"Say 'Yes, Mistress,'" she tells me, rubbing her feet up and down on my hard cock. "And open your pants."

"Mistress," I say. "I'm not done with your foot massage."

"Yes you are," she says. "Open them."

So I do. I unbuckle, unbutton, unzip. I pull my jockey shorts down and circle my cock with my fingers.

Rhonda's feet shove my hand out of the way. She pushes her feet together, with my cock trapped between them.

"Pervert," she smirks at me, her voice rough with pleasure.

She leans in, bracing herself on the edge of the sofa. I steady myself on the coffee table not far behind me.

With her ass on the edge and her knees bent, Rhonda gets plenty of leverage. She crushes my cock between her feet. She watches me as she does it.

It's easier than I expect. Her feet are still slightly wet from my spit. She knows what she's doing. It only takes moments.

I cry out. I come. She watches me closely as I shoot my load all over her feet.

Rhonda purrs, "Now you can kiss them again." Laughing, she pushes her feet in my face.

"Of course, Mistress," I say. I think it surprises her slightly when I start to do it.

"Really?" she says, no longer perturbed—just surprised.

"Really, Mistress," I tell her. My tongue strokes her arches, and this time she doesn't giggle.

BEAR CLAWS IN THE MORNING

Sommer Marsden

B rought you bear claws," Bobby said.

I dropped the sponge I was using to wipe down the kitchen counter and turned, stomach growling. "Gimme."

He was watching me intently with his dark-blue eyes. So dark they almost looked brown. I never tired of looking at them, especially when I caught a hint of amusement in their depths. When I reached for the box something slid and rattled.

"I thought you brought me bear claws," I said, my stomach rumbling again, prompted by words that implied food.

"I did." He cocked an eyebrow and watched me.

I took the pink bakery box and something repeated the pattern—slid, rattled, thumped.

"Bobby..."

"Just open the box, Penelope."

I untied the butcher's twine and pulled the lid up. From inside, two sharp claws regarded me.

"Oh my god." I touched them. My fingers were trembling from the force of adrenaline in my system. "Are these the ones we saw at—?"

"Aaron and Rebecca's barbeque? Yep." He grinned.

We'd been at our friends' house weeks before and when I'd gone to help Rebecca with the food, she'd had these things. Bear claws, they were called. Made from hard plastic, they were designed for the user to slip his fingers into the grips and then pierce, pick up or shred cooked meat. I'd been fascinated by them. Turning them over in my hands, touching the sharp but not dangerous tips. Rebecca had been clueless, rattling on about the sump pump in their basement. But Bobby...Bobby had watched me. Smiling wryly as I stroked the hard plastic implements.

"Your very own set. Because remember—"

I turned to him so fast I knocked the bakery box from the counter. "Are you going to ask me if I remember coming home and confessing to you how much these things turned me on? How I imagined them scraping along my body and up my thighs? Or how you fucked me after my confession? Is that what you're going to ask if I remember?"

He gave me a knowing smile, a little smug, a lot sexy. Before he could answer I was thrusting the claws into his hands and nodding. I pulled my tee over my head, pushed my gym shorts down. It was cleaning day, and I was dressed like a raggedy person but naked was naked and that's what I was within thirty seconds.

He licked his lips. It was a predatory move.

"Yes, I remember," I said, dragging my fingers over his Sunday sweatpants. Worked in, paint stained, seen better days... and perfect to accent a spectacular erection.

"Hurry," I said, and then stared at him.

He eyed me up, and I felt on display—studied. It made the wetness between my legs that much wetter. It made the craving in my belly that much stronger.

"Turn around," he said.

"But—"

"Oh, no. I have the claws, Penelope. I'm telling you to turn around. Hands on the counter. Glad you cleaned it." I heard him chuckle even as I obeyed.

Facing the wall, I placed my hands flat on the counter and when he took his knee and knocked my legs wide I found myself chewing my lower lip. Worrying it with my teeth because the force of my pounding heart was suddenly dizzying.

I heard him squat and then exhale deeply. "You have the prettiest skin. So pale and perfect." As he said it I felt the claws touch down. Cool, impersonal plastic that glided along my skin softly at first. It almost tickled. When he reached the backs of my knees my legs dipped from the sensation.

Bobby chuckled. "Stay still."

When he scraped the claws up the opposite way, from ankle to ass, he did it with a heavier touch. My pulse began to slam in my temples, my throat...my cunt.

He did it again but on my outer thighs. From hip to ankle. My skin began to sing with fire. The firmness of his stroke with those wicked-looking things varied from featherlight to menacing. Bobby stopped and I found that I was struggling to breathe, clutching the counter as I hung my head and fought not to babble and plead.

"Turn around."

I did it willingly—eagerly—spinning so my back and ass were flush to the counter. The claw marks on the backs of my legs ached and tingled. He pushed his face to my pussy and licked me.

"They have done a number on you," he said, spreading my thighs wider with his hands. Hands still wearing those intimidating claws. "So, so wet..."

"*You* have," I gasped. He licked me more, dragging his tongue—broadened and flat—over my clit. I nearly came. "You've done a number on me," I said.

He began a slow, rhythmic motion scratching me from my inner thighs to outer thighs as he ate me. The mix of the softly stroking scratches and the wet ministrations of his tongue had me half-drunk with arousal. I arched my hips to meet his mouth but it amped up the force of his scratches. My thighs buzzed with blood and my stomach felt as if I were in free fall.

"I'm—"

He shushed me, lips still against my pussy, and the vibration worked through me. He slid the sharp, cold plastic up until the claws dragged along the fragile place where thigh met groin. "Come when you want," he said, lips still pressed to my nether lips.

I came, pushing my hands into his dark hair, holding on as the first sweet spasm shook me where I stood. He kept going, licking me with a force that staggered me even as I insisted it was too much.

"It's not," he said. He dragged the bear claws softly along my belly, over my hip bones, down my flanks. When I came a second time, he stood fast, claws still on, scraping my upper arms as he turned me. He knocked my legs wider again and I moaned.

He entered me fast, his hands slipping beneath my breasts and holding me that way. The sharp yet smooth plastic biting against my nipples. The tips pressing into my flesh whenever I breathed.

I hung my head, surrendering to his grip as he pulled my body back to take his. We had all day. We had a new toy. I had marks on my body and his cock inside me. I was blissed out in a way I hadn't been in ages.

"Fuck," he laughed softly. "I wanted this to last so much longer. But with you all striped up with scratch marks like my own little candy cane…" he trailed off.

I found my still-thumping clit with my fingers as his tempo amped up and when he roared, very much like the bear he was pretending to be, I managed to come with him. A small, sweet shudder of an orgasm that had me laughing wildly as we came to a stop, stilling there in the tiny silent kitchen.

"I brought you bear claws," he repeated, chuckling.

"I love them. Reusable, washable and no calories."

He kissed the back of my neck. "And now that I have them you just never know when they'll make an appearance, little girl."

I shivered in his arms. "That's my favorite part."

BLUE DENIM PUSSY

Clarice Alexander

I want your honest opinion," Sasha said, twirling around in front of Colin, letting him see her colt-like legs, haughty ass and slim waist, all contained in a pair of new and tight-fitting dark denim jeans. He didn't respond immediately, taking in the way she looked. Sleek in her long-sleeved black blouse, her birch-colored hair up in a ponytail, gray-green eyes wide while she waited for his answer. Still, he couldn't actually think of anything to say. Nothing except the fact that he was going to fuck her. Here. Now.

"Tell me," she urged, tilting her head to look past him at her own reflection in the dressing room mirror. "I mean, what do you think?"

Remaining silent, he took one step toward her in the small space and grabbed hold of her hand. His fingers slid upward to close firmly around her delicate wrist, like a pair of handcuffs snapping shut. Something in the gesture made Sasha forget what she was asking and pay attention to the look Colin was giving her.

"Come here," he said, and she closed the space between them as he placed his free palm over the crotch of her jeans and let her feel his large hand against her cunt. Instantly, she rested her pussy on his hand, pressed into him, and he began to do the most intricate, marvelous things with his fingers. Dancing them up and down. Massaging her pussy through the denim. Stroking just hard enough for her to lean her head back and sigh.

This was obviously the response he was looking for, and Colin quickly sat on the padded bench running the length of the room and moved Sasha so that she was cradled on his lap. Slowly, but firmly, he continued to rub her cunt through the jeans. He paid attention to every touch, obviously on a mission. She helped, letting him know exactly what she wanted, pushing up with her hips to meet his stroking fingertips as he responded to each move. Focused on bringing her pleasure, he worked harder, firmer, then slid one finger between two buttons in the fly to touch her naked skin.

The feel of his hand on her was electrifying. Just his finger on the space above her pubic hair. Yes, of course, he'd touched her there before, but this was different somehow. Being fingered like this with her clothes still on made Sasha feel the urgency in what they were doing. He pushed down, searching, and his fingertip plunged into the wetness that had already seeped through her nether lips. Withdrawing his hand, he licked his finger clean, then resumed his pussy massage through her jeans.

Closing her eyes, Sasha stifled a moan. Christ, it felt amazing. If he touched her clit with his middle finger, pressed it right up against the seam of her jeans, she could come. Colin appeared to guess this, and he sat her on one hand and did exactly what she wanted. Tapping against her clit, harder as she got closer to climax, he stroked her cunt until she was almost there. Almost—

"Take them off."

Sasha opened her eyes, stunned, at that point of almost coming that had made her brain slow down in direct correlation to the rate that her heartbeat had speeded up.

"Just to your knees. Now."

The urgency had her fumbling. She stood, a wreck, and tried to unbutton the jeans, but found her fingers useless. Colin did the job, pulling hard and popping them open before sliding the tight jeans down her lean thighs. He went on his knees in front of her, pressing his lips against her white panties, breathing her scent in through that sliver of cotton. Then these were pulled down, too, and he pushed her up against the cold glass of the dressing room mirror and licked at her pussy with his eager, ready tongue.

Sasha gripped on to Colin's shoulder, breathless, as he made those crazy spirals around her clit. She'd been on the brink from the decadent pussy massage, and now Colin was replicating those actions with his tongue. Around and around the tip went. Teasing and tricking, bumping up against her clit and then leaving it alone to throb desperately, urgently. He kissed her inner thighs for a moment, to give her a chance to miss him. Then, back at the game, he nudged her clit, pushing, before finally ringing her pulsing gem with his lips and sucking. Just sucking.

Oh, yeah, Sasha thought, too tongue-tied to say the words out loud. *Oh, yeah.* Captured by the jeans and held upright by Colin's hands around her waist, she let her body relax into the climax. Sliding into it. Drifting into it. Helpless to stop herself. But then, she didn't want to stop. Did she?

When she opened her eyes, Colin was still helping—helping her take off her jeans and folding them into a neat square. "We'll get these," he said. "Because if you didn't guess from my response, I like them."

Then he was turning her, hands flat against the mirror, his body behind her, letting her feel the promise of his cock pressed against her ass. Letting her know with a single look at her eyes in the mirror exactly what was going to happen next—

HUNGER

Emilie Paris

*Y**ou want it but you can't have it.*

This concept is my favorite form of sexual torture. It's why I like being tied down, why I fantasize about people who are out of my reach. I am fascinated by the eroticism of denial, of hunger as an aphrodisiac. Yes, I ultimately succumb to my cravings, but I wallow in the euphoria of holding out as long as possible. Denying myself makes the first bite, lick or taste that much sweeter. Who doesn't crave the forbidden—be it food or fantasy?

What food is forbidden? Not apples, of course. Not since Eve. Not anymore. But sweets. The seductive dark, sticky treats. Sugar-glazed and rich in butter, dripping with icing and freshly whipped cream. And what X-rated acts are forbidden? The same sort, of course. The type you crave late at night, when you've exhausted all of the many possibilities on cable. Images bubble up in your mind, unplanned, unwanted, unexpected. If you give in to them, you might never be able to get back. *That's* the fear that binds me to the good-girl track.

Denial, I remind myself. *Hunger, as an aphrodisiac.*

It's my mantra. It keeps me in place. At least, it does so until the urges become too strong to ignore, and I'm forced to dress, hurriedly, to make my way to the car, to drive out on the empty streets until I reach his house. (Who can explain why desires are always so much stronger at night?) I knock on the door, just loudly enough to make him hear me. Then I stand there, head down, and wait for what I know he has to say.

"No, baby. No."

At his words, that unquenchable yearning overwhelms me and makes me fall to my knees on his porch, desperate. He is the man who has drenched me in chocolate. Who has squeezed the juice of the ripest berries over my naked skin. He is the man who has taught me to eat at his feet, mouth open, waiting. The one who has made me so fucking hungry.

I've been good for so long, I think. I've denied myself for so long. I need to devour a feast—not of food, but of him. I don't mean simply sex—but the dirtiest, stickiest sort of sex, dripping with icing, sugar-glazed. Rich, too rich to handle.

"Please," I say, knowing how it sounds and how it looks. Here I am, again, in the middle of the night, on his porch, and he and I both know that I'll do anything to make him take pity on me.

"Baby," he says softly. "No."

I think of the weeks that have gone by since I last had him inside me. I think of the intense cravings that keep me up late at night, cravings that I try to control with thoughts of why the two of us can't be together. And all the reasons that sound so good and honest and smart in the daytime, fade to nothing when I am hungry for him. One of us has to be strong. Is that right? One of us has to be the one who remains unmoved.

But not tonight.

I shake my head, muttering under my breath. I'm not crazy. I'm hungry. That's what I say, looking up at him and realizing somehow that he was waiting for me. It's 3:00 a.m., but he's not in his sweats. I didn't wake him up. He's in jeans and a T-shirt, and I can tell by the way he's staring at me that he was wide-awake before I came rapping at his door. He was awake and thinking of me, and that's what gives me the edge.

I smile, because it's almost as if I can smell the sex now, smell the scent of our sex and how good it will feel and how fulfilled I will be. I smile and shake my head, because I know he's taunting me by keeping me out here in the chill predawn air, but that he's going to give in. He's as out of his head with yearning as I am. His cock is as hard in his jeans as my pussy is wet. I lick my bottom lip when I look at the bulge in his slacks.

"Let me in—"

"You shouldn't be here."

So he's right. So fucking what? "Shouldn't" doesn't mean anything to me right now. "Shouldn't" is like a made-up word that has no translation in my language. I reach forward, and he steps away.

Denial, I think. *Hunger as an aphrodisiac.*

The words have lost their magical power. I can't hold myself back. My desire is too strong. I sigh as I remember everything he and I have done together. Oh, we've been dirty. We've played with olive oil, with butter, with icing. We've played with ripe fruits and slippery vegetables. With whipped cream. With wine. With everything. We've been the messiest of lovers and now we're tangled in a mess that's far worse than any kitchen disaster we could have created ourselves. And truly I don't give a fuck. Because without him, I can't eat and I can't sleep and I can't even think straight. And I know somehow that it's the same for him.

"I'm so hungry," I say, and he furrows his brow, but I know I'm going to dine tonight. I know that my appetite will be momentarily satiated when he reaches for my hand and leads me into the apartment.

PINK ELEPHANTS

Eric Williams

Don't think about white elephants. Or pink elephants. Or whatever. When someone makes that comment, you can't help but think about them, right? Enormous, hot-pink elephants immediately bebop through your mind. If you ever served time in marching band, the parading pachyderms quite possibly will dance in your head to the tune of "The Baby Elephant March." Except, this evening, the concept was a little different. Try, "Don't think about getting a hard-on." I mean, don't even fucking think about it. Insert a bitter laugh track here, because, of course— bam. There it is. Mr. Happy. Straight standing and ready to go.

The main thing to understand is that I had nothing to do with the situation. I wasn't involved in the preparations, didn't plan the outcome. That might sound callous, but it's true. Trix had to comprehend the full range of possibilities when she brought another girl into the scene. She's aware of my history, of the little nuances that fire those erotic synapses in my fucked-up brain. In fact, she's memorized every one of them.

"A slumber party," she said, innocently. "You won't mind,

right, Colton? Me and Reese, hanging out." I knew they'd be watching a romantic comedy or some other chick show, but my mind basically shut down at "slumber party." I could see it all. Tall, blonde and beautiful Trix and the sleek, dark-haired Reese lounging about our living room in their little see-through nighties, replete with ruffled edges, or trimmed with marabou fluff straight out of an X-rated, drive-your-man-crazy catalogue. I've always had a major weakness for feathers.

From the moment she told me that Reese was on the way, I owned instant visions. There they'd be, sitting on our sumptuous gold-velvet love seat, drinking some pink concoctions, doing their nails or talking about bras. Whatever it is girls do to have fun.

But, really, I didn't have to fantasize too hard about that. I know all about what girls do at slumber parties because Trix and I hooked up at one. Got to know each other deep down and personal during the course of a friendly little sleepover. A sleepover in which nobody got any sleep and nobody gave a fuck. At the time, I was dating someone else, an uptight career girl who had a penchant for wearing her hair in a Victorian-style bun. Maybe "uptight" is not the right word, exactly. "Fully wound" would be a truer description. A serious multitasker, she never really relaxed.

I thought I could melt her. From the first time we met, I had plans of helping her let her hair down—literally. Of spreading her out like some Botticelli model, those loose gingery curls framing her perfect face while I finally changed that serious expression.

That's why I suggested the threesome. I wanted to place her in a lushly decadent position, wanted to see her truly enjoy herself for once. All right, and I'll be perfectly honest here—I wanted to see what her sultry friend Trix looked like beneath her street clothes. Amazingly, it didn't take a lot of convincing before Julia agreed. So maybe she wasn't that uptight after all. Or maybe she was multitasking, once again. Taking care of my needs while exploring her own bi-curiosity. And let me tell you, it was amazing. Me and Julia and Trix all spread out on our king-sized bed. Bodies overlapping. Hands busy. Tongues working. Let your mind go. Pink elephants, man, forget that. Try *not* to think about two beautiful women licking each other, topsy-turvy in a sweet sixty-nine. Instant mental picture, right? Instant fucking hard-on.

In the morning, the truth was obvious to all of us. Julia was gay. Trix was into me. And I was in a quandary. What to do? What to do? Move in with the feline blonde with the killer body. That's what I did. And now that same filthy-minded minx was suggesting we do it all over again? Actually, from the sparse amount of information given to me, I couldn't be sure exactly what was on this evening's agenda. And I knew that if I asked— if I put it flat out there on the table and said, "Do I get to fuck Reese, or is this just a girl-girl thing?" Well, then I'd look lame, wouldn't I? For not knowing, not having the wherewithal to figure the situation out for myself.

So, I did what any guy in my position would do. I got a raging hard-on the size of a rocket ship, and I waited impatiently to see what would happen. Waited for Reese to arrive with her little lavender overnight backpack slung insolently over one arm, tripping up our stairs in her high-heeled red-gingham slingbacks. Waited hungrily for Trix to offer the invitation, if there was going to be one.

By midnight, I was pretty sure I'd misjudged the party, pretty sure I was going to be spending the night alone in our big bedroom, fulfilling my fantasies with one knowledgeable hand and a bottle of Trix's vanilla-scented body lotion. And that is precisely when my lady strolled down the hall, totally naked, and said, "What are you, crazy? We're *waiting*—"

Still, I could tell from the pleased look in her large eyes that I'd done the right thing. Behaved like a gentleman. If I'd obviously expected it, or been overly flirtatious with her friend, then she would have dissed me. No pussy for Colton. But because I'd played it cool, at least on the exterior, I was offered a free pass into heaven. And let me tell you, heaven looks a whole lot like my girl fucking her best friend. With a strap-on.

Trix had the evening well choreographed. I'll give her that. As soon as I arrived in the living room, I saw the white twisted candles lined up on the mantel, saw our leather sofa bed in place, made up with cherry-pink satin sheets. And Reese, the black-haired vixen, was right in the center of the mattress, burgundy lipstick already slightly smeared around the edges of her full mouth. Some kissing had definitely been going on during the past hour, but I didn't worry myself about that. Girls getting ready. That was all. Of course, Reese was wearing exactly the type of come-fuck-me confection that I'd imagined. Sheer and feather trimmed. What a knockout.

When she moved, looking over my way, she gave me the kind of dirty wink that would have made me instantly hard on any other occasion. As it was, I simply got harder. Staring fixedly at the seductive scene, I stopped at the threshold, knowing that instructions would be forthcoming. Silently, I watched as Trix slid into a dainty leather harness and climbed onto the bed with her buddy. Reese sighed and said Trix's name quietly, reaching forward to trail her fingers over the pink plastic tool before closing her hand tightly around it in a fist.

All right, so I had a moment to wonder how long this evening had been in the works. Trix had to go buy sex toys in preparation for the event. What did that say about my powers of observation? But then I stopped thinking about anything, as I watched my girlfriend play the aggressor in bed. First, she kissed Reese's neck, slowly, lingering as she made her way down her best friend's body. I took a step closer to the bed, wanting to see, wanting to really see. Trix pushed that transparent nightie up and out of the way, not bothering to take it off. Little nibbling bites to Reese's nipples made the brunette bombshell moan and toss her head.

Now, we were looking straight into each other's eyes again, and I found I couldn't look away. Not even when Trix continued down the valley of Reese's concave belly to her waiting pussy. Oh, I wanted to watch that. I wanted to observe each motion as

Trix parted what I imagined were Reese's plump nether lips and got busy between them, but something happened to me. Rather than lose myself in the pure porno aspect of the evening, I was captivated by the look of unadulterated pleasure in Reese's gold-flecked brown eyes. And I just couldn't look away.

"Colton," she murmured, and I moved even closer, so that we were one hot breath away from each other, and she reached out and put two fingertips on my bottom lip. Soft, girl fingers rested there so sweetly. I flicked my tongue out to touch them, to draw them into the warmth of my mouth, and I could tell that at this exact moment, Trix began tongue-fucking her. Reese arched her back and her eyes glazed and I couldn't help myself. I leaned forward, cradling her head, wanting to fiercely kiss her, to bite her bottom lip. Necking can be so sexy sometimes. And as Trix continued to play her probe-the-pussy games down there between Reese's lean thighs, I kissed her friend. Tongues together, breathing meshed. She was so sweet, so ready. And fuck, I could have kissed her for hours.

But Trix had other plans. Sitting up in bed, she slid Reese's legs over her own and plunged inside with her strap-on tool. Reese gasped and pulled away from me, head back on the shiny pillow as Trix brought her hands up to caress her small breasts. Again, I was the observer, and I couldn't tear my eyes from how decadent Reese looked.

"Your cock," she suddenly murmured.

Yeah, my cock. I'd forgotten about it for the moment, but at the words, that thing throbbed hard against my thigh.

"I want it," Reese whispered. Somehow I knew exactly what she meant. She didn't want me to fuck her, because Trix was taking care of that need with perfect ease. She wanted something to suck on. Well, I could help her out. I lost my black boxers in a heartbeat. Climbing onto the mattress, I positioned myself right next to the wild beauty and waited as she turned her head toward me, as she parted those stunning lips and introduced my cock to the warm, wet pleasures within.

And what pleasures. Reese had a gentleness to her, a cool quality that had made me peg her in the past as a shy creature. Those large dark eyes, long lashes, sideways glances. But I was wrong. Nothing shy about her. Just a quiet depth, a sweetness to the way she played dirty. With her lips tight around my tool, she sucked hard, and then as she pulled her head back, she carefully grazed my cock with her teeth. Oh Christ, it felt good, and I pushed against her, wanting more, but she shook her head.

Her speed. Her methods. No pressure.

So I had to close my eyes and wait. To let her take her time, now licking my balls, moving to get right in there. Making Trix move with her, pulling out and getting behind so that she was taking Reese doggie-style.

Reese looked beautiful. Legs spread, hands steady, holding herself in position as Trix pumped hard inside her. Then lifting her head and parting her lips, so that she could draw my cock back down her throat. I stroked her soft hair away from her face, staring down at her, seeing that other slumber party in my mind. That night in which Julia had fucked Trix, my lover's hair finally down from that severe style, tickling over her breasts as she gripped into Trix's slim waist and ravaged her. Julia had looked the way I'd always imagined she could, untamed and out of control, but as I'd watched her, I'd realized she was looking like that because of someone else. Not me.

Now, Trix was taking over that dominant position, firmly fucking her friend while I got to enjoy the wet wonders of Reese's mouth. She gave Reese a tentative spank on her heart-shaped ass, and I felt the vibrations on my cock as Reese swallowed hard at the sensation. Oh, the girl liked it, and Trix immediately slapped her ass again, leaving a matching pale-purple print on the other side. My cock stirred at that image, because I knew immediately what it would be like to be in Trix's place, taking over the job. Slapping that firm, haughty ass while fucking Reese. Or even better, I understood what it would feel like to take the luscious raven-haired stunner over my lap, to flip up that faux-innocent nightie and give her beautiful bare ass the serious and thorough spanking it deserved.

Yet just as I pictured this, Reese changed the game. She pulled off of Trix, slid back from me, and motioned with her head for me to move.

"What—" I murmured. Then, "Where?"

"Take my spot—"

I wasn't sure. Did she want to watch Trix fuck me? Was I going to like that? But as I hesitated, I saw her slip her delicate fingers over Trix's hips, unbuckling that harness, removing the toy. With calm movements, she put the slicked-up tool onto herself, and then waited. Trix and I stared at each other. What was going on? How had Reese so easily managed to usurp Trix's power?

In truth, it didn't really matter how. The intensity was too great to start deciphering the situation, analyzing who should do what to whom and why. We simply followed Reese's instructions, Trix taking the spot on her back on the bed and me sliding on top of her, my cock automatically finding its way inside her thrillingly wet pussy. And then Reese—sweet, innocent-looking Reese—was behind me, maneuvering into proper position, her fingertips spreading my muscled asscheeks, trailing down the split between. And then her cock, well lubed from her own pussy juices, pressed aggressively against my asshole.

Oh fuck. What was going on?

She slid on in, despite the fact that my body tensed instantly. I turned my head to look over my shoulder, wanting to see her face. She drove forward, as if she'd been ass-fucking men all her life, and I had to take it. Had to, because I wanted it like I'd never wanted anything before. Reese with her rhythm, slip-sliding her way inside me, and me, forgetting who I was or where I was, automatically fucking Trix. Just fucking her. Because I had to.

The three of us, connected—interconnected—worked in synchronicity. Trix, with her eyes shut beneath me, taking the double-force of being fucked by two people. Reese would thrust and I would thrust and Trix would groan. Then Reese would pull back, sliding almost all the way out, and I would pull back, so I wouldn't lose contact with her, and Trix would groan again. My mind was filled with gray fog, with white noise. I looked up at the mantel, staring at the candles flickering there, trying to figure out how we'd gotten to this point so quickly.

"Don't try so hard," Reese whispered in my ear, as if she knew exactly what I was thinking. "Don't even try."

Then she ran the tips of her fingers along my shoulder blades and leaned all the way into me, so that I could feel her body pressed along my back. Her breath on the nape of my neck, her mouth opening, teeth searching for purchase on my skin. *Wild thing,* I thought, as she bit me hard. *I guessed wrong. I didn't know.*

What I did know was this: it was only the beginning. This was going to be a long, raucous evening of fun. I saw it all in my mind. But I saw something more. In this position, Trix and I could gaze at each other, staring, and I wondered if she knew what was going to happen. Knew the way I knew.

Because, really, it wasn't my fault. I didn't plan it. Didn't ask to be invited to this bedroom tryst. But in the morning, as Reese packed her tiny nightie away and gave the two of us quick hot kisses good-bye, I understood that I'd be packing soon, as well. That within a week, I'd be at Reese's door, my heart racing as I pictured the way her body would feel next to mine. As I imagined her buckling on a black leather harness, taking me for another ride.

Trix should have known better. Should have understood what it would mean not only to invite a girl into our bed, but into my head.

Pink elephants?

No, man. Just the taste, the glimmer of something new, something that won't let you sleep until you have it again.

DIRTY PICTURES

Beau Morgan

Jesse won't meet my eyes.

"Pretty girl," I say softly, "look at me." She doesn't, but I come in close with the camera, anyway, wanting to capture that vulnerable expression, the shyness that surrounds her. Her full lower lip is plumped out, pouting. She tosses her long hair so that it falls into her face instead of away. Wisps of soft gold streak over her cheeks and mouth.

"Don't be ashamed," I tell her. "This is art. There's nothing to feel bad about."

She won't lift her face, despite my patience, my soothing tone. Instead, she actually does the opposite of what I want, burying her face into the pillows in the center of the bed. The brass bed is in the middle of the room. It's not mine, a piece of furniture borrowed for the shoot. But the bed works with the lines of her body, with the shape of her face. There's something old-fashioned about Jesse, an aura from another time. As a backdrop, the brass bed complements her.

I put down the camera, walk over to her, slide my hands

through her blonde hair and pull it off her face. I tilt her head back forcefully, and she gives me a frightened little half smile, as if she thinks I might kiss her, as if she might like that.

Stepping away again, I frame her with my lens, catch her naked breasts, her flat belly, the rise of her slender hips. The sheet covers the lower portion of her body, and she hasn't allowed me to pull it off her. Each time I artfully arrange the cotton sheet to reveal more of her naked from, she moves, slips back underneath, begs me to give her just a little more time.

"Look at me," I say again, and now she doesn't lower her chin, but she closes her eyes. I take the picture anyway. Her long lashes stand out against her pale skin. Her chin is at an angle I would consider defiant if I didn't know how scared she is.

Sometimes when you shoot real people, not models, they freeze. Jesse is not a professional model. She's a nineteen-year-old, young looking for her age, but with the perfect appearance for my patron. I try to help her relax by flattering her, by encouraging her to talk about herself.

"You never thought you'd be a pinup, did you?"

She doesn't answer.

"You know you're beautiful," I try next. Despite my best efforts, Jesse won't relax. It's time to choose a different method.

"Lie down," I say, still using my most patient voice. I stand beside the bed and take the sheet all the way off. Jesse tries to cover her nakedness with her hands, crossing them over her bare pussy, shielding herself from me. She leaves her breasts uncovered, and I take the picture like that, on the bed looking down at her. One shot. Then she turns her face to the left, tucks her chin against her shoulder. Her cheeks are flaming. I can't remember ever being that shy. I feel ancient compared to her, even though I'm only six years her senior.

"Move your hands," I command, bending on my knees and coming to rest between her legs. I want a picture taken up her body, up the line of it, catching her shaved mons, her concave belly, the curve of her breasts. The curlicues of brass that make up the headboard are behind her, the pattern of metal a tangle in soft focus. I visualize her hands gripped into the railing, my body pressed hot and hard against hers. The image is only in my head. I've got work to do.

She fans her delicate fingers apart, but doesn't take her hands away. I shoot the picture, then cradle my camera in one hand and reach to grab hold of her fingers, to move them, to arrange her as I want.

"Please," she says softly, "another second."

Squeezing her fingertips, I set her hand on her hip, release it, and take the shot like that, one palm over her cunt, her other hand away, a half-revealed picture of her pussy. At the camera's click, she moves her free hand back, hiding again.

I stand and go to my wardrobe, rifling around for a sheer silk scarf. As I drape it over Jesse's naked body, I imagine the photographs I would like to take of her: Jesse bound, her hands over her head, a rope—not handcuffs—capturing her wrists to the bed frame. I picture her blindfolded while the flash catches her off guard, the white light reaching her even through the blindfold.

The scarf seems to help her. Even though it doesn't hide anything, it's a layer of protection between her body and the camera. She breathes deeply and then sighs. I take hold of her wrists and bring them over her head.

"Stay," I tell her. The pose elongates her body. Jesse trembles, but keeps in place for me. Perhaps, all I needed to do was talk rough to her, talk straight. She locks her wrists together, one over the other, as if they actually are bound together. Maybe we're both visualizing the same things.

I take the picture, then have her roll onto her stomach, and I crouch over her to take a close-up shot between her spread thighs. Her ass tightens, and I tell her to relax, then move around her, staring at her, finding each shot and taking it.

My patron adores girls like this one. The shy young flowers. The nubile princesses. I have Jesse get on all fours next, staring at me, directly at me. I remove the scarf, pause to admire her stark naked form. This is the hardest for her, the most difficult, meeting my gaze while I invade her with the lens. She shuts her eyes. I won't have it.

"Look at me."

"Please..." she says.

"Now."

Something in my voice makes her obey. She opens her eyes wide and I take the picture. When I develop the black-and-white prints, her blue eyes will turn a clear gray. I focus on them, reading the embarrassment in them, shyness mixed with longing.

For the last shot, I move behind her. She can't see me. I get close to her body, close enough to smell the sweet scent of her sex. I use my hands to stretch her legs even wider. I take a picture on my back, beneath her, looking up. A tight shot of her pussy. The hungry mouth between her legs open and ready, willing. The muscles in her arms start to tremble. I visualize fucking her with my camera, spreading her lips wide apart around the lens, sliding the black tube inside her.

Taking the picture.

EROTIC
EXPLORATIONS

Julia Moore

I just came. My fingertips still smell of my fragrant juices and my legs are trembling and weak. It's always the same for me right after I climax. I feel washed out, limp as a rag, but relaxed, as if I've just received a long, hot oil massage. In fact, when I *have* treated myself to a real massage, I never feel quite as refreshed afterward as I do following a mind-shattering, body-shaking orgasm.

Usually, I have my best climaxes while astride my husband's cock. I know precisely how to do it. I climb on top of Alex's firm body with my slender thighs spread apart, and I pump, sliding my wet pussy up and down his straining hard-on. He reaches out and touches my firm breasts, pinches my nipples, makes me arch my back as I work him. I like being on top, riding him, like being able to watch the expressions change on his handsome face. His dark brown eyes stare into mine, and his lips pull back in a sort of grimace, as if the pleasure is so strong that it's almost painful.

But just now, I used my favorite vibrator, climaxing with that instead. Or, rather, climaxing with that *first*. My special toy is a small, battery-powered job only slightly bigger than a tube of lipstick. However, the size is deceptive. Although small, the toy is one powerful fucking machine. You can hear the engine throbbing away clear down the hall, which is why I masturbate only when I'm alone.

At least, I did before tonight.

I've been married for nearly three years. We have a vibrant sex life, my husband and I. We work hard to make each other's fantasies come true. When Alex confessed a desire for doing it in public, I treated him to a wild time in the back row of our favorite theater, making absolutely sure that we saw none of the movie. And when Alex learned my weakness for fucking under the spray of a hot shower, he surprised me one morning, climbing in behind me and making me late for work in the most pleasurable way possible.

But Alexander's job takes him out of town often, and this is why I bought myself the sex toy. Not as a cock replacement, you understand, but as a way to pass the time while he's gone. I didn't tell him I'd bought it, never used it with him, or when he was in town.

Never, until tonight.

Alex was due back from his latest trip tomorrow. We'd had steamy phone sex each night he was away, and I had every intention of picking him up at the airport tomorrow evening, dressed only in a long black trench coat, stockings with garters, and my favorite spike heels. I'd choreographed the scene in my head, visualizing us fucking against our convertible in a deserted corner of the parking lot. I could see each step in my mind: Alex lifting my coat in back, slipping his cock between my thighs, taking me hard and fast. Maybe I'd planned it too well, because simply the thought of what I was going to do had me all excited. So excited that I decided to take care of my urge with my special toy, sliding the vibrator deep inside of my cunt and letting the mechanical vibrations throb through me.

This is exactly how Alex found me.

He'd changed his plans as a surprise, cutting his trip short and arriving a day ahead of schedule. Rather than call from the airport, he took a taxi home, only to discover me in the center of our bed, my long red hair fanned out on the pillow like a gingery halo, my legs spread wide apart as I worked the vibrator back and forth between them. Yes, I should have heard him unlock the front door and call out my name, but I didn't. This is because I was wearing a headset and listening on my Walkman to a woman's voice describing a particularly dirty act. What a treat. I'd never listened to a sex tape before, but I'd bought one on a whim, and now, my vibrator charged up, my body ready, I'd given in.

And it had turned me on.

When Alex walked into the bedroom, suit jacket over one arm, tie askew, I'm sure he thought he'd sneak up on me in bed, fast asleep, curled up with one arm hugging a pillow. Instead, he was greeted with the vision of me in the throes of passion, ferociously fucking myself with a vibrating wand while listening to the husky voice of a nameless, faceless storyteller as she purred her way through an X-rated fantasy. And when he found me like this, all he did was watch. Silently, hungrily, standing in our doorway and staring in awe. Staring with such intensity that suddenly, I opened my eyes, sensing his presence. For some reason, I wasn't frightened or embarrassed at all, just startled and about one millisecond away from coming.

"Don't stop," he said, loud enough now for me to hear him over the tape. "Keep going. Keep going for me."

I couldn't have stopped if he'd paid me. The urgency of the impending climax was simply too much to deny. My body started shaking with the powerful vibrations and I came, staring into my husband's deep-brown eyes, listening to the woman on the tape talk about how a big, fucking cock was going in and out of her. Plunging into her dripping snatch until she could feel it at the back of her throat.

I've always had a thing for dirty talk. Hearing these words while on display for Alex made me climax more fiercely than I ever had. But when I was finished, I did start to feel slightly odd. I'd never thought about sharing this part of my sex life with Alex, never had tried to imagine how he would feel about it. Flicking off the vibrator and shrugging off the headphones, I waited to see what Alex would have to say about his discovery. He didn't say anything. Not a word. He simply undressed in a hurry and came forward, still staring at me as if I were some fantasy creature who had appeared in his real-life bed. The look on his face made me aroused all over again. This time, I was ready for his cock. And, oh man, it was ready for me.

"You're so fucking sexy," Alex said, reaching the bed, as if pulled toward me by the strength of his rod. "I've never seen you look like that." He paused, searching for the right word. "Untamed." He said it as if he were naming me, and then he climbed on the bed and took hold of both my wrists in one of his hands. "But, baby," he said, positioning himself over my body, "I know something you don't."

I looked up at him, waiting, sensing that his cock was just a sliver of space away from my slick pussy lips and desperate for his skin to meet mine. "What do you know?" I asked, when it became apparent he wouldn't continue until I spoke.

"I know how to tame you." Then he was moving forward, his body against mine, opening me up with his throbbing rod and sliding inside of me. Automatically, my pussy welcomed him by squeezing, and he sighed and then grinned at me. As if saying that he understood I was testing him, and that he knew he'd be able to pass. Did he ever. He took me for a wild ride. Long and hard, as I'd imagined he would outdoors at the airport. It was his way of saying he'd missed me on his trip, that he'd been desperate to fuck me each night he was gone. His eyes closed and he leaned back, so that I could see the long line of his neck, the taut muscles clenched in his jaw. He was almost there; I sensed it. But I sensed wrong.

Pulling out, Alex moved away from me on our king-sized bed.

"I want to see you do that again."

"What—?" I panted, not understanding.

"Touch yourself for me. This time, with your fingers, while I watch."

I got it now, but I had something of my own to add. "You, too," I whispered, my voice like the woman's on the tape, a cat's purr. At my request, Alex nodded, as if that part of the bargain was understood. He would stroke his cock while I tickled my clit. Slowly, I brought my hand to my cunt and parted my nether lips. While he watched, I fingered myself, gently because I'd already come once, and softly, because I wanted to make it last. I could feel Alex watching me, his gaze moving from my face to my body, his eyes lingering. It was as if he couldn't decide which part turned him on the most. Watching my expressions change as the arousal worked through me, or staring as I played with myself. Taking it all in, he started to move his hand on his rod, slicked up from my pussy juices.

That turned me on more than I'd have thought. We'd never even come close to doing this before. Sure, I knew that he must occasionally masturbate. I mean, I do, so why wouldn't he? I didn't have a problem with the concept of him jerking off while he was on the road, but it wasn't something we'd discussed, or something we'd ever shared. Now, I wondered why we'd waited this long. It was amazing to see his hand moving up and down on his cock, faster and harder than I'd ever have had the nerve to touch him. When I give him hand jobs, I am careful not to stroke too hard, to hold him too tightly. Now, I had to get closer, to really see his method. He seemed to squeeze the tip when he reached it, then loosen his fist for the ride down, pumping up again and then sliding down. The sound was arousing, as well, a clapping noise as his hand met the skin of his lower belly. I was so mesmerized that, for a moment, I forgot to touch myself. Forgot, until Alex said, "Don't stop—"

And then I remembered. My fingers picked up their circles, round and round, just barely brushing my clit, and then faster and tighter until I had gotten to the point where I could take a firmer touch. While Alex stared hungrily I used four fingers to give my clit little love taps. This move pushed my husband over the edge.

"Christ, spank it," he urged, his hand a blur of motion against his throbbing tool. I followed his command, slapping my fingers harder against my clit, and coming from a combination of this and the way Alex watched. This climax was nothing like the first. The power radiated throughout my body, from finger-tips to toes, shuddering through me and leaving me breathless. And, although we came separately, both bringing ourselves to climax, I felt that we came together. I sensed that Alex felt the same way because he moved to hold me in his sticky embrace, limbs pressed against each other, bodies still trembling.

"I never knew—" Alex started, turning my head so that he could stare down into my eyes. I nodded, because I understood. Never knew that it would turn me on so much to watch him turn himself on. And vice versa. But now we know—how to do it, and how to watch, and I can't wait to turn him on again.

FOCUS OF ATTENTION

Shane Fowler

The woman's body was wrapped in shiny black vinyl, and her dark hair was piled high up on her head. I sat one table away, watching her. Staring. She wore a zippered dress, tight collar and knee-high boots. You could have stood her under a shower and the water would have rolled off her clothes. I liked that mental picture, the spray from the shower beading up and streaking, like teardrops, down her water-repellent, bondage-inspired outfit.

Daniel didn't mind that my attention had wavered from him. He poured us each another glass of champagne and then clinked our glasses together, saying softly, "Cheers, baby." I didn't respond.

The object of my desire had midnight-black hair and bright green eyes. Her full lips were slicked with a deep berry-red stain. Instantly, I imagined that lipstick smeared along the flat of my belly, and lower, decorating my shaved pussy with ruby streaks. I pictured her crouched between my thighs, the juices of my pleasure adding shimmer to her lips, her sea-green eyes warm and liquid, radiant with want and need.

"Cat got your tongue?" my husband asked. He reached out and stroked the back of my hand with his fingers. "You'd like that, wouldn't you? You'd like it if that particular pretty pussycat had hold of your tongue...right between her legs."

Maybe this wasn't appropriate chitchat for dinner at a fancy French restaurant. But I was pretty sure that the other diners wouldn't care in the slightest. First off, few spoke English. But more importantly, this wasn't your average restaurant.

Daniel and I were ensconced in a corner table at a decadent nightspot in a popular district of Paris. A club *privé,* or *private* club; you need to look like you belong in order to be granted access. The hostesses wear tiny dresses that show everything when they bend over: inner thighs, naked ass, hair or bare. The dimly lit rooms are decorated in black, and the ceiling, with a glistening plasticine material stretched over, rolls like water. Cut-glass mirrors in the dining room reflect the patrons, letting you get a good look at those around you while you eat, but before you *dine.* The mirrors throw a multitude of rainbow lights dancing around the room, and the effect is like being inside a kaleidoscope, twinkling, glimmering, surreal.

But I know the place. I didn't need to observe the exotic decor, the gorgeous waiter-girls. I only had eyes for her.

She winked at me. Her long, mascara-drenched lashes fluttered, and I suddenly knew what she would look like when she came, knew that those ocean eyes would glow even brighter. I could picture her on the bed in the center of the other room, me on top, her crimson, spade-shaped fingernails creating designs down the skin of my naked back.

One of the oddities at this particular club is the double bed in the center of the second room, a room that serves as both bar and dance arena. Rich velvet curtains from the canopy above the bed shield a mattress sheathed in black satin. In my fantasy, I was the star, grabbing the zipper nestled between this lovely woman's breasts and undoing her dress with my teeth, peeling off that layer of vinyl to reveal her tender skin. I visualized her body as pale all over, no tan lines, no piercings, no tattoos. She didn't need additional adornments. She made the ultimate fashion statement with the collar encircling her slender throat.

Daniel clinked our glasses a second time and I turned toward him. "Are you hungry, Katrina?" he asked me. "Or are you thirsty…?"

My husband has always wanted to see me eat another woman's pussy. In fact, it's his number one fantasy. When we fuck, he describes what I will look like, the way my face will be coated with her sticky sweet juices. The way I'll know exactly how to make her come, spreading the lips of her pussy, using my tongue and my teeth to find her clit, to tug on it gently, to nip it and give it sloppy, wet kisses.

"Thirsty," I answered, knowing what he meant, what he wanted me to say. I lifted my champagne and took a sip. The wetness on my lips was her wetness, the taste her subtle blend.

Daniel sat back again and said, "So look at your little friend again. I know you want to. Stare at her, make goo-goo eyes at her, tell her silently how much you want to eat her, how much you want to press your face into her sopping cunt and make dessert from the creamy nectar of her sex." He smiled at me, his face coldly handsome, his eyes on fire. "You'll know just what to do when you get there, Kat. Stop worrying so much."

As I looked back at the woman, I realized that Daniel was right, I would know what to do to her, how to do it. And I wanted to start doing those things immediately.

At the club, it's couples only. The woman's mate, an older Frenchman with thick silver hair and an athlete's build, watched me lose myself in his wife's beauty. After our dinner plates had been cleared away, he leaned toward me, pointed to himself, and said, "Jean-Pierre." I held my breath as she followed his lead, touching the valley between her breasts with one cardinal-red nail and saying, "Claudia."

Jean-Pierre grinned as my gaze flickered between them, from her to him, then back again. He nodded, approvingly, at my own special outfit. I wasn't dressed in the S/M bondage queen gear that Claudia had on, although my trousseau did contain plenty of vinyl. This evening, my husband had chosen a more romantic look for me. Before leaving the hotel, Daniel had brushed my long, chestnut curls, running the boar's-bristle brush through my crowning glory until my tresses gleamed. The silky loops fell loose down my back, free-falling over the straps of my floral sundress. Beneath the short dress, I wore white stockings, high heels, and a pair of virginal white panties.

Most girls go pantyless at the club, for easy access, but Daniel likes to pull my panties down my thighs before we make love, revealing me slowly. I *know* that most girls go without undergarments, because this was our second trip to the night-spot. The first time we visited the club was a year ago. We'd been discussing it for months ahead of time, ever since Daniel had spotted a reference on a kinky website. My interest was piqued by the idea of a civilized club created solely for intro-ducing couples to couples, a place that allowed people to strip down and fuck while others watched.

From the moment the hostess looked us over through her peephole and opened the door, we were comfortable at the club. The surroundings are subtle; the patrons unusually good looking. On our first visit, we ate a sumptuous meal, made our way into the second room to drink and size people up, and then waited to see what would happen. We wanted to understand how the place worked, what the rules were, the social clues.

In the bar/dance area, we settled ourselves on a deep red sofa and made casual eye contact with the couples nearby. We drank glasses of champagne, watched a few brave dancers grooving on the slick floor and continued to wait. After listening to several songs, we noticed a trail of couples slowly making their way down a winding staircase to…we didn't know what. Finally, we followed, walking across the dance floor to the stairway. I felt the eyes of other patrons watch me as I reached out for the cool metal railing to guide our way to the room down below.

On the second floor, things were much simpler. There was no more of the blasé flirtatiousness of the room above. Women were seated on the floor, nursing from their lovers' cocks. Men had bent their ladies over at the waist and were taking them from behind. It was a debauched underground etching from the 1890s come to life. And for us, it was fantasy turned to reality.

I think my husband would have come in his pants if I hadn't pulled them down his thighs and gotten in front of him, mouth open, tongue out to stroke the straining shaft of his powerful rod. As I sucked him, Daniel staked out the room, and once he'd come for the first time of the evening, he moved us into position next to a beautiful threesome. The group consisted of two women and one man, and I watched, entranced, as the blonde vixen dined on the brunette's pussy. The fourth member of the party, probably the husband of one of the girls, stood a few feet back, also viewing the grope-fest, his own hand wrapped around his meat, pulling and tugging. I understood why he was content with being an observer. The X-rated scenario was extreme. Their moans and sighs, slurping sounds. The way the women treated each other, at first touching tentatively and gently, but giving way to heated strokes as the intensity built.

On our left, a beautiful woman in tight leather slacks knelt on the floor, pleasing her man with the skilled affections of a ravenous mouth. Her lover's attention was captivated by another couple, next to him, and his hands were full with the breasts of a woman not his own.

Daniel and I were among the youngest of the crowd, but we were not the most outgoing. Couples in their fifties and sixties got comfortable on the leather couches and pleasured each other. At first, being a part of the action was too intense for me. I wanted to watch, but not take part. I wanted to *be* watched, but not be taken by anyone but Daniel. He shielded me in the beginning, using his body as a buffer zone. He bent me over a plush, padded seat and fucked me doggie-style, and when he began to find his beat, his hand only naturally connected with the naked skin of my ass....

All heads turned at the noise. All eyes looked up.

"That got their attention," Daniel said. I blushed so hard that my cheeks felt illuminated in the dim light. Spanking must be a no-no at the club, or if not a faux pas, then a very rare event. But rather than turn away, the patrons moved in closer. Daniel, always in charge, spanked me again. Harder. Louder. I gripped on to the seat and steeled myself for the ride. He pumped me, bucking his hips into mine, grabbing my long hair and wrapping it around one fist. He used my curls to keep me steady, pulling my head up so that I was forced to see the people watching, insisting that I open my eyes when he realized I had squeezed them shut.

"They're watching you, Kat," Daniel hissed.

I didn't answer.

"Open your eyes, baby. You're the show tonight. You're on center stage."

People moved in closer, tight around us. Hands reached out to touch me, to stroke the skin that he was spanking. And despite my shyness, despite my earlier reservations, I found myself enthralled by the feeling of so many fingertips on me, so many probing hands.

Daniel grabbed my hips and fucked harder into me, my cunt making a sweet slurping sound each time he connected. There were women at my level now, on their knees next to me, peering at my face, kissing my cheeks, watching my reaction each time Daniel's strong hand connected with my quickly reddening ass. There were men close by, pinching my nipples until my skin seemed to scream, digging their fingers into my heated flesh.

"Kiss her back," Daniel said, indicating the woman closest to me, a knockout redhead whose lips were mere millimeters from my own. I bit my bottom lip instead, dying to kiss her, but scared again. I looked into her eyes, then turned my head to look over my shoulder at Daniel as I came.

He said, "Kat...okay, Kat," leaned his head back and followed me, diving deep into bliss.

We left right after, confused and excited. Fueled with enough fodder for a year's worth of fantasies. I remember that the women were lovely, but I can picture no faces, only the heat of the bodies and the warmth of their touch.

But that was last time.

On our return trip, things were different. We were more experienced and I was less bashful. And then there was Claudia. I simply could not turn away from her. She had that entrancing look of a lusty vampire. With me in my pristine outfit, and her in bad-girl black, we made an interesting couple. Now, really, Daniel and I make an interesting couple. He's six three, with auburn hair cut short, a goatee that frames his fierce smile, and gray eyes that only come alive after dark. Wolf's eyes. He has a way of looking at me that lets me know what he's thinking. Usually, he's thinking about sex, so my life as a mind reader is pretty simple. I'm twenty-eight and I have a petite build—five three, 105 pounds. Daniel can lift me over his head as if bench-pressing me.

But Claudia and I, well, we would *scream* as a twosome. We'd fit together with ease, my face between her legs, her thighs wrapped around my body, limbs entwined, hair spread about us like the glossy coats rich women wear.

Even so, I had the problem of communicating this to her. The majority of the club's patrons are French. It's not a place that many Americans know about. On the nights Daniel and I have visited, we have been the only native English-speakers. So everything I wanted to tell Claudia, I needed to do with gestures, with kisses, with my hands on her pale skin. Before dessert was served, she and her husband had slid closer to us. She put her hand on my thigh, beneath the tablecloth. He leaned toward us and watched as she turned my chin toward hers and kissed me.

All fear fell away. I embraced her slender body and held her to me. I kissed her deeply, then let my mouth move from her

lips to that beckoning charm dangling from her collar. I bit this
and tugged, my teeth gripping into the cold metal loop, pulling
her upward by that slim circle of silver. She moaned loudly and
I could feel myself smile. Then she took one of my hands and
placed it on her lap, and I let my fingers wander down to the
hem of her dress and between her legs, discovering not only that
she had no panties on, but that she was shaved bare, like me. I
let my fingers move down farther, stroking her knee-high vinyl
boots, slipping my fingertips along that sleek material and then
back up to her supple skin again.

When it looked like I might unzip Claudia's dress and take
her right on the table, the hostesses swarmed around us, urging
us in French and broken English to move into the second room.

"Come—"

"This way—"

"*Si vous plaît*—"

It was obvious they didn't want us to fuck in the dining
room. My hand tight in Claudia's, we followed, but rather than
seat ourselves on the banks of cloth-covered sofas, we moved
directly to the bed.

Other diners had already settled in this room, but no one had
yet dared climb onto the mattress beneath the canopy. Claudia
pressed me forward, onto the bed, and then climbed on top of
me, straddling me at the waist. She grinned, batted her smoky
eyes at me and leaned her head back. Knowing what she wanted
me to do, I slid one pinky into the mouth of her zipper and
pulled down until her dress was completely open. She wriggled
out of it, now astride me only in her collar and her boots. I
began to touch her, rubbing her pert nipples with the balls of my
thumbs, circling her waist with my hands.

I'd been correct in my fantasy assessment. She had no tattoos,
no piercings other than the small silver hoops in her ears, which
I licked and kissed when she bent down to me. Her white skin
was striking against the black canopy above us and the black of
her boots. I liked the dangerous feel of the vinyl boots against

my own skin. It felt untamed, as if I were a pony and she my Mistress, taking me for a ride.

Others gathered around us. The music, which had been subtle during dinner, now shifted to the throbbing rhythm of rock and roll. *American* rock 'n' roll was playing as my dream lover bent forward and kissed me, offering her ass to her husband, who stood behind her. I held her as Jean-Pierre fucked her. I kissed her raspberry-hued lips, licked the rise of her cheekbones, pressed my mouth to her smooth forehead. I stroked her hair, wrapped it around one hand as Daniel likes to do with mine, pulled and made her bring her face down to me.

Even as she kissed me, she arched her back so that her husband could get in deep. She wrapped her arms around my neck and held me as he impaled her with his cock. I moved with his rhythm, felt her body press against mine and rock with the force of his thrusts. I didn't look around for Daniel, sensing that he was close by, watching, approving. Claudia's husband pushed her forward, joining us on the bed until his hands were on either side of my head, the three of us merged into one wild creature. He spoke halting English, his breath coming hard and fast, "She likes you. Claudia likes girls, she likes guys, she likes everyone. Don't you, Claudia?"

My baby mewed, like a kitten. Her husband sped up the ride, fucking her ravenously and then slowing and pulling out of her. He stood above us, still jerking on his cock, milking it until he sprayed his come over her naked back. Daniel, at my side now, was quick to rub that lotion into Claudia's skin, to croon to me as he did so, "You liking this, baby? Your wish coming true?"

I grinned at him over her head, still holding her, not needing to respond. She and I stayed together for a moment, and then Claudia murmured something and her man decoded the words for me. "Take her into the bathroom. Wash her, bathe with her."

I didn't need any other instructions. The club's bathroom is unisex and it's located along one side of the dance floor. A high-tech fantasy creation, the room boasts black-painted stalls, chrome sinks, and a shower walled in on three sides with glass, but open on the fourth. No door. No curtain. There were couples grinding beneath the silver disco ball, and Claudia and I made our way through them to the shower.

Some of the patrons had watched our escapade on the bed. Others seemed oblivious, but noticed us immediately when they saw Claudia, naked save for her boots, moving in sultry dance steps across the floor. Her image was reflected in the mirrors on the walls, and I saw people turn to stare, to try and find the real Claudia and not the reflection as we disappeared into the bathroom. A few lovers followed us. Claudia and I were sending off signals that were difficult to ignore.

Black tiles framed more mirrors above the bank of sinks. Claudia leaned against one wall and watched as I removed my rumpled dress, my panties, garters, heels and hose. Then she stripped off her own shoes and collar, took my hand and entered the shower with me.

Inside the glass shower, we turned on the multiple shower-heads and began to wash each other. There were bars of honey-scented soap and I lathered up with the luxurious suds and then ran my hands over Claudia's naked body. Her skin grew slippery with the soap and water, and she pressed against me, slid into me, pushed me back against one glass wall. I looked over her shoulder, saw Daniel standing in the opening of the shower, watching. I called out for him to join us, but he shook his head, satisfied with being in the audience instead of partaking in the pleasure.

He motioned, like a film director, for me to kiss my newfound girlfriend. Holding her in my soapy embrace, I dug my fingers into her thick, wet hair, met her slick lips with my own. She kissed me back then reciprocated the body-washing, lathering my breasts, my thighs, between my legs. She dropped the soap and neither of us thought to pick it up. I was lost in the heat of the shower and the heat of her mouth. I turned our bodies, pressed her back against one of the walls and kissed her pouty lips, the hollow of her neck, her breasts. She was mooning the dance floor with her lovely, pale asscheeks, and it drew even more faces into the opening of the shower.

The steam from the shower made me feel thick and hot, but the glass walls were cool and comforting. Claudia took control, turning me around again, my back to her this time. I was happy to let her take charge, to let my brain go on autopilot and my body swim in the need to do what she wanted me to. She pressed the flats of my palms against the glass and began to rub her body along my back. Then she went down on her knees on the wet tile floor and began probing me with her tongue, losing her fingers in my pussy and her curious tongue in my asshole. I gripped for purchase on the walls, but found nothing. I looked back over my shoulder for Daniel, but couldn't see him.

Claudia moved between my legs, turning her body so that her mouth found my clit and her fingers were now spreading my asscheeks. Her tongue mimicked the rhythm of the rock music pouring in from the dance floor. Claudia's mouth took me higher, her knowledgeable tongue, her fingers tickling my asshole. And then I heard my husband's voice, felt his cock pressing there, felt Claudia continuing with her tapping on my clit, and I started to moan. I ran my fingers through Claudia's wet hair, curling from the steam and the heat. I pressed my cunt forward, thrusting with my hips against her mouth as Daniel fucked my asshole hard and savagely.

The soap on my body was the only lubrication he needed. He grabbed on to my shoulders and moved his hips back and forth, leaving the head of his cock in my ass, but rocking the shaft in and out. I was finding it hard to breathe. I looked down and saw Claudia's eyes locked on my face, her lips pursed around my clit. Daniel's body continued in its easy rhythm, the feel of his intruding cock making my heart beat faster, but the force of it welcomed by my body. Having Claudia working my clit relaxed me enough to really enjoy Daniel fucking me there. Usually, I need him to talk to me while he takes my back door. I need him saying things like, "Aren't you a naughty girl, liking it this way?" I need him to paint some sort of picture, some fantasy scenario, ass-fucking me as a way to show his power. Now, I only needed the real feeling of Claudia's mouth bringing me outrageous pleasure, and the knowledge that our act was being witnessed by a crowd of excited couples.

As I neared climax, Claudia's husband moved into the shower, standing close to me, deciphering things his wife didn't even have the time to say. "She wants you. She wants to see you come." I granted her wish before I could even think about it, my body throbbing, my heart beating so hard I could hear it. "She wants you to make her come..." he continued, while I was thinking *Of course, of course, now it's her turn,* and quickly Daniel was pulling out and I was on the tiled floor with Claudia, turning in a sixty-nine, burying my face into her shaved pussy. I looked up once and saw that both Daniel and her husband were stroking themselves, and that Jean-Pierre, who, unlike Daniel, had not even taken his clothes off, was standing in the spray of the shower, drenched totally, enthralled.

Claudia didn't let up with her tongue. Even though I'd already come, she seemed devoted to making me climax again. I did my best to please her, lapped at her pussy lips, found her clit between my teeth and nipped at it. But no matter what I did, she just kept working me and her body showed no sign of reaching her ultimate peak.

Finally, her husband bent on his knees and said, "Roll over. You go on the bottom, let Claudia be on top."

I maneuvered our bodies as he said, never relinquishing her pearl from between my lips. As soon as we were situated, I heard the sound of skin hitting skin. My body responded instantly, pushing up at Claudia's mouth, drenching her with the juice of my cunt. I love the sound of a spanking. Claudia's husband continued to smack her wet, naked ass while I worked her jewel, and between the two of us, we quickly had her body trembling with a powerful climax. Daniel, watching the festivities, shot his load against the glass of the shower and Jean-Pierre followed a beat later, coming on his wife's well-heated ass.

On shaky legs, we rinsed off a final time, then stepped aside and dried off, Daniel holding a towel out for me as soon as he'd gotten back into his clothes. The hostesses were at our sides, giving Jean-Pierre a robe to wear, leading us to the bar as if we were celebrities.

Over champagne, Jean began telling us more about himself. But especially about Claudia. "She needs a little bit of spanking in order to come, a little shock of pain," he said. "She likes the rest. Claudia likes everything. But she needs that spark to get her over the top."

"Katrina, too," my husband said. "But your wife captivated her. She lost herself in Claudia's beauty."

I could tell Claudia understood because she blushed—the first time I'd seen her do that. Jean-Pierre continued. "You're the only other couple we've ever seen here who spanked." I looked up at him, startled, but he went on. "Last year, almost exactly this time. Downstairs." He spoke directly to Daniel. "We watched very attentively as you gave your wife a spanking. We've been coming back each Saturday since then."

Daniel grinned at Jean-Pierre. "I told her, but she wouldn't believe me. It always pays to get people's attention."

GAMES
PEOPLE PLAY

Isabelle Nathan

You never know what's going to happen when you go out with Molly. She likes to be in charge, to set a mood and carry it through. So on Saturday night, when my best friend called and said to meet her at her apartment, I agreed without question. When Molly makes decisive statements, I rarely argue. It's how she's gotten me into the strip clubs out near the airport, specifically to the one geared to lesbians. It's how I once ended up doing tequila body shots with three very attractive strangers: knocking back the liquor, licking the salt off warm skin and sucking the lime out of one new acquaintance's peony-lipsticked mouth. And it's how our picture appeared on the cover of a weekly paper for a piece about lesbians who were hip before certain celebrities made it hip to be a lesbian.

But I had no idea what was on Molly's mind this evening. All she'd said when I arrived was this: "You won't believe what I have in store for you tonight." And now she seemed secretive and pleased with herself, which made me unbelievably nervous. I'm a shy sort of girl, myself. Shy, with a dirty mind.

Was Molly going to make us enter a wet T-shirt contest? Or buy us red-eye tickets to Vegas? What was her plan? I stood in her bathroom, looking at my reflection, wondering whether I'd have the stamina to keep up with her tonight.

"What are you thinking?" Molly called from the bedroom. I turned to look over my shoulder at her. She was sprawled on her back on the bed, doing her best to zip herself into a pair of unbelievably tight jeans.

"Why don't you put on something comfortable?"

"These *are* comfortable, once I get them on," Molly groaned, "and that's not what you're thinking is it? That I should dress in a sack? If it is, I want you to lie to me and make something up."

"I was actually thinking that I look washed out," I announced, not willing to tell her my real worries about what her secret plans were.

"All you need is some sexy lipstick." I watched as Molly inhaled deeply, got the zipper the rest of the way up, then stood and admired herself in the mirror across from the bed. Her ample ass looked divine in the denim. She grinned at me in the mirror as she gave herself a few light pats on the rear and then turned to poke through her jewelry box on the dresser. "You know where it is, Sidra. Top drawer on the left."

I pulled out the drawer to inspect Molly's collection, or, really, the evidence of her obsession. There were at least fifty tubes inside the drawer, all stacked neatly with their labels facing toward me. I didn't know where to start.

"Grab the one in the cobalt-blue case." I fumbled around until I found it. Of course, Molly had chosen a darker color for me than l normally would have, but when I put it on I discovered I liked the hue, getting into the look of myself staining my lips a deep ruby hue. I felt Molly approaching, and I turned to look at her for approval. She stood in the doorway, staring at me. "Is it too dark?" I asked.

"Did you know that women in ancient Egypt wore blue-black lipstick? I mean, like 6,000 years BC."

"How do you come up with facts like that?"

Molly shrugged. Her shoulder-duster earrings swung back and forth. "I don't know. Lipstick trivia interests me. The Egyptian women would think you look too pale; *you* think you look too dark. Call it a draw, and let's go."

She took a step toward me, dug her fingers through my hair and then pressed her lips firmly against mine. I leaned back against the porcelain sink, startled, my heart racing. She smelled of sandalwood and talcum powder. Her hair tickled my cheeks and I thought of putting my hands around her and pulling her even closer to me, of opening my lips to meet her tongue with mine, of sliding my lips down to the hollow of her neck and licking her there, biting her. Before I could do any of these things, Molly quickly backed away from me, slid her lips together and glanced at herself in the mirror. "We'll both wear the same color," she said, and then registering my surprise, added, "Can you think of a sweeter way to put on lipstick than kissing it from a friend?"

I just shrugged. Molly's best feature is her ability to surprise. She is known for being daring. It's why her shyer friends, myself included, are pulled to her. And I wondered, excitement building inside me, what Molly would find for us to do tonight. As she reached for her purse, I noticed the pair of handcuffs hanging casually from the strap, but I thought it best to ignore them. Sometimes, all Molly needs is an opening to change the entire course of an evening.

Still, once she'd kissed me, couldn't I have guessed where she was headed? Was I that dense? I don't know why I couldn't have figured out her plans, but I didn't.

"Molly—" I started, uncertainly. I like to be prepared. It is one of my main quirks. I always need to know what's going to happen. This odd character flaw explains why I quiz friends about movie plots before heading to the cinema, why I can't make it through a mystery without flipping to the back of the book and reading the ending. Now, I had nothing, no inkling as to what was going on in Molly's X-rated mind.

"On the bed, Sidra." She tilted her head toward her brass bed, which was covered with a shiny, satin comforter and mounds of multicolored velvet pillows. Then she continued to stalk forward, like a cat, making me walk backward until I bumped into the edge of her mattress and sat down. "Lie on your back with your hands over your head," she commanded. The sight of those silvery cuffs in Molly's hands made my pussy throb. I could imagine what the metal would feel like against my skin, what it would be like to have Molly in charge. Doing all the things she wanted to—and all the things I wanted her to do. But I needed her to vocally tell me, to spell it out before I acquiesced.

"What are you doing, Molly?" I whispered. "I mean, what are you going to do?"

"I'm going to fuck you," Molly explained, as if it were the most normal thing in the world for one best friend to seduce another. As if I were a little bit slow not to have figured this out for myself.

It had literally been years since Molly and I were an item. I was sort of interested in what it might be like to sleep with her. More than interested; the looks she was giving me were making me hot. I could feel my heart beating, and I focused on that sensation as I stared at what Molly was holding in her hands.

"But why do you need the handcuffs?"

"That's the twenty-thousand-dollar question," she said, smiling, "isn't it?"

As it turned out, Molly didn't *need* the handcuffs at all. She wanted them. There's a big difference in the world of bedroom play. I got the feeling that she would be perfectly adept at making love without toys, but the addition of extra paraphernalia added to her excitement. And this added to mine. Naked and secured to her bed with the cold steel cuffs around my wrists, I waited for her to join me. For those few moments, I wondered whether Molly was going to peel off the pants she had worked so hard to get into. Or would I be the only nude player in this scenario?

For once, I didn't ask. It felt as if I were in a dream, and I didn't want to ruin the magic of it. Yes, I like to ruin the endings, but I suddenly thought that maybe this was something I should work harder to change. Perhaps if I let myself go without knowing how a situation would wind up, I would have more fun during the actual experience. So I spent my time staring at Molly, seeing her in a different way than usual. More than my sexy best friend, now my sexy bed partner. But when would she stop staring at me and join me under the sheets?

She took her time, sitting on the edge of the bed and running her long crimson nails up and down the insides of my calves. This odd tickling sensation was entirely unique. I shivered each time her fingertips found virgin territory.

"For years I've wanted to..." Molly started, now bending on the edge of the bed to kiss where her fingers had been mere moments before. Oh, I would melt. The feel of her warm, wet tongue on me had me straining against the handcuffs, which I'm sure was exactly what Molly had hoped for.

"Wanted to what?" I managed to whisper.

Molly didn't move her mouth from my skin when she spoke, which made it difficult for me to understand her answer. I repeated the question, and she removed her lips from me for a second, murmuring, "Wanted to taste you again...Candy."

Molly has called me that since school when I'd had a thing for cherry lollipops. I'd always sucked one during English comp, and Molly had thought it was a cute habit. Turned it into a nickname. At least, that's what I'd originally thought. Because, as I said, this wasn't the first time Molly and I had been bedmates. It was the second.

On our last day of summer before starting college, she had come to my house to say good-bye, a bouquet of red cherry suckers in one of her hands. We'd gone up to the attic together, to an old sofa, and she had unwrapped one of the lollipops and had me suck on it while she'd eaten me out. I'd ended up coating her with my sweet, sticky juices. As I'd climaxed, she'd whispered, "I knew you'd taste like candy between your legs."

But why had it taken us so many years to try again? Molly explained now as she continued stroking me. "We were never free at the same time. You were with Toni, then Michelle, then Brenna. I was with Simone, then Georgia...."

She'd left out a few names, but I realized that she was right. When one of us was free, the other almost always had a girl-friend. And vice versa. Now, Molly continued her licking games up my body.

"But I can't wait anymore," she sighed. "It's been too long. I really need to have your flavor on my tongue."

I couldn't have fought her if I wanted to, and I didn't want to. I lay back and savored the moment as Molly brought her pouty lips to my delta of Venus, spread my nether lips with her fingers and went to work. Or play. Or whatever you call it when your best friend goes down on you. And oh could she go down. Molly knew all the tricks, the special make-it-last tricks that you only learn after years of cohabitating with women. She pressed the flat of her tongue against my clit, firmly, until I groaned as I felt the first flicker of sexual fire burn through me. Then she left my clit alone completely and made darting circles around it until I arched my hips on the bed, trying to connect more firmly with her mouth.

This was why she had chosen to use the cuffs. They gave me a little room for action, but mostly left her in charge, which was exactly how Molly liked it. I realized once again that she was still dressed, while I was nude, and that made me wetter still. Molly was intent on bringing me pleasure, in the slowest way possible, stretching it out until my whole body seemed to vibrate.

But finally, she seemed to want to feel my skin with her skin. And she stood and stripped, losing her clothes much more quickly than it had taken for her to put them on. Naked save for her long earrings, lying on the bed next to me, her pale skin seemed to glow, like the inside of a seashell. So white that it had a sheen to it. Unlike tanned L.A. starlets, her body seemed purer for the lack of color.

I wished my hands were free so that I could touch her. But Molly didn't seem to mind, getting her body next to mine, caressing me with her skin. She arched her back, rubbed herself on me, worked in a way that made me think of a panther, stalking along the mattress toward me. As she moved up the bed, I stopped thinking and lost myself in the feel of her, the scent of her, the warmth of her body on mine. But when she moved to the side of the bed to kiss me, I looked down and saw that her cranberry lipstick was smeared along my lower belly. This is what made me come. Lipstick kisses on my skin, prettier than anything I'd ever seen before.

I threw my head back and let the swells of pleasure break over me, burst inside me like the surf pounding against the Santa Monica shore. They shook my body from the inside out, took me away and then gently, slowly brought me back down again. Into Molly's loving arms.

This evening, for all my fears of what she had in store for us, her plans had involved nothing but her, me and a bed. Nothing else was needed.

THE SEX TEST

Alison Tyler

M y best friend Roxanne and I share everything, from secrets to lipstick to the occasional man. Years ago, we had keys made to each other's apartments, for those fashion emergencies when she desperately needs to borrow one of my leather jackets and I'm out of town. Or the occasions when I want to lift one of her treasured heavy metal LPs and she doesn't answer my text. We lend, give and trade items all the time. So when she brought over a stack of magazines that she'd finished reading, I thought nothing of it.

Looking back now, there *was* something odd about the way she handed the magazines to me. A subtle rosy blush colored her normally pale, freckled skin. A strangely charged heat shone in her dark-green eyes, and she ducked her head rather than staring at me straight on. "Don't worry about giving them back, Jodie," she told me. "I'm finished."

I hefted the stack and then fanned out the top few, looking them over. She had all the girly genres covered—a gossip rag, a fancy foreign number and a famous one devoted to helping women transform themselves for men.

"They're just fluff," she continued, sounding somewhat embarrassed. But then, as if she couldn't help herself, she added, "Who knows, maybe you'll learn something." She motioned with a casual nod to my faded blue jeans, long-sleeved white T-shirt and battered boots. I'm no gambler when it comes to my wardrobe. I like the clean lines of denim and a tank top, the soft caress of well-worn leather, or a sharp-looking suit when I need to dress up.

Roxy's the opposite. We are both long and lean, but my best friend tends to dress more exotically, choosing splashier colors, tighter fits. She's gone through all of the trendy phases—punk, femme, even the military look that was the rage again this year. Her spunky attitude takes her through even the most outrageous fad, and sometimes I've actually been tempted to join her on a fashion adventure. Nobody but Roxy could get me to trip along after her in a pair of dangerous high heels instead of my normal motorcycle boots, but she's done it. No one but my best friend could cajole me into wearing a bright lipstick-red sarong at the beach, and Roxy's done that, too.

"Have fun," she grinned, watching as I set the magazines on my glass coffee table. "I'll call you tomorrow." Then she kissed me good-bye, trailing her fingertips through my shoulder-length brown hair, holding me close so that I could smell the perfume of her skin. Yes, we give each other bear hugs and friendly kisses all the time, but this embrace was filled with a little more longing than a regular good-bye smooch. I stared after her, wondering exactly what was going on, but not able to guess.

After she left, I got comfortable on the white leather sofa in my living room, perusing the various magazines in the fading summer sunlight. Outside my open window, I could hear the sounds of happy voices overlapping, couples giggling together on the gold-flecked sands of the beach. By myself that Friday evening, I was thrilled to have such mindless reading matter to fill my time. It would keep my thoughts away from the fact that I was dateless.

The first magazine was a slim volume filled with gossip about celebrities I didn't know. I flipped through it in no time. The second, a slick European edition, took me longer. I daydreamed my way through the four-hundred-plus pages of the spring fashion bonanza, pictured myself in the different designer suits, tried to imagine which pieces would look better on me and which would be more flattering to Roxanne. Not difficult at all. She'd wear the beaded ball gowns, the fantastic, frilly confections made of fluttering lace. I'd accompany her in the sleek black suits, the wide-legged crepe de chine pants, the butter-soft black leather.

By the time I'd visualized each of us in all of the different outfits, it was getting late, and I decided to move to my bedroom. First, I poured myself a glass of chilled white wine, then changed into a black tank top and a pair of gray silk boxers. In my bed, I slid beneath the covers and reached for magazine number three. This was a famous one, known for articles filled with sexual ideas, innuendos and reader confessions. I consider it the equivalent of eating some brightly colored, lip-staining drugstore candy made entirely of synthetic ingredients. Not good for you, but oh so sweet going down.

I worked my way through slowly, as if reading about an alien culture. As I flipped the shiny pages, I learned the proper way to wear sheer pink lip gloss (as if I'd ever give up my trademark hue of deep, true crimson), read the amazing statement that "navy blue is the new black"—I still don't get that—before finally coming to a quiz in the very center of the magazine. *How Much of a Risk-Taker Are You Beneath the Sheets?* the headline queried. Below, was the interesting subhead: *What Your Secret Fantasies Reveal About You.*

Well, I'm not a risk-taker at all. I didn't need a stupid quiz to tell me that. I'm the type to weigh my options, dipping my toes in the shallow end to test the temperature first. It takes a while for me to make decisions, and once I do, my mind is set. But before I could simply turn the page and move on, I noticed that

Roxanne had already filled out the questionnaire. She'd used a fine red pen, circling the different letters of the multiple-choice answers. I wondered whether I would be able to guess the way she would respond to each query. That was the *real* test.

Still, I hesitated for a moment before starting. Would she want me to know her innermost fantasies? That was easy to answer: Roxanne and I tell each other everything. This would simply be a fun way for me to exercise my brainpower, trying to guess how she would fill in a silly sex test.

The first question jumped right into the subject matter: *Choose the fantasy that most describes your hidden desire: A) Taking the upper hand in a bedroom situation. B) Sharing the power with a partner. C) Letting your lover set the stage.*

C was circled twice.

Hmmm. That one took me by surprise. My instincts told me that she'd have chosen *A*, for sure. Roxanne has the type of firecracker personality that often accompanies bright-red hair and golden-freckled skin. I'd assumed that she would be the one on top in any situation—between the sheets or otherwise. With a bit more interest, I read on.

Question two asked the test-taker to put the following fantasies in order, with the one that was the most arousing at the top.

Role-playing
Exhibitionism
Voyeurism
Food play
Bondage

Roxanne hadn't bothered ranking them at all, as if the concept didn't interest her in the slightest. Instead, underneath the different choices, she'd written in the indecipherable statement: *Being found out.*

Now what did that mean—and why would it be a turn-on?

I took another sip of wine, considered calling her and asking her about her answers, and then decided to simply keep on reading. This was the most exciting stuff I'd found all night.

The next part of the quiz was made of several phrases, requiring the reader to mark a *T* for True or *F* for False. *I have participated in the following activities:*

- *Played with sex toys*
- *Acted out role-playing fantasies*
- *Tried a ménage à trois*
- *Experimented with bondage*
- *Been with another woman*

Each statement had a *T* next to it, and the final one had an exclamation point written in by hand. From sharing stories in the past, I knew that Roxanne was in no way a tentative lover. She'd told me about the time she'd taken her thong off in the window of a café on Main Street. Without thoughts of reprisals, she'd spread her slim legs so that her date would be able to see her pantyless pussy when he returned from feeding the meter. He'd paid the check immediately, hurrying her out behind the restaurant for a bit of public sex in the parking lot, so excited that he couldn't even wait until they got home. Which was exactly what Roxanne had been hoping for.

Then there was the lover who'd liked to dress her up. They'd often enjoyed decadent fantasies come to life in the guise of a dean and coed, or kinky nurse and shy patient. She had thrown herself into the fun of make-believe, dragging me along with her to thrift stores downtown in search of the perfect costumes.

"I need a cheerleader skirt," she'd confessed. "Something short and pleated."

We'd spent hours perusing the racks at all of our favorite haunts until she'd come up with the perfect red-and-white-pleated number. "Dan's going to flip when he sees this," she'd said, pleased, before correcting herself. "Well, I'm actually the one who's going to flip for him, and he's going to come from watching." She did a mock cheer to show me exactly what she meant.

Roxanne never seemed to feel awkward talking about sex with me. She'd even called me late, late one night, needing to immediately share an encounter she'd had with two of her coworkers. After a daylong, stressful meeting at the ad agency, the threesome had gone out drinking to one of Roxanne's favorite watering holes.

It was that season when brushfires plagued this most wealthy of communities, and from the bar located on the top floor of a hotel, they had watched the mountains burning. Something about witnessing the destruction of all that valuable real estate had made Roxy hot. She'd found the nerve to come on to both of her handsome and receptive coworkers. They'd paid for their margaritas and gotten a room in the hotel. There, these lucky men had spent several hours making her sexual sandwich fantasy come true, with Roxy in between as the filling.

But somehow even knowing all of these stories from her past, I'd never have guessed that she'd been with a girl. Or that she'd tried any sort of bondage. I couldn't envision her captured, her wild, untamed spirit reined in. Where had I been? Had she tried to tell me but felt that I wasn't willing to hear?

I was anxious to find out what else I'd missed hearing about. Yet another stab of guilt at reading the quiz stopped me. How would I feel if Roxy had stumbled on my own filled-in questionnaire? That was an easy question to answer: I'd never take an idiotic test like this, wouldn't think to waste my time on one. If I had, though, I definitely wouldn't mind Roxy reading my answers. There was nothing about me that she didn't know already. So taking another sip of wine, I quickly got over my moral issues and plunged on.

Question four focused on dirty movies. Next to the titles were brief write-ups, in case the questionee hadn't seen the flick. I'd seen them all. And I knew Roxanne had, as well.

Which erotic movie would you most easily see yourself starring in:

- Basic Instinct *(Dominant woman)*
- 9 1/2 Weeks *(Submissive woman)*
- Bound *(Lesbian relationship)*

The second and the third titles were underlined, letting me know that she wanted to try a submissive role in a girl-girl relationship. Suddenly, instead of simply acting like a private detective, peeking into my friend's hidden fantasy life, I found myself getting aroused.

Oh, Roxanne, I thought. *You naughty, naughty girl.*

Now, the way she'd acted earlier in the evening made sense. She'd been revealing herself in an unexpected manner. Carefully, cautiously. And that wasn't like my Roxanne at all. A born risk-taker, she was used to spelling things out clearly from the start. With any other potential lover, she'd have been bold and outspoken. Not with me. The lengths she'd gone through to get into my mind were both surprising and flattering. How she'd bookended the magazine between the others, using them as innocent props, knowing that I'd reach for this one later in the night, guessing easily my routine of climbing into bed to enjoy the frivolous volume.

Oh, Roxanne, I thought again. *You aced that quiz, didn't you? You're the number one risk-taker of all. Go to the front of the class, girl.*

But what did it all mean? She was coming on to me. That was for sure. Yet why hadn't we gone this route before? She knew full well that I like both men and women, and she also knew that I play the top role whenever possible. My personality may not be that of a standard risk-taker, for I am methodical in my dealings. From my work to my social life, I enjoy order, calm and the power of being in charge. It floods through me in a rush, from my very center outward to the edges of my body. Bringing someone else to that highest point of pleasure, being in charge of her fulfillment, that's what makes me cream. If submitting is a turn-on for a lover, it works well with my need for dominance.

Sprawling against the pillows, I slid a hand under my nightshirt, finding the waistband of my charcoal silk boxers and then stroking myself lazily through the material. My thoughts were entirely of Roxanne, of me and Roxanne, playing the way she obviously wanted to play.

In my fantasy, I saw Roxanne letting go. Tied or cuffed to my bed, her supple body trembling, her head turning back and forth on my pillow, that long glossy hair of hers spread in a fiery mane against my white sheets. I saw myself, not undressed yet, still wearing a pair of my favorite faded jeans, a tight white tank top that perfectly fit my lean, hard-boned physique, and holding something in my hand. Closed my eyes tighter, as if that would make the image come clearer to me. Ah, yes, it was a crop, and I was tracing the tip of the beautiful weapon along her ribs, down the basin of her concave belly. A belly I've admired so many times in dressing rooms, or out at the beach, although never have I let my fantasies get away from me.

Now, I did, seeing in my mind as I parted her pretty pussy lips and slid the braided edge of the crop up inside her, getting it nice and wet.

My hand pushed my boxers aside, needing direct finger-to-clit contact. Slowly but firmly I made dreamy circles around and around. I thought about Roxanne's tongue there, working me when I finally joined her on the bed. She'd still be tied. Bound to my silver metal bed frame. But her tongue would be free to act how it wanted to. I'd bring my hips in front of her, use my own fingers to part my nether lips, let her get a good look at me inside before allowing her to kiss my cunt.

When she was ready, and I was dripping, I would press myself against her face, would let her tongue-fuck me until I could hardly take the pleasure. Only then would I turn around, slide into a sixty-nine, reward her with the present of a well-earned orgasm. I'd eat her until her whole body trembled, slip my tongue up inside her, paint invisible pictures on the inner walls of her pussy—

With a harsh intake of breath, I stopped. Stopped touching myself. Stopped fantasizing. What if I was wrong? Maybe she had simply filled out the quiz for the hell of it, had forgotten all about it and given the magazine to me in total innocence. What if I was the one reading things into this, making the wrong assumptions? Yes, it looked as if we'd be perfectly matched in the bedroom, but perhaps that wasn't what Roxanne had in mind at all. Hell, maybe she hadn't even been the one to take the quiz.

Feeling an unexpected sense of panic burst through me, I reached for the magazine again, skimming the remaining questions for signs that Roxanne was the test-taker, and that she'd been answering the queries for my eyes only. It didn't take me long to find the proof I needed. There, as usual, at the end of the quiz, were the directions for tallying the results, followed by three different write-ups explaining the scores: *Cool-headed vixen*, *Hot-blooded mama*, and *Bungee-jumping badass babe*.

A heavy-handed X had been drawn fiercely through the three different write-ups, and Roxanne had inserted a new one in her careful handwriting in the margin. It said, *Frisky Femme Feline: Loves her friends, and loves to take risks, but sometimes doesn't have the guts to say what she wants. Which is this: You. I want you, Jodie. Call me and let me know if you will play the way I like. Will you?*

Would I?

Now, it was my turn to forget my careful, plodding manner, my style of weighing all facts and figures before making a decision. I picked up my phone and dialed her number. Maybe she wouldn't answer—she'd said she had plans for the night—but I'd leave a message.

I didn't have to. She answered on the very first ring, as if she'd been waiting for my call.

"It's me," I told her.

"Hey, Jodie," she said, her voice ultracasual. She didn't know if I'd read the test. That was obvious from her tone.

"Where are you?"

"Why?" she asked, still playing the innocent.

"How soon can you be here?"

Now, I heard her laughing, relief in the quickness and ferocity of her giggles, and then I heard another noise that made my heart race. The front bell. She was right outside. A risk-taker to the very end. Risking her heart. Putting herself out for potential embarrassment, but probable pleasure.

Tossing the phone on the bed, I hurried to the front door, just as she let herself in with my spare key.

"Get over here," I said, motioning with my head toward the bedroom. But we didn't make it that far. We couldn't. Roxanne and I only had the patience to shut the door, to stop in the center of my living room and reach for each other. My hands worked quickly to undress her. Hers helped me as we got the white peasant blouse over her head, pulled down her faded cutoffs, revealed the wonder of her body as she kicked out of the navy lace thong she had beneath.

"Navy's the new black," I muttered to her as I pulled my own clothes off.

She gave me a quizzical look, but didn't speak.

"That's one of the things I learned from your magazines."

As I spoke, I pushed her back against the leather sofa, making her knees bend as she sat on the lip of it. I took my spot on the floor in front of her. Unlike the cool quality of my fantasy and the steely way in which I held out her pleasure until the end, I needed my mouth on her pussy immediately, needed her taste on my tongue, her sweet, tangy juices spread over my skin. Slow and steady, as always, I worked her. She was divine, sublime, her cream like nothing I'd ever tasted before. The way she moved, her hips sliding forward, her hands lost in my hair. Every touch, every moan let me know how right we were together.

Now that we were really in sync, I found that I could start to relax. Roxy was almost desperate, yearning, wanting me to let her climax. I decided I would, if she could answer my questions. Lifting my lips away from her sex, I started off.

"A) You want my mouth against your pussy—"

"Oh, yes."

"Let me finish," I admonished her, and when I looked up into her eyes, I saw that she was paying me careful attention. "A) You want my mouth against your pussy, or B) You want to roll over on your stomach and let me play back there."

Roxy sighed hard, understanding what I was offering, and she answered by moving her body, rolling onto her stomach and pressing her face against the smooth surface of my leather sofa. Quickly, I parted her rear cheeks, touching her hole with my tongue. Just a touch, but I felt the electrifying shudder that slammed through her body. Roxy, my bad girl, loves to be explored like that—she'd told me so once when we'd stayed out all night drinking. Confessed exactly how much she liked it when a lover licked her between her heart-shaped cheeks.

My fingers slid under her hips and up in her snatch while my tongue probed and played. I ate her from behind for several minutes, and when I was ready to move on, I leaned back and asked question number two.

"You planted the test where I could find it—"

Again she interrupted me, sighing the word, "Yes," as if it were an entire sentence. "Yesssssss."

"Not finished, baby," I told her, and she shook her head, as if she knew she'd done something wrong. I could tell that she was dazed by the proximity of her orgasm, and that was exactly why I wanted to keep teasing her. My main talent in bed is the ability to hold off. To force myself to wait for that final release and to help my lovers wait for it, as well.

"You planted the test where I could find it—" I said again, watching as Roxy, with her head turned to the side, bit her bottom lip to keep herself from responding too early. "Rather than simply telling me what you wanted because you thought that I might punish you for playing dirty."

"Oh, true," Roxanne purred. "True, Jodie. True."

That was all I needed to hear. I brought one hand against her ripe, lovely bottom, spanking her hard on her right cheek, then giving her a matching blow on the left. Roxanne sucked in her breath, but didn't move, didn't squirm or try to get away. How pretty my handprints looked against her pale skin. I wanted to further decorate her, but I couldn't keep myself from parting her cheeks again and kissing her between. Roxanne could hardly contain herself now. The spark of pain mixed with the pleasure confused and excited her, and she ground her hips against the edge of my sofa, wordlessly begging for something. For more.

I gave her more. Alternating stinging, sharp spanks with sweet, French kisses to both her ass and her pussy, sliding my mouth down along her most tender, private regions, pushing her further toward the limits of her pleasure.

Once again, I stopped all contact, sensing exactly the right moment to ask the final question on my own, personal Sex Test. "You're about to come on my tongue," I said, my mouth a sliver away from her skin before I brought her to climax. "True or false?"

"Oh, yes, Jodie," Roxanne whispered as the pleasure rose within her. "True—" She dragged out the word, as if it meant something else.

I brought her to the limit, and then was silent after that. There were no questions left to ask. Only answers, given silently by her body, and by my own.

NAKED NEW YEAR

Dante Davidson

On New Year's Eve, Nicole told me to meet her at our neighborhood park at half-past eleven.

"Is there a party?" I asked.

Her glossy dark hair flipped around her face as she shook her head. "Not a *party* party," she explained, a little half smile touching her lips.

"Then what?"

"Just be there. By our bench. And be on time."

Although I thought the request was out of the ordinary, that didn't mean I found it any less erotic. Nicole has her own sorts of ideas for how to celebrate the holidays. Rather than gorging on turkey on Thanksgiving, we shared a night filled with giving thanks in all sorts of wanton ways that would have made the Pilgrims spontaneously combust. There were no red construction-paper hearts on Valentine's Day, but pretty twisting candles dripping white wax upon our naked bodies. The Fourth of July was celebrated with sexual fireworks so great it took days for us to get our strength back. So knowing Nicole, I had the feeling that her idea of a New Year's fiesta was going to be a whole different sort of party than one in which the ball dropped.

And I was right.

At the designated meeting time, there was Nicole, waiting for me on the wooden bench where we had shared our first kiss nearly a year before. The park was deserted at this hour—there is a posted sign near the front parking lot stating NO USE BETWEEN SUNSET AND SUNRISE, and the atmosphere was dreamy. This was our place. For our own private use.

Nicole had on a long black coat pulled tight around her slender waist, but she shifted her legs as I got closer, letting me see that she was bare beneath the sumptuous fabric. That made me harder than I'd been on the walk over. Harder than I thought I actually could be.

"What time is it?"

"Half-past," I told her, "just like you said."

"But *exactly* what time?"

I checked my watch again. "Eleven thirty-two and eighteen seconds. Why?"

"The countdown," she explained matter-of-factly.

"You want to go home and watch on TV?" I was baffled. Why have me meet her here if she didn't want to stay and play?

"A different countdown," she explained. "Our own special way to celebrate."

I slid a hand into the opening of her coat, and my fingers met the warm, soft flesh of her breast. God, did her skin feel delicious. I wanted to pounce right on her, wanted to tear open her cloak, spread her out right there in the chill night air and have my way with her, but Nicole's dark eyes flashed at me in the moonlight, and I didn't move.

"What way?" I asked finally, since that's what she seemed to want.

"We'll have our own countdown," she said, "a countdown to coming."

Ah. That made sense. That sounded like my sweet little sex

fiend. "You're not talking only about a mutual orgasm, are you?" I asked.

She shook her head.

"You want us to really ring in the New Year."

Now, she nodded.

"That's going to take some precision."

"Then we'd better get started," she said, parting her coat completely and letting me see the wonders of her naked body, all agleam against the velvet background. I knew she must be cold, but she didn't tremble at all. Her cheeks were rosy from the night air, and also from the excitement of being outside, in a public place, about to do a very private thing.

Even though I knew we were all alone, I turned my head to make sure. Way across the grassy space, there was a row of houses. Some were festively lit, and I could hear the sound of muted music. Half a football field away in the other direction was a public pool, closed for the winter months. Everything else was quiet and empty.

"Ready?" Nicole whispered.

I nodded and dropped to my knees, leaning into her, drinking in her scent before bringing my mouth to her split. She twined her fingers in my hair and pulled me back. She wasn't going to let me start with dessert. That was clear from her take-charge attitude. Reluctantly, I moved upward, positioning myself between her legs as I started by kissing her collarbone, then her breasts, one then the other, spending time to warm her all over as I made her wait for the pleasure of my tongue. Or, really, she made *me* wait. I knew this wasn't difficult for her at all. I was ravenous, ready to dine, but Nicole was enjoying the suspense. She likes the thrill of the buildup. She's taught me a lot about waiting in our eleven months together. I should have known she'd want to make this evening last.

As Nicole made soft cooing noises, I continued my tantalizing trip down her body. When I brought my mouth forward again, I expected to feel her fingers in my hair, slowing me once more. But no. Now that I'd kissed my way along the treasure map, I was allowed to open the box and see the jewel within.

Nicole sighed and shivered as my tongue flicked out to touch her clit. I could feel how excited she was and that made me even more aroused myself. I was getting into this delayed gratification kick, and I teased her by moving away again, kissing her inner thighs, working down her lovely legs until she said, "No, please, baby. Don't be cruel…"

Back up I went, nipping at her pussy lips gently before ringing her clit with my lips. I expected to hear sighs of contentment, maybe a chorus of "ohs" and "yes, baby, yes'es." What I heard instead was, "Wait, Damon. What time is it?"

I held my watch up for her to see while I continued to flick my tongue against her clit, moving more rapidly now, trying to make her scream, or at least make her forget all about the coming New Year—or the New Year's coming. But I had no luck. Nicole can remain contained for the longest time. I like to make her melt, like to take her outside of herself.

"We have twenty minutes," she said, and I did catch a waver in her voice, so I knew my ministrations between her thighs were having some effect. "Here, come up on the bench with me."

She stood, spread her coat along the bench and then moved aside. I quickly lay down on top of the velvet-padded bench and took her back into my arms, but now, we were in a sixty-nine, with Nicole popping my fly and releasing my more-than-willing hard-on. Her ruby-slicked lips embraced the head of my cock, and I leaned back on the bench and swallowed hard. God, does my girl know how to give head. She's so talented that for several moments I forgot what I was supposed to be doing. But then I felt Nic's body wriggling on mine, and I realized how cold she must be, and I went back to warming her up with my mouth.

She was deliriously juicy and wet, and I licked and lapped at her as she introduced my cock to a series of generous head-bobbing sucks from between her gorgeous lips. I was moaning now, and I knew Nicole liked the way my voice vibrated against her. I could tell from the way she wiggled her ass back and forth, and then pressed herself firmly down on my mouth. I found the silver rings adorning her pussy lips and licked and tugged at these until Nicole groaned. Then I thrust my tongue deep inside of her and fucked her like that, my hands on her ass, spreading her cheeks wide apart and strumming my fingertips against her asshole. In response, Nicole rubbed her head back and forth on me, so that I could feel her hair tickling my most sensitive skin as she continued to give me the blow job of the year. She tricked her tongue up and down my shaft and then drew the rounded head between her lips once more, sucking fiercely.

I would have loved to have relaxed right then and come deep down her throat, but now I was into the game, and I brought my wrist up and flicked the button so I could see the time: 11:49. We had eleven minutes left, and there was no way I was going to give in to her before midnight—or let her give in to me.

I pulled away from her and put my hands around her waist. "Off," I hissed.

"You want me to stop?" She sounded startled.

"I want you to stand up and bend over the bench. I want your naughty ass high up in the air, so arch your back for me."

She moved quickly into position. I stood as well, kicked off my boots and stripped out of my shirt and jeans. Now, we were two naked beings, wild things in the middle of this deserted space. I anchored her with my hands on her hips and slid the head of my well-moistened cock between her thighs. Nicole sighed harshly and pushed back against me, and I sensed that she was testing me when she slid one hand between her thighs to cup and cradle my balls. That wasn't playing fair. We had nearly eight more minutes of prime fucking time. If she teased my balls like that, I wasn't going to last. But I wasn't going to tell her to stop, either, because it felt amazing. So I played dirty, grabbing hold of her long dark hair in one hand and pulling her head back. Nicole likes when I manhandle her, and I turned her head to the side and roughly kissed her, making her forget that she was trying to push me over the edge.

When she was breathless from the kiss, I released her and started to stroke her, in and out, but now I punctuated each thrust with a stinging spank on her upturned ass. Nicole loves a good spanking, especially when she's being fucked. She groaned at the feel of the punishing blows, and then rewarded me with pulsing contractions of her cunt. Each thrust won a spank. Each spank won a squeeze. We were trying to lustfully outdo each other, until I forgot all about the little contest of wills and could think only about the outrageous pleasure.

And that's when Nicole hissed, "Damon—wait!"

I looked down at my watch, and said, "No, baby. It's okay. Come on. Ten, nine, eight…"

She shuddered all over. I could see she was trying her best to obey.

"…Seven…six…five…"

We could hear the noise from the neighboring party increase in volume, and then we were coming together, riding together, fucking with as much force as I could ever imagine. It was as if I could see a halo of fire around us, our energies connected as we brought each other over the crest…and into the New Year.

"That was amazing," I sighed, aware that I could see my breath in the air. I reached down and quickly bundled Nicole up again in her coat. Then I slid my own jeans back on and took hold of her, bringing her onto my lap for a warm embrace.

"Yeah," she purred back at me, head resting on my shoulder. "But if you think *that* was fun, just wait until you see what I've got planned for Groundhog Day."

IN PROGRESS

J. Richards

I realize now that at the beginning Colette was simply taking things slowly, being easy on such a wild stallion as myself. She thought if she moved too fast she might scare me off and into the arms of another, less-focused Mistress. And she was right. Had she spooked me with constant discipline, with too-soon, too-hard punishment, I would have fled. But instead, she teased me, taunted me, until I found myself asking her for it. Begging her for it.

Standing in front of the refrigerator, reading over Mistress Julian's comments in a column cut from *Bad Girl*, feeling the heat and wetness start to flow at my core...that's when I began to understand the structure of a D/s relationship. Lowercase *s*, always, head bowed, eyes lowered. Humble. I wasn't humble, clad in tight black stretch pants and a Lycra running top, my hair a jumble of windswept curls, my cheeks flushed from my morning run. I wasn't humble as I poured my juice into one of our vintage jelly glasses and prepared to make a single slice of toast.

Humble means getting Colette's meal first, bringing it on a

tray to her bedroom, serving her with head bowed and then asking, in my softest voice, if there is anything else I can get for her. Humble means sitting on my heels on the floor by the bed, shoulders back, body arched, waiting for her to choose to feed me a bite of her toast, a bit of her muffin, a sip of her juice.

No, I was not humble. I was wild and spirited, unbroken and untamed. But I was searching. My day job, my real world, my nine-to-five life is perfect for that type of personality—though I lie, it's never nine-to-five, it's all-consuming.

I'm an artist, fairly successful for one so young, my work shown in many of the downtown galleries and quite a few of the private, wealthier estates in our community. I have a luminous quality to my art, they say, I have a free-flowing hand, a lack of inhibition when it comes to paints and brushes and colors in tubes. I have no fear of light or dark, of shading, of muting, of brightness, of screaming.

On the canvas, that is.

But alone, in bed, with my Mistress, I am out of control, all over the place, my strokes too heavy or too light, my body contorting in a vain effort to find peace. I need control here, where I have none. My breathlessness of art does not serve me well. My constant moving, shifting and gliding, my colors as they burst free—each one a different shade, a different hue— these take me further from my goal, not closer to it.

Colette sees this all, and she knows, and she ponders the best way there is to rein in a free spirit without damaging the soul. Her blue eyes flash with ideas, with concepts, but she doesn't rush into anything. She would not have me destroyed; she would not have the filament that glows inside me damaged; she would only have me tamed, when I am in her arms in bed. She would only have me find the peace that I so crave.

I used to be envious of those who possess that peace. I used to talk to girls on the bus who ferry themselves from job to home to TV dinners without so much as a thought to art or life or pleasure or pain. They were the lucky ones, I thought, without the need inside them that burns inside me. The fire that causes me to toss and turn restlessly in my Mistress's embrace—the inner rage that never lets up, that never finds its mark.

Sometimes, I'd talk to them, asking what they did for fun, flirting casually, easily, searching for the answer. Why were they so different? They seemed like creatures in a zoo, under glass, pinned down. I wanted to observe them, wanted to find out what was missing inside them that could enable them to enjoy watching soulless movies, empty TV, overly bland theatrical performances. What was it? What was it?

Ah, maybe you've already guessed. It wasn't a lack in them, wasn't something they'd been born without, but something that I had been born with. Something that I had no control over, the heat, the fire, the need to create. And creating takes that extra bit and builds it up until it is a constant vein of life pulsing beneath the skin. You can't turn it on when you're in slump, you can't turn it off when you want to sleep. The paintings call you, the paintbrushes speak, the tubes of color wake you up.

Come and create, they whisper. *Forget food. Forget sleep. Forget love. Forget life. Come and make things of us. We need freedom. You can give us that freedom.*

Doomed, head bowed, for me my Mistress is my art. She calls to me and I go. She beckons me, and I am hers. I walk on heavy feet to the studio and open the door. The light is just right, streaming through the window in curtains of yellow and gold. The paintings stand against the wall, mocking me, howling at me: *Finish us! What do you think you're doing? Sleeping? No sleep. No time. You don't have enough time.*

There is too much art in my head.

It must come out.

Colette knows this, she strokes the side of my face when I sleep, she kisses my lips and tastes the life there; she uses a cool rag to wash the paint from under my nails. She bathes me. She feeds me. She keeps my outer workings in healthy order so that someday, sometime, I may find peace.

No peace while those voices call to me.

Come to the studio, there are ideas here. You can let them out. You can be free of them.

The stallion inside me bucks and raises its head. I moan and look at the clock. "It's too early," I say to no visible creature. "Too early to start work."

No, those voices chide at once. *It's too late.*

I pull on my robe and wander to the studio, opening the door and staring at my works in progress. They call to me, like hungry children, *Feed me, finish me, use yourself up to make us whole.* I find strength as I begin to mix the paints, my palette a ray of sin and light, of dark and heat, of wet and dry. I do not think in terms of colors, do not know the names of the tubes, but, instead, the feel of them in my hand. How much of this one has been used up, how much of that? The crinkly metal folds and condenses, that looks so strong, but, once empty, is weak and brittle.

I gather my strength and I begin to paint, the moonlight playing melodies on my ghostly form. The sound of my feet as I shuffle on the wood floor a rhythm that matches my heartbeat.

Colette knows—her blue eyes appear on my canvas, watching—Colette knows, and she tries, so hard, to understand. But she is not one of the artists, the few, the chosen, the cursed. She is not one of us. But she tries, she comes to stand in the doorway of the studio, her nightgown hanging long and loose down her body, her hair a tangle of gold spun from straw. She watches me work, never speaking, never interrupting, and I know—in a split second of wisdom—that she is as envious of me as I am of her.

She is complete. She is finished. She will never be anything but who she is.

While I...I am a work in progress.

YOUR WISH IS MY COMMAND

N. T. Morley

'm not sure I want to do this," said Parker.

"You have got to be fucking kidding me," Vanessa answered, in a pique.

"No," snapped Parker. "I can't do it."

"It was your idea!"

Parker was blushing, but then she'd been blushing for an hour. She looked at her friend hopelessly. Vanessa gave her a look that would have melted chromium steel.

Vanessa's lithe body—raised to well above six feet on the heels of the boots she was wearing—was garbed in a rubber catsuit so tight that it showed every detail of her body. You could even see her nipples through the rubber—though part of that was because the breast cups had sculpted nipples. Vanessa had actually had to shave herself to get into the damn thing, it was so tight, and she'd complained about it endlessly to Parker.

Vanessa was in no mood for a reluctant partner. "You are not backing out of this," she snarled, her face livid with anger. "I am sweating my fucking tits off, Park-ker, and you are not backing out of this, Park-ker!" Vanessa always accentuated both syllables of her best friend's name when she was really pissed off. And she was pissed off with good reason—it *was* Parker's idea to dress up like this for the charity auction. And of course Vanessa was sweating more than Parker—no wonder she was bitchy. "And my fucking feet are killing me—who the hell wears six-inch heels, anyway?"

"Oh, I think they're hot," said Parker nervously, trying to change the subject.

Vanessa responded by tapping the leather riding crop on the inside of her palm a few times—and then whacking it so hard that Parker jumped. If Parker couldn't manage to weasel out of it, Vanessa was going to do horrible things to Parker's ass— and in front of a hundred screaming frat boys.

Well, they weren't all frat boys, sure. The AIDS charity auction was sponsored by a number of campus fraternities, but it was also sponsored by the campus gay and lesbian organization. A lot of the fraternity brothers had declined to work alongside their more Greek-inclined associates. But some of them had put their prejudices aside and volunteered for the auction, no doubt thinking it would make the chicks think they were "sensitive."

Outside, the booming voice of Big Teddy Gumdrop, DJ at the town's only gay bar, was introducing the act before Parker and Vanessa.

"And now, let's have a big hand for LaKisha Swanson wearing a dress made of condoms!"

There was a round of halfhearted applause as LaKisha strolled onto the runway. Teddy gushed gloriously about the condom-dress—"Made of *both lubricated and unlubricated* condoms, so you can let those dirty mouths wander—cuts down on time running to the medicine chest!" He got some scattered laughs.

Jesus. A dress made of condoms. That was maybe the only thing Parker could think of that was more humiliating than what she was wearing: a plaid rubber schoolgirl skirt—micro-mini was understating the matter—and a white latex blouse that hung open, showing her black leather bra. Her hair was up in those goofy pigtails, sticking out obscenely from the top of her head. If they followed the plan—which Parker was trying to figure out some way to avoid—when the announcer called their names they were going to walk out on the runway to the sound of Vanessa's favorite metal song and prance around for thirty seconds before Vanessa forcibly bent Parker over the high stool thoughtfully provided, and whipped the living tar out of her.

Well, that wasn't the idea. It was supposed to be just a couple of whacks, gentle ones, Vanessa had promised. But from the way Vanessa was tapping that riding crop, Parker wasn't entirely sure her best friend wasn't going to go a little overboard. *Maybe a lot overboard*, Parker thought as Vanessa scowled.

"You were the one who came up with this whole idea," said the annoyed Vanessa, as if in answer. "You were the one who thought it would be really fun to dress up like schoolgirl and dominatrix and—"

"Vanessa, I know."

"—go out in front of a million horny frat boys and every gay student on the campus and—"

"Vanessa, I know!"

"—lift your skirt and let me spank the shit out of you—all in the name of safer sex, mind you, good clean fun for the betterment of society, something I guess you read in a left-wing sociology textbook—"

"Vanessa! I know! I know it was my idea! I'm just a little freaked out, is all! Do we have to do the spanking thing?"

"Yes," growled Vanessa. "We have to do the spanking thing. What else are we going to do if I don't spank you?"

"I don't know—dance or something?"

"Dominatrices and schoolgirls do not dance," said Vanessa primly.

"You're a good dancer," said Parker weakly.

"Flattery will get you nowhere."

"Couldn't I just, like, get down on my knees in front of you or something?" The instant Parker had said it, she'd regretted it. Oh, *that* was a fucking bright idea.

To Parker's horror and dismay, Vanessa's face brightened. "Hey, that's a great idea. That would be hot. Total schoolgirl submission thing. The frat boys will love it. You sure you don't mind?"

"I—"

"We're going to have to sit out there when they're auctioning off the outfits anyway—you can just stay on your knees in front of me the whole time! That would be so hot!"

"Oh god, look, I wasn't thinking about that—"

"*Sold! To the gentleman in the pink tux!* Please see the cashier, Pinkie. Ladies and gentlemen—"

Parker felt like a knife had just been jabbed into her guts. She almost doubled over in pain. Her head swam.

"Calm down," whispered Vanessa, her voice cutting through the haze of fear. "Just calm down!"

"Now we have a very special act for you, something I'm sure all you fraternity pledges will drool over! Showing the many faces of latex, we've got—"

"Oh god, oh god, oh god…" Parker knew she was going to throw up. She just knew it.

"Mistress Vanessa and her Slave Girl Parker displaying latex fetishwear from Gothic Dreams!"

As they strolled out onto the runway, they were met with shocked faces, horrified and disgusted at the vileness of Parker's half-naked body and the scandalous nature of her outfit. Frat boys and gay boys alike started screaming and throwing things—popcorn, water bottles—pelting Parker with garbage. Parker felt her stomach seizing up as Vanessa tightened her grip on the leash—"Parker! Parker! He called our names! We have to go out there."

"What?" Parker was in a daze, still overwhelmed by the fantasy of being covered in trash.

"It's time. We have to go out there." Then Vanessa leaned close and whispered into Parker's ear: "I'll be gentle."

Maybe it was the warm feeling of Vanessa's breath on Parker's ear. Maybe it was the tender way Vanessa spoke to her—with a feeling of closeness, tenderness, even caretaking. Maybe it was just that in the midst of the vortex of terror she was experiencing, Parker felt so dazed that she let her eyes wander slowly up and down the length of Vanessa's rubber-sheathed body, and realized, for the first time in her life, that her best friend was fucking *hot*.

"Yes, Mistress," Parker heard herself saying, the terror surging up as she curtseyed, the way Vanessa had taught her. "Your wish is my command. I hear and obey."

"Don't be a smart-ass," said Vanessa, and swatted Parker on the ass.

"Here they are!" said Teddy, laughing a little nervously. "Girls, we were beginning to wonder about you—we thought you got started on your act a little early, ha ha ha..."

Parker's head spun at the sudden wave of silence that filled the auditorium as Vanessa led her onto the stage. Vanessa strolled with power in her gait, her long legs making Parker practically run to keep up. How the hell did Vanessa walk like that in six-inch heels? Parker was surprised to be struck with the sudden curiosity—maybe Vanessa had had more practice than she let on.

The silence overwhelmed her. Parker felt a wave of fear—they hated her. They despised her. They were disgusted.

Then the cheers started. The sounds washed over Parker and Vanessa as they grew in volume. In a few seconds, Parker's ears were hurting.

Vanessa stepped aside and displayed her schoolgirl, posing with her tits sticking out—sculpted nipples and everything—as Parker curtseyed again, bringing a series of whoops and howls from the crowd. She curtseyed twice more as Teddy spoke.

"That's right, give it up for Mistress Vanessa and Slave Girl Parker. You college kids have it so easy! Back in my day, we *never* had dominatrices and latex schoolgirls on campus, just acid and 'ludes!"

The crowd's cheers rose in volume—whether because of the series of curtsies Parker had given or because of Teddy's cheesy drug quip, Parker couldn't say. And she didn't care.

Her eyes were dazzled by the bright lights, but she could see the men and women in the audience howling with laughter, cheering and pointing at her. For an instant she wondered if they were laughing at her or with her, and then she realized that it didn't matter—they were captivated, unable to look away, and that was what mattered.

"Ladies and gentlemen, if there are any of you out there, Mistress Vanessa tells me that Slave Girl Parker has been a very, very, very, verrrrrrrrry bad, bad, bad slave girl. Isn't that right, Slave Girl Parker?"

Parker blinked as Teddy shoved the microphone in front of her mouth.

"I said isn't that right, Slave Girl Parker?"

"Y—yes," said Parker nervously. "I've been a bad, bad girl."

"And what do we do with bad, bad slave girls, Slave Girl Parker?" giggled Teddy.

"Uhhhhh..." Parker groped for the words.

"We spank the living shit out of them," said Vanessa as she grabbed the microphone from Teddy, her voice low and husky—a voice Parker had never heard from her best friend before. "Isn't that right, Parker?"

Parker put her lips to the already spit-slick microphone, feeling a little creeped out by swapping spit with Big Teddy Gumdrop and her best friend at the same moment. But she managed to say it.

"Yes, Mistress. Your wish is my command."

This time the cheers were so loud they made the microphone feed back.

The riding crop came up, and down again. Parker jumped, but Vanessa was just tapping her shoulder. Vanessa spoke into the microphone: "Then bend over, Slave Girl!"

The crowd went crazy with screams, laughs and cheers as Parker nervously turned around and then stepped up to the stool that had been arranged for just this purpose. She had known this was coming, but she wasn't prepared for the wave of fear she felt as she slowly bent over, placing her belly above the seat of the stool.

Damn it! She was too tall! She couldn't lean on the stool properly.

"Spread your legs," hissed Vanessa, covering the microphone with her hand—but then the microphone started to feed back. Parker didn't move, so Vanessa spoke into the microphone this time: "Spread your legs, Slave Girl Parker."

Damn it, that's right! They'd tried it with this stool before, and it was too low for her if she kept her legs together. Had she really agreed to fucking spread her legs in front of all these fucking screaming frat boys? She must have been smoking crack. Parker's head spun as she tried to figure out how she could get out of it now.

But she couldn't.

"I said, 'spread your legs,' Slave Girl Parker," snapped Vanessa into the microphone. "Are you disobeying your Mistress?"

She stuck the microphone into Parker's face, and Parker squeaked "No, Mistress. Your wish is my command."

And then she spread her legs, and the crowd erupted like it hadn't done before.

And Parker spread her legs wider, and snuggled down onto the stool, listening as Vanessa gave her the next order.

"Now lift your skirt, Slave Girl Parker."

Oh god, oh god, oh god. She couldn't do that! She was wearing underwear, sure, but what difference did that make? Besides, it was latex underwear—she was sure the crowd would be able to see everything.

"Lift your skirt!"

"Yes, Mistress. Your wish is my command."

Parker's hands were shaking as she reached back and lifted the plaid latex skirt. The crowd howled.

Parker felt more exposed than she had ever been before—because she was. She was standing in front of hundreds of frat boys, legs spread wide, her skirt lifted and only the thinnest, skimpiest latex panties between her and them. Between her vulnerable, exposed body and theirs.

God, what had made her think of that?

At least she wasn't wet. She was much too scared to be wet. Much too freaked out. It was just an act. It was just a game. It had nothing to do with sexual interest. Parker knew she was straight, and besides, even if she hadn't been, Vanessa was, too. And none of these guys would have wanted to fuck Parker anyway.

"Damn!" giggled Teddy. "That's enough to make me straight—almost. Wouldn't you boys like to take that home?"

The crowd erupted again in cheers and shouted encouragements, and Parker realized with horror that she could hear feminine voices among the shouts—"Work it, girl," and "Pussy Power!" in particular.

Parker wondered for the hundredth time how she got into this.

"Are you ready for your spanking, little girl?" Vanessa's voice had a quality to it that Parker didn't recognize—a commanding nature, and a husky sensuality that made her shiver.

"Yes, Mistress. Your wish is my command."

WHACK! Parker jumped at the loud sound—and heard herself screaming.

"If you think that's hard, little girl, wait until you find out what happens when you don't clean up your room!" It was Vanessa, laughing cruelly, sneering down at Parker as the schoolgirl looked over her shoulder at her best friend. But Parker realized that her ass didn't hurt—Vanessa had barely hit her at all.

Barely tapped her. She'd just held the microphone so close to Parker's ass that the crop-crack had sounded like a gunshot. How the hell did the crazy bitch think of that trick?

Then she did it again, and even though she knew it was coming, Parker jumped again. The crack rang like a gunshot through the auditorium, and the crowd roared. The microphone whined, and Vanessa put it to her lips again.

"Say 'thank you, Mistress,'" she purred, and Parker felt the microphone against her lips again, slick with spit.

"Thank you, Mistress," Parker heard herself saying, her voice as much a purr as Vanessa's. She couldn't be wet—she was much too freaked out to be wet. Maybe she was just sweating.

"Spread your legs wider, Slave Girl Parker," ordered Vanessa. Parker hadn't realized that when she'd jumped, she'd snuggled her thighs back together. Without even hesitating for an instant, she spread her legs wide, pulled her skirt up farther and listened to the crowd cheering.

WHACK! She wasn't wet. *WHACK!* They were all looking at her. *WHACK!* Looking at her ass, getting hard and wet as they watched her being punished in front of everybody. *In front of everybody. Is Vanessa wet, too? No, no, I'm not wet. I can't be wet. I'm totally straight, and this doesn't even interest me, it's just fun to have all these guys looking at my ass. Fine, then, I'm not wet, but I wonder if Vanessa's wet. She did make that comment once about her boyfriend Todd's girly magazine... God, could Vanessa be getting turned on by this?* Parker squirmed and whimpered into the microphone as she felt the barely there taps on her ass—and found herself wishing, all of a sudden, that Vanessa was hitting her harder. *Not that I'd like that,* thought Parker. *But it would be more realistic. For the crowd, I mean. I wonder what that would feel like? It feels kind of good being hit light like this—I wonder what it would be like to be spanked hard—really, really hard...*

"One last time," cooed Vanessa into the microphone. "Beg me for it, Slave Girl Parker."

No way, Vanessa couldn't possibly be getting turned on by this. She was just acting for the crowd. Parker's mind was working so fast she almost forgot her line. "Please, Mistress, may I have another?"

Then it happened. Vanessa brought the crop down, hard this time, so hard Parker didn't just jump; she practically screamed. Which was probably more about the fact that Parker had decided, this time, to obediently lift her ass for her Mistress's crop, and had done so just as Vanessa brought the crop down. As a result, Vanessa had nailed Parker's pussy dead-on, right between her swollen lips—swollen from heat, of course, being imprisoned in the latex panties, and spread apart only from the tightness of the unbreathing garment, of course—and the pain exploded through Parker's body. Even through the latex panties, it felt like Vanessa had just given Parker a stiff kick from those pointy-toed boots right in Parker's unfortunate cleft.

Vanessa handed Teddy the microphone and leaned close to Parker's face, so close Parker could smell her sweet breath, feel it warm on her face. Could even smell Vanessa's sweat a little—she was sweating as much as Parker was under these hot lights in these latex clothes—and the sharp chemical tang of the latex, like ammonia and condoms mixed together. Parker took a deep breath, scenting her best friend's sweat as she squirmed in pain, shaking her ass to cheers from the audience.

Vanessa's bitch-persona had turned into the worried best friend in an instant—as soon as she realized she'd missed Parker's ass and hit her pussy. "Oh god, sorry, sorry, sorry—oh, I'm so sorry, baby, I didn't mean to hit you there—oh god, are you okay?"

Through stars and whirling pain, Parker felt a trickle of moisture escape the crotch of her latex panties and run down her thigh. *They can see it*, she thought as she savored the pain radiating outward from her tortured pussy. *It's just sweat, it's just sweat, it's just sweat, but they think it's something else. It's so hot under these lights, it's so hot inside these panties, I'm* sweating. *I'm just sweating. I can't believe my whole body isn't pouring sweat. But they think it's not sweat. They think it's something else. They can all see how wet I am—dripping wet, gushing down my thighs. I'm humiliated. I'm totally humiliated, and god, that hurt like a motherfucker. That bitch Vanessa, how dare she do that to me! Why didn't she watch where she was hitting me? Right on the clit—she hit me right on the goddamn pussy. Oh god, I've got to get backstage and masturbate.*

"No," moaned Parker softly into Vanessa's too-close face. "I think I'll be fine."

A horrified look crossed Vanessa's face, as Parker stared into her eyes. She had never really noticed how beautiful her friend was—except in the jealous way that came from Vanessa getting all the guys. But now...it didn't bother her at all.

"Ooooh, that's gotta hurt!" Teddy was laughing. "All right, now that our slave girl's had her spanking, you two just sit there and do your thing while we finish this little bit of business, then you two sizzling-hot girls can go backstage and slide right out of those slutty outfits—hey, there's a thought, now, guys!" The crowd erupted in cheers. "And yes, you naughty boys, you get *these* outfits, fresh off our little sluts' bodies... Let's start the bidding!"

Obediently, Parker got off the stool, looked into Vanessa's eyes and saw the fear and discomfort there. Then what Parker did shocked her. Tenderly, to screams from the crowd that drowned out all previous cheers, Slave Girl Parker stood up on her tiptoes and placed a kiss on her Mistress's mouth, not even closing her lips when she felt the full swell of Vanessa's lips against hers, and lingering when she felt the electricity going through her body.

Vanessa didn't kiss back, but she didn't pull away. The crowd's cheers were deafening.

Meekly, Vanessa sat down on the stool, her latex-sheathed thighs pressed tightly together.

And meekly, Parker said, "Your wish is my command,

Mistress," and lowered herself to her knees and put her head in her best friend's lap.

The two outfits went together for an obscene sum. Some silver-spoon frat boy was going to have a hell of a charge to explain on his father's credit card bill next month—"No, really, Dad, it was a charity auction. For...uh...starving children in Uganda. Yeah, organized by the Campus AIDS Project."

But not before he and his friends put this outfit to good use, Parker thought wickedly.

After they got backstage, Parker was sure she was going to be able to wait until she got back to her dorm room, but she wasn't. The second she got inside the little backstage bathroom, pulled down her latex panties and sat down on the toilet, she started. She didn't even know she was doing it, really, she just thought how bad she needed to piss and then she was rubbing her clit, feeling her pussy all swollen, sliding one finger down to her pussy between strokes on her clit. Sliding one finger, then two, inside her, discovering only then that she really was wet—wetter than she'd ever been or ever thought she could be—and it wasn't just sweat, though there was plenty of that, too, sheening her whole body under and around the latex schoolgirl outfit. Sweat dripped from her in steady streams onto the toilet.

But what was really embarrassing was that Vanessa wouldn't have suspected anything if the first orgasm hadn't just primed Parker's need for more—and it took her five minutes to come, the second time, rubbing her clit in big circles and leaning back on the toilet so she could work a finger into her pussy. She came so hard she cried out, sounding like a sob, and Vanessa knocked fervently on the door.

"Are you all right?"

"Uh...yeah..." said Parker nervously, her voice shaky as the orgasm echoed inside her body. "I just...I think I'm kind of sick from being so nervous."

"Do you need help? Do you want me to come in?"

Jesus, thought Parker. *Do I ever.*

"No," she sighed. "I'll be out in a minute."

Vanessa needed Parker's help getting out of the catsuit, which had decided to stick to every inch of her skin. Parker even had to unzip the crotch and peel the latex down off Vanessa's ass, and that didn't help matters a bit.

But she didn't say a word, even when she was bent over Vanessa's upthrust buttocks, even when the thought occurred to her that a real slave girl would have shown her submission by licking her Mistress's ass in front of that whole auditorium— now what had made her think *that*?

"Pull harder," said Vanessa, and Parker did. The latex suit came free with a wet noise, and Vanessa giggled.

"Our reputation is sealed," said Vanessa miserably, dipping her French fry in ketchup. "We're the sluts of the whole campus. I hadn't expected to attain that honor until my junior year at least."

"There are worse things, aren't there?" said Parker, lazily toying with a fry.

"And the lesbos. I swear, next time we go to a party, everyone there is going to expect us to make out for them. Nice fucking touch, pervert, kissing me in front of everyone."

"Oh, come on, we didn't do anything they can't see on TV."

"Yeah, right," snorted Vanessa. "Except we gave it to them live."

"Come on. Guys will be begging us for dates."

A crowd of frat rats came into the diner, spotted Vanessa and Parker and recognized them instantly. They started pointing at the two girls and laughing.

"See?" said Vanessa. "They're going to be making fun of us forever. We'll never live this down."

"Come on, we're celebrities. We're people's heroes."

"Yeah, especially those dykes in the front row."

"So? I think it's pretty cool we had the guts to actually go through with it in front of everybody."

"Oh yeah, right! You're the one who almost chickened out! If I hadn't pushed you out there you'd still be cowering backstage!"

"And I love you for it," said Parker, and Vanessa looked shocked. As if to defuse the loaded statement, Parker grabbed her tits and stuck out her tongue at Vanessa, and the tension dissolved into giggles.

Suddenly, a frat boy appeared at Parker's elbow. Vanessa looked at him angrily.

"You were the girls—"

"Yes," snapped Vanessa meanly. "That was us. What do you want?"

"I was wondering…" the frat boy said, holding out a napkin and a ballpoint pen to Parker. "Could I have your autograph?"

Vanessa started laughing hysterically, but Parker didn't think it was very funny. In fact, she thought it was very fucking cool. Which is why Parker just smiled demurely, looked at the guy—who was hella cute—and said, "Your wish is my command."

She took the napkin and signed her name, while Vanessa laughed her ass off.

JOINING THE CLUB

Lisa Pacheco

'm sure you've heard of the Mile High Club. Personally, I never saw the point. *What's so cool about having sex in one of those miniature bathrooms?* I wondered. Slammed against the mirror with your legs spread wide, trying to avoid plunging one foot in the neon-blue toilet water while keeping your ass out of the sink. I like comfort. I like plenty of room. I like to make noise.

But on our recent flight from New York to San Francisco, Sam and I found ourselves in a new predicament. We fell asleep, my head resting lightly on his shoulder, his strong arm wrapped firmly around my body. And once asleep, I began to dream.

Have you ever had a sex dream so real that you were certain the person you dreamed about must have shared it with you? This one was like that—an image of us from recent memory. Raw. Outta control. It was a vision of Sam fucking me on the hood of my car, my legs hooked over his shoulders. Staring down at me in the dimly lit parking garage, that greedy look filling his eyes, whisper-hissing, *"Like that? You like it like that?"* with each forward thrust.

"Yeah…"

"Oh, I know you do, my hungry one. I know all about you."

I stirred on the plane, feeling the flushed, embarrassed heat in my cheeks, the wetness between my legs from just a dream. Then I looked at him. His eyes were open, watching me.

"You're beautiful when you sleep."

I smiled and then told him about my dream, and he leaned back in the seat and said, "I wish we were somewhere we could turn that into a reality." I checked my watch. We had three more hours of flight time.

"Do you want to…?" he finally asked, motioning toward the rear of the plane. And there it was—I suddenly understood the whole concept of doing it on a plane. I unbuckled my seat belt and walked back to the lavatories. He followed.

When you hear people bragging about their indoctrination into the Mile High Club, they don't usually mention the amazing difficulty it can be to get two people into one bathroom. We are both full-grown adults and airplane restrooms were built for miniatures. Despite the close quarters, Sam pushed me into the lavatory, followed me in and shut the door behind us.

In a flash, I was up on the rim of the sink, back against the mirror, legs splayed—forgetting all about my previous misgivings. I hiked my black skirt as high as it would go and slid my cream-colored panties to the side. Sam was ready, pressing forward, cock plunging inside me.

And *that's* when the turbulence hit. The little red warning light flashed, commanding us to return to our seats. The pilot's manly drone insisted that our belts be buckled. Sam kept right on going. It was like taking a ride on the top of a washing machine, the motion of the plane, the delicious friction of his body against mine. Disregard everything I said about the tiny compartment, about the foul blue water, about the sink. My breath caught in my throat, my hands gripped the edge of the steely counter for leverage. My mind was consumed entirely with want.

There was a knock on the door. "You have to return to your seat…"

"I'm not feeling well…" I hissed, my voice heavy and dark with urgency.

"Oh," she left it alone, not wanting to get involved.

"Ohhhh…" I murmured, echoing her. "That's right. *Yeah,* that's right."

Sam grabbed the back of my hair, lifting my face upward for a kiss. We tried, but missed, as the plane suddenly bucked and we were thrown against each other. Now I was pressed against him, feeling his hands cradling my ass, plunging me up and down on his rod. The red light continued to flash. The captain continued to speak over the intercom, describing exactly what was causing the pockets of rocking air. Didn't matter. Nothing mattered except the way it felt to be in Sam's embrace, the way the motion of the plane worked with the motion of our bodies.

Sam turned in a tight circle, so that his back was now against the rim of the sink and I was still in his arms. I could see my reflection in the mirror. My blue eyes glowed in the fluorescent light. My cheeks were rose tinted, fever flushed. My teeth bit hard into my lower lip, smearing what lipstick I still had on.

"Now," Sam said.

"Now," I agreed, and breathed a harsh sigh of release, relief, as we came together. The vibrations worked to set me off, those, and the last wild jerks of the plane caught in a violent burst of air. Then, as the turbulence lessened, slowed, and the air became calm…so did I.

Sam set me gently down on the floor. Cautiously, he slid the door open and then quickly slipped out and closed it behind him. I re-latched it, cleaned up and then joined him back at our seats. No one saw, but the flight attendant came to my side after a moment, handing me an extra airsick bag, with the words of caution, "Just in case…"

MERRY MERRY

Sommer Marsden

He hums when he binds me. Whether it's leather or rope or ribbons or…whatever. Joshua hums.

This time as he winds Christmas lights tight around my ankles, he hums a carol. He loves Christmas. He likes to do something clever and step back to admire me with a sigh.

The green electrical cord with small white bulbs traps my ankles together. I can feel that it's knocked my back-seamed thigh-high stockings askew. My pussy grows wet; my mind grows blank. As he winds it higher and higher, I let go and surrender to the white empty space in my head that brings me calm.

When he binds me, he finds peace. When he binds me, I do, too. "Ready?"

I nod. It's really not up to me. This is bondage, after all. The *B* in BDSM. He's the *D* and I'm the *s*. He's the one in charge, I'm the one surrendering.

My thighs are shaking just a bit because they're trussed so tight and I'm on four-inch stacked heels. I wiggle my toes just a tad to give myself the illusion of freedom. To calm the thing that often starts to crawl and twitch deep inside of me when I cannot move. That thing reminds me to go back to that white place in my head and trust that Joshua will take care of me.

"If you behave," he says, threading the string of lights carefully between my legs to begin wrapping it around my waist. "There will be a reward. All good girls get a reward if they are good come Christmastime."

He puts specific emphasis on the word *come*.

I watch his handsome face, lost in thought as he begins to wrap up over one shoulder and then loops down the other way. Before I know it, my chest bears a big *X* of Christmas lights, my breasts still exposed on either side of the crossed bulbs.

He cocks his head and lets the loose end of the lights dangle.

"Garland or ribbon?" he asks. I don't answer. He's not asking me. He's asking himself.

"Ribbon seems best. More festive," he says. This time he looks at me and reaches out to pinch my nipple. He compresses his fingers slowly. Keeping that hard tip of flesh trapped between his digits. He squeezes slow and steady until it feels as if all blood is absent from my nipple and it aches from the lack. I lick my lips, breathing through the pain. A small bead of sweat pops out on my upper lip and he leans in to lick it off.

I don't make a sound and he nods at me, smiles, his green eyes shimmering with happiness. He releases my nipple and blood flows back in, fast and painful. I manage to suppress the urge to sob.

"Good girl," he says.

A rush of fluid slides from me and I am grateful that he has me trussed up in indoor/outdoor lights because at least I know they're waterproof.

Joshua goes to gather the ribbon and I watch him move. He's big and he's bulky but he moves with a grace that few people possess. Like a cat. A big muscle-bound cat with a buzz cut and feline green eyes. When he laughs softly to himself, that laugh skitters up my spine, raising goose bumps along the way. I love to fucking hear him laugh. It means he's happy. When Joshua's happy, I'm happy.

The ribbon is red and he grins at me as he comes forward. "Front or back?" Again, he's not talking to me.

"Put your hands out in front of you, Merry," he says. He sings softly as he knots the ribbon before tying it in a big impressive bow. Then his finger dips between my legs, lightning fast, finding the wet and slippery center of me. He strokes my clit with practiced ease and my knees dip a little. I fear falling and stabbing myself with hundreds of tiny white lights. But he grabs my elbow to steady me.

"You're extremely wet. Is something turning you on?" He chuckles softly and I feel a small smile pull at my lips. "Maybe I should turn you on," he says.

He finds that swinging loose end of the lights and plugs me in. I come to life. A breathing Christmas ornament. An aroused Christmas angel. Santa's dirtiest little elf.

I look down at myself all alight, wrapped with a bow and a warm glow, and pride flexes in my chest. Right behind it is a bit of anxiety at not being able to move. But I remind myself that's only temporary and Joshua will have no problem distracting me from my situation.

"Now for some decorations." But before he moves away to grab god knows what to adorn me, he pauses before me, runs a proprietary finger over my skin so I tremble. He leans in as if to kiss me but nips my bottom lip between his sharp teeth and makes me hiss.

But I don't cry out.

"You're so good at this, Merry," he says and licks the flesh he's just bitten.

I watch him, trying now to keep my balance. The way I'm bound I have the sensation of swaying a bit like a tree in high wind. My ankles ache from the unnatural stance. I have developed an itch behind my right knee. My ears are ringing and my mouth is dry. But between my legs, I'm wet like nobody's business.

"Here we go. Jingle bells," he says, carefully applying one

nipple clamp to my right nipple. The alligator clip gnaws at tender pink flesh and shoots a jagged shard of pain into my chest. But the pain slides slowly into a dull and aching pleasure in my cunt.

I try to shift just a little—just for some sensation that could bring me sexual pleasure—and I fail. The way he's bound me, I won't feel good until he makes me feel good.

That thought creates a burst of pride on his behalf. My clever Joshua. Friend, lover, Master, artist, occasional god of small situations. Like whether or not I can part my legs. For the record, I cannot.

"And what else? Oh," he says, laying an almost chaste kiss on my lips. It makes me quiver and my cunt flexes deeply, wanting to feel his mouth on me somewhere else. Wanting him to push me and pull me and stretch me and bend me and fucking take me until I cry.

Instead of showing that in any way, I take a deep and steadying breath and watch him wander off like the absentminded genius he can often be.

He comes back with a plain alligator clamp that he's tied with tinsel. He applies that slowly—perfectly cruel—to my other nipple. And now the ache and thump is marching under my skin all around. I feel crazed and kinetic. I feel as if I will simply shatter at his feet, a heap of tinsel and ribbon, lights and bells. Christmas debris accented by shards of woman.

"You have so much control, Merry," he says. "But sometimes your stellar control is too much, yeah? Sometimes you just need to let go. Don't you think that would be a good thing to do?"

He turns away from me and comes back a moment later with a butt plug. A lively shade of red like the bow, it is glistening with lube. He smiles at me and that smile invades my bones, winds its way into my blood.

His thick fingers find my pussy and he strokes my plump lips slowly so I relax. I can't help but relax under his touch despite knowing what's coming. He penetrates me with a finger and then the finger becomes two. He levers me forward a bit and when I shiver in his arms, dependent on him for my balance, he slides the butt plug in nice and easy.

"You're such a snug fit," he says in my ear.

And then I do sob. Some of my stellar resolve crumbles and he nods.

"You know my greatest job is getting you to let go. It's not about being strong right now, Merry. It's about being strong enough to break."

He stands behind me and rubs his hard-on—still sadly trapped in very nice trousers—against the butt plug. With every thrust of his fake fuck he nudges that thing deeper into me. His fingers find my clit and he rubs. I'm warm from my lights and my breasts are singing grand opera from the alligator clamps.

It only takes the feel of his lips and then his teeth on the back of my neck and a few more flicks and drags of his finger before I'm coming with great sobs. My body bending and bowing, completely at his mercy to hold me up or let me fall. I'm off balance and if he saw fit to throw his hands up there is no doubt I'd topple like a discarded Christmas tree.

"See, now that's what I wanted. That was my goal. Now I can unwrap my present," he says. But he pushes against the plug again and says, "But not this part. I like this part right where it is."

First he plucks the bow and pulls it apart, dropping it on the ground. Then he starts at my feet and unwinds me that way. Freeing my ankles and then my knees. I feel itchy and tingly when the lights are removed. The heat and the constriction had become normal. Now they are gone.

He unwinds the cord from between my legs and starts to undo the X he created. The ball of lights grows bigger and bigger in his hands. It's awkward and I wonder why he doesn't just unplug me. Until he finally gets me untangled and tosses the bright ball in the corner.

"Ambiance," he says and winks.

He pushes my shoulders steadily. Not too rough but the command is unmistakable. I am to kneel. I do so quite willingly, my nipples still aching and throbbing from the two decorations he's yet to remove. I try to ignore the insistent pain from them as it gnaws at me.

He takes his pants off slowly. Then his tee. Under his gray trousers he's bare. His cock stands out hard and straight and I lick my lips when I see it.

"I know. Almost there," he says as if reassuring me I'll get my treat.

He steps forward, runs the smooth crown of his cock along my lower lip and I dart my tongue out to taste him. Musky, salty, warm...Joshua.

He finesses his way into my mouth, dragging out that point in time like it could last forever. With my mouth full of him, my throat full of him, the pain in my nipples becomes an odd mix of discomfort and pleasure. My stomach flips like I'm on a roller coaster.

"You're a good little cocksucker."

The plug in my ass makes my body thrum. I want it out. I want it deeper. I want something but it's all swirling together and I can't pinpoint my desire. So I focus on licking the length of him, tasting his skin.

He puts his hand on the back of my head, propelling me forward while steadying me. He drives into me with ease because we've learned to work in tandem. Him taking pleasure, me giving it. Giving him pleasure makes me wet, makes me needy, and when I get too far gone, he brings me down by giving me what I want. In spades.

"Enough of that."

I almost keep going, but he's already given me an orgasm and I want another. I'll behave. I pull back and look up at him. He smiles, thumbs my cheek, says, "Such pretty blue eyes. No wonder they named you Merry. You always look that way. Even when your nipples are blanched out from clamps and you're trying not to focus on the pain."

He gestures with a toss of his head and I lie back. I get his little mannerisms and the unspoken directions. The soft white carpet licks at my back as he gets down on his knees. He tweaks one clamp and I whimper. He tugs the other and I go light-headed. But then he takes it all away by getting between my thighs and putting his face to my needy pussy. His tongue swirls along my folds, nudges my clit, laps at me so I'm restless.

He looks up then, green eyes dancing with happiness. "By the way, this time, since it's Christmas, you may come when you like. No permission needed."

I'm momentarily stunned, then giddy, then slightly nervous. I don't want to come too fast. I want to make this last.

From the apartment upstairs I hear a familiar beat of a holiday song. Then Joshua's sucking my clit and my brain shuts down.

He reaches up—still pushing me, I realize—and opens a clamp, taking his own sweet time. The blood starts to flood back into my deprived flesh and when he finally takes pity and pulls it free, I find myself crying out.

I almost come. That was the point. But I bite my lip, sharpen my focus, grip the thick carpet like a lifeline.

"So well trained," he chuckles.

His tongue drives into my slick opening. Joshua fucks me with his tongue and I am torn between focusing on that sensation and wondering when—for the love of Christmas—he's going to take pity on me and remove the final clamp.

He moves his mouth deliberately. My pussy is slick and swollen and it's hard to tell what he's doing just beyond putting his mouth on me. I am one giant nerve ending trying to hold on. Trying to maintain. Then he captures my clit with his teeth, reaches up, pulls the clamp off so it scrapes my tender flesh until the very last second that it's cleared. He drops it without ceremony. Quickly, he shoves three fingers in my cunt, curls his fingers and I come. Like a shot being fired into a bright blue sky, I come.

And, oh, all that is holy, is it good.

He fucks me with his fingers until every tiny twitch has passed. When he speaks, his voice is a growl. "Turn over, Merry."

Gone is the fun singing and the teasing and the mirth. Now he sounds like busted glass and gravel. He sounds like tires on a worn-down road. A growling in the dark. It sends a shiver racing up my back. When that shiver reaches my scalp, it makes it prickle.

I turn on hands and knees. Present my ass, my pussy, and clearly see where this is going. He nudges into me slow enough to make me squirm. I'm full all over, the plug in my ass already filling me so that every inch he penetrates me is a blissful intrusion. When he's in and my clit thumps erratically along with my heart, he starts to move. Slow—agonizingly so—pressing his thumb on that plug all the while.

I gasp and grind back. I put my forehead to the carpet, fist my hands in the pile. Pray for him to move faster or slower—anything but this taunting half tempo.

His free hand smoothes my lower back, strokes my asscheek, grips my hips roughly. A good hard thrust jolts me, makes me groan.

He's pressing that plug again and the pressure in my back hole and his thrusting in my cunt have my poor clitoris throbbing with blood. I feel like I could claw and chew at the fucking carpeting if I let myself go. Instead, I simply imagine him moving the way I need. Call it positive thinking.

A smart smack to my bottom and I jump. The plug jostles, his cock slides deeper, I inch closer to another release. I am climbing steadily to a peak...on my hands and knees.

Another smack, a grunt from him; he's gone from clever man to intelligent beast. He's watching my ass shake, I know. Watching the color bloom on my skin.

"Nice," he growls and smacks again.

I clench my pussy tight around his driving cock and he makes another noise. A darker one. It rumbles from his chest and makes me hold my breath.

He presses, presses, presses that damn plug and I clench up tight around him. He gives me three fast blows on the ass and I yell out my orgasm into the thick white carpet that reminds me of snow.

"Good. Girl." The words are guttural and then he's gripping me tight, driving into me hard and fast, trapping that plug deep. He spills into me and then there is silence.

"Merry...Merry," he whispers. "You are still the best present to unwrap."

GETTING STARTED

Thomas S. Roche

Have you ever tried to get a threesome started? It's much more difficult than just negotiating the damn thing and getting to it. There are all these weird, unspoken cues that are hard to predict. Players don't know what to do until they do it...and then, they're not sure if it's the right thing to have done. Until suddenly, you're past all that, and everyone's sure about everything. Then nothing has to get started; it just surges along, with a sense of ease. And then, it's all fucking worth it. *More* than worth it. It's worth all the stress and the worry about how to get things started, about whether such-and-such thing is the right thing to do. It's worth *everything*, because threesomes are like having all of your candy and eating cake, too.

My girlfriend Becca and I had placed a personal ad for a woman to have a threesome with us. We're not a bad-looking couple. More importantly, we're up front, fairly queer savvy and not too obnoxious. I think that puts us miles ahead of many of the straight couples placing personal ads for girls to fuck them.

It was a pleasure screening the applicants. Other couples I've talked to have said such things can be an ordeal, but that wasn't my experience at all. I found it *hot*. It felt intimate, by which I mean it intensified the connection between Becca and me. It was amazing.

There were far more responses than I thought there would be, and far more of them seemed both hot and interesting than I ever could have hoped or prayed for. There were many different women from twenty to forty, and we showed no particular preference for women toward the younger end of our spectrum. In fact, when we selected five interested parties to chat with on the phone, all were in their thirties...except for one: Summer. She was a twenty-year-old junior at State, less experienced than the other respondents. Becca was suspicious of her, even though she agreed she was the cutest (from her pictures) and the most up front (from her email).

But when Summer turned out to be the first choice for both of us, Becca had second thoughts. She observed that she seemed pretty young.

Becca said. "She'll be *clueless*."

Having had more experience with women than my girlfriend, I think I was more forgiving of a young woman's cluelessness, as young women had repeatedly been fairly forgiving of mine. Becca was more suspicious of young women, not for competitive reasons but because she is easily bored by them (younger men bore her even more thoroughly).

I had to agree with her that selecting an age-appropriate third was important. But Summer was too good to pass up. That bright smile in her photos, the flash of fire in her eyes, the freshness in her email and her voice when we talked to her on the phone, all helped me convince Becca to make a date with Summer.

Unlike the other women who'd emailed us, Summer was relatively inexperienced. She said she was just starting to explore "the idea" of her bisexuality. Before long, that exploration took the form of sitting on our living-room couch looking very, very nervous.

That is not to say that Summer didn't look incredibly fetching with that bright red flush to her face. It could almost be construed as a flush of arousal. Even if it wasn't, sexual embarrassment has always struck me as kind of hot.

Summer wore a pair of torn blue-jeans and a tight white T-shirt. Her breasts were smallish but very nice, especially in that tight T-shirt, for she was not wearing a bra underneath, and her firm nipples were quite erect. Her hair was short, bleached blonde and spiky. Her face was pretty, her lips full. She had a nostril ring and, she had told us, one in her navel.

"Do you want to, maybe, watch a video?" I offered, as Summer and Becca looked back and forth from each other to me, not sure who should start the proceedings.

"I...I don't think so," said Summer uncomfortably. She began to say something else, but quickly stopped—my girlfriend's tongue was suddenly in her mouth. Becca kissed Summer hungrily—and to my surprise, Summer responded in kind, sinking into my girlfriend's arms and kissing her back, passionately. The two women embraced. After a moment's kissing, Becca began to pull up Summer's tight T-shirt, lifting it over the girl's small breasts. Summer moaned softly as Becca began to suckle on her breasts. I came around the side of the couch and sat down next to Summer; she turned her head toward me and met my exploratory kiss eagerly, her tongue teasing mine as she nibbled at my lower lip. I put my arms around her from behind and began to kiss her neck as I fondled her firm breasts, feeling my girlfriend's lips and tongue nipping at my fingertips between licks at Summer's hard nipples.

Somewhat awkwardly, Becca and I undressed Summer. She allowed us to do all the work, but her soft moans of pleasure as we disrobed her told us that she was enjoying herself, perhaps more than she suspected. When we had her pants off, I began to stroke her pussy through the thin, white cotton panties she wore. "Shall we retire to the bedroom?" I asked, and Summer nodded.

My girlfriend and I took Summer to bed, removing her panties and then undressing ourselves. Nude, we pressed our bodies together on the bed, Summer in the middle, her eager kisses moving from one mouth to the other as our hands wandered over her slender, tight young body. I slipped one finger inside her and found her very wet. To my surprise, Summer reached out and took hold of my cock, which was rock hard by that point. She bent over and began to suck it, licking all over and taking it into her mouth.

In a moment, my girlfriend's face was between Summer's legs, and she was eating the girl's pussy hungrily. Summer relaxed into the sensations, spreading her legs wide—but then, "Is it okay if he fucks me?" she asked.

"More than okay," laughed my girlfriend. Becca nudged me on top of Summer, perhaps a little insistently. As Summer spread her legs, Becca reached down and guided my cock between Summer's slick lips. As I slid into Summer, the girl let out a moan of pleasure, one which Becca matched as she ran her fingers over the place where I penetrated Summer. Becca slid up fully against Summer and began to kiss her as the girl's body twitched and heaved with pleasure, her hips finally settling into a pumping rhythm which met each thrust of my cock into her body. She was gasping, groaning as I rhythmically penetrated her, thrusting and bringing her closer to orgasm with each stroke. Becca reached down between us and began to stroke Summer's clitoris with her spit-moistened finger—that did it. I felt Summer's pussy contracting as she let out a sobbing moan of ecstasy. My girlfriend kissed our lover deeply as the girl climaxed—and then, as I continued fucking her, thrusting in and out of her body, Becca began kissing me—her tongue slipping deep into my mouth as I gasped with pleasure and shuddered atop Summer, my cock pumping into her. My cries and gasps of pleasure made Summer clench her knees tight around my back and beg me to come deep inside her.

I did. She and I slumped, soft and sweet, together. Becca was up against us both, kissing and caressing. Her hand felt the place where Summer and I joined, still wet with my seed and her juices. Becca touched that place with a sense of excitement, like she'd found something sacred. And maybe we had.

Soon my hands wandered, too, all over Summer's luscious young body. Summer's hands, too. We all stroked each other. We kissed again—all three of us, trading off. Seeing Becca and Summer make out with the fervor of girl-on-girl virgins may have been the hottest sight I've ever seen. It was magnificent.

It didn't take long before I was hard again, and they were atop me—mouths, hands and wet pussies seemingly everywhere.

The three of us rolled into a passionate tumble and—what do you know? The three of us started making love all over again. Before we knew it, we were going at it again, eagerly, all three of us tight in a clinch, kissing and grinding and ready to fuck, to do all sorts of naughty, nasty things to each other. There was no doubt about getting started, now. Every touch, every tease, every look, every breath, seemed to spawn another...to bring more heat, more arousal, more excitement. The intimacy built between us, till all three of us breathed in concert, flesh slick with sweat and tingling with pleasure. We were out of control, but we liked it that way. Our passion surged on through the night.

Sometimes when you get started, I guess, there's no reason to stop. So we didn't.

THE GAME

Alison Tyler

Angel called that first party, almost two years ago, a trial by fire. Having to meet the entire band at one time. But, honestly, I preferred it that way, plunged into the group without a chance to step back, to move away from the flames.

Still, I was scared. I tried to control my nerves as I slid off her motorcycle and then waited while she set her gloves and helmet on the rack. We'd parked her bike in the circular driveway, already filled with other, more decadent bikes, and we walked past them to the front of the house.

"Guess we're the last ones here," Angel said, leading me up the stairs and into Deleen's Hollywood Hills estate. "That's good. You'll get to know everyone in about five seconds flat—then you can stop trembling and enjoy yourself." I nodded and gripped her hand. As a model, you'd think I'd be used to meeting celebrities—especially since I'm considered one myself. But I was fairly new on the scene. And meeting the members of Objects—the band with the most number one hits in the country—was disconcerting, regardless of how many fashion shoots I'd done.

Angel pulled me along behind her, whispering assurances: "You'll do fine. They'll love you." We brushed past the multi-colored balloons that filled the entryway, the orbs lolling against the molded doorways and fluttering softly up to the ceiling.

A poster of the new album cover, *Objects of Desire,* was taped to one wall. It showed Angel, Deleen, Beauty and Arianna totally nude with graffiti–style arrows pointing to their breasts and cunts. Lola, the cherub of the group with her blonde ringlets and innocent smile, sat naked in her wheelchair, staring up at the rest of the group.

As I looked at the picture, I realized how each band member derived power through individuality. Angel's tattoos were starkly severe in the black-and-white photo, as if they'd been carved into her body. Arianna had painted stars and stripes on her breasts to make them more patriotic. Deleen was like a mad sorceress. She winked at the camera with an almost evil smirk, and rubbed her hands together with glee. Beauty, who's half German and half Native American, had braided her thick, black hair into a solid rope—it made her look dangerous. She stood sideways between Deleen and Arianna, and her braid hung down her back, past her shoulder blades, almost to her waist.

"That's the uncensored version," Angel told me. "The public receives a model with black Xs covering the indecent parts."

I stared, fascinated by the curves and dips of the women's bodies, their unique shapes, but Angel pulled on my hand, leading me into the sprawling living room. The lights were dimmed, and I almost stumbled over a white cat walking up to greet us.

"Hey, Mister." Angel picked up the kitty. "I'd like you to meet Katrina."

I shook a fuzzy paw, and Beauty, staked out on a matching sofa said, "Where are your manners, Angel? You introduce your lady to a pussy before us?"

Angel shrugged, set the cat gently on the ground, and said, "Everyone, I'd like you to meet Katrina. Katrina, this is everyone." She looked around the room, "Well, almost everyone. Where are the hosts?"

Arianna, reclining on a matching red leather chaise lounge with her girlfriend said, "Somewhere in the kitchen." She was covered by a petite Asian beauty named Sara, draped casually over her like a shawl.

"You should check out the spread," Beauty told us. "Ellis got the Sleeping Buddha to cater."

Angel and I turned as Ellis appeared in the doorway, caught beneath the iridescent light filtering through a gathering of balloons. Ellis is a true Irish redhead, her ivory skin sprinkled with millions of freckles like golden confetti. They seemed to sparkle across her nose and shoulders and over her cleavage, and I wondered if they covered her entire body, then blushed at the thought.

Deleen came up behind her carrying a glass of champagne in each hand.

"Hey, Angel. Who's the babe?"

"Deleen, really," Ellis admonished. "You're frightening her."

"This is Katrina," Angel said, her arm behind me, pushing me toward them. I shook hands with Ellis. Deleen, passing the champagne on to Arianna and Sara, took one of my hands in both of hers and kissed my fingertips.

"Charmed," she smiled.

"Help yourself to food," Ellis said, ignoring her flirtatious lover, "We've got a feast spread out in the dining room, buffet style."

Angel and I piled up plates, then walked back into the main room and settled onto the floor against a flood of satin pillows. Ellis came to sit by my side. She had on a strapless dress with a black bodice and a short skirt of fluffy lace. Her slender waist was accentuated with a wide velvet ribbon. I complimented her on the look and she said, "Thanks. Easy on, easy off," and then leaned across me to ask Angel a question, rubbing her breasts slightly against my knees.

I wondered if she'd done it on purpose, and then looked at her startled as she asked me a question.

"I'm sorry, what?"

"Do you know Lola?"

"No. I know *of* her, but we haven't met."

"She should be here later," Ellis said, looking at Angel to include her in the conversation. "Lo was meeting with a publisher in New York about doing a book of photos." She paused, as an idea came to her, "You know, she ought to take some of you." Ellis said.

"The two of you together," Deleen interrupted. "Now, *that* would be a picture."

I saw Angel nodding in agreement, but turned when Arianna leaned up on the sofa, Sara moving with her lover's body as if she were another limb.

"Add Sara, too," Arianna insisted.

"And, um," Beauty fumbled as a gorgeous strawberry blonde strolled in from the kitchen holding a bottle of mineral water. She walked up to Beauty and snuggled against her.

"Liz," she purred.

"Yeah, and Liz," Beauty finished, lamely, and the rest of us laughed, transforming an awkward moment into a rather silly one. Liz didn't seem to mind. She curled her long limbs around Beauty's, protectively, like an owner.

"I wouldn't get too comfortable if I were her," Ellis whispered to me. "Beauty left her last girlfriend on the plane when she met this one," Ellis nodded to Liz who was now kissing Beauty's earlobe. "Beauty's always had a problem with the word *commitment.*"

Angel excused herself then, to get more food, and Ellis took this opportunity to lean even closer to me. Her body pressed against my side so that I could feel her fragile ribs, the warm, bare skin of her upper chest on my arm.

"How long have you two been hiding out?" she asked me when Angel was out of the room. "We haven't seem much of Angel since the recording ended."

"A month," I told her, thinking in my head that it was thirty days exactly since she'd come with Melanie to the fashion shoot at *Zebra*.

"And you met …"

"Through Melanie at *Zebra*." I waited for the recognition to appear in Ellis's eyes.

"The journalist?"

I nodded.

"You're on the cover of *Zebra* this month, aren't you?" she said, getting it.

I nodded again, giving her a quick version of the smoldering look they'd had me do for the shoot—the one currently appearing on every newsstand. Lashes lowered, head tilted, lips pouting.

"You seem different in person," Ellis said, smiling at me. "So much younger."

"That's the makeup," I explained. "But it's what Angel said, too. It's what she liked about me, I think, the person beneath the image." Everyone in the business knows about it, but only a few people allow others into their shell.

Angel had said, "Can I talk with you?" And I told her, knees trembling at the thought of talking with the lead singer in the hottest band in the country, "Hang out until I get this makeup off." She'd waited outside the dressing room, chatting with Melanie who kept yelling for me to hurry up. I came out in a T-shirt and ripped jeans, my normal attire, and Angel looked me over and shook her head.

"You're younger than all that, aren't you?" she asked, glancing toward the lights and the fancy dresses hanging from a metal pole in "wardrobe." "I'm the same age underneath," I grinned, "You just have to look beneath the surface."

Angel had nodded, moving in close to me as Melanie withdrew to answer her cell phone in private. "Yeah, I would like to do just that, Katrina. I would like to see what's lurking beneath your surface, peel you open, spread you out, learn each of your secrets for myself."

Then Melanie had returned and things continued as normal—at least until the next time Angel and I were alone. Still, I didn't say any of these things to Ellis. She would know all about duplicity, two-faced worlds, being the partner of Deleen— someone whose little black book contained the number of every "in" person in Hollywood.

Angel came back then, now sitting on Ellis's side, and she gave me a look over Ellis's head that I took to mean, "How are you holding out?"

I shrugged back at her and then said, "Please," as Deleen stopped in front of me with a fresh bottle of champagne. It surprised me at first that there wasn't any "help" at the party, but I was glad for it, glad for the low-key atmosphere. I could tell that these people were for real—not needing the constant stroking of fans or media.

The house—mansion, really—was as kickback as they were— set up for comfort, not appearances, although all was stylishly done. There were pillows everywhere, velvet and satin striped, with butter-soft leather sofas. I hoped to decorate my own place in a similar fashion someday, wanting to be able to walk into a room, eyes closed (or blindfolded), and enjoy the surroundings by touch only.

By my third bubble-filled glass, I was leaning against the cushions, listening to Montage croon on the stereo, drifting in a warm fulfillment. I paid scant attention to Angel and Ellis who were discussing the promotion for *Objects of Desire*. I watched as Arianna and Beauty gossiped across the space between their sofas, Sara describing her latest nude centerfold in *Planet X* magazine, and Liz, a first-class cabin attendant, explaining how Beauty had stolen her heart at 32,000 feet.

I wondered what had happened to the girl Beauty had been with, and I thought about asking Ellis, but she left to fetch a joint. When she returned to the living room, she was tottering on her spangled high heels.

"Want some, Angel?" she asked, collapsing on the pillows

on Angel's left side, turning my lover into a "person sandwich" with Ellis and me the bread.

"Naw, I'm saving my voice."

"Katrina?" she asked.

"Sure."

Marijuana goes to my head quickly, especially when I'm drinking, so I only took one hit. But Ellis apparently had been smoking in the bedroom before coming out. She was flying, and while I lit up, she leaned seductively against Angel and said, "You have the most beautiful eyes, Angel. You know it?"

Angel tried to brush her off, nicely, by saying, "Deleen's the one with the killer eyes." Angel turned to me and said, "Did you know that Del's eyes have no color?"

I was more stoned than I'd thought, because this statement tripped a string of bizarre images in my mind. "What do you mean?" I finally managed to ask.

"They're almost perfectly clear. She usually wears shades or colored lenses to hide them. Del!"

Deleen looked over from her lazy-lioness position in the hammock chair.

"What's up?" She was gone, too.

"Come show Kat your eyes."

"Send the kitty over here."

I got up, also a bit unbalanced, and wove my way to Deleen's corner. She turned a floor lamp around so that the light shone directly in her eyes, and I drew in my breath. They were like glass, perfectly clear irises with liquid black pupils in the center.

Deleen smiled at me and said, "I always wear contacts for public appearances. I wouldn't want to scare anyone."

She put her hand out to steady me. I'd been rocking in place, and her fingers were like flames licking at my skin. Startled, I stumbled back to the pillow corner. Ellis was now in Angel's lap, her dress hiked up to her thighs exposing the purple ribbons of her garters as she straddled my lover. Angel didn't seem uncomfortable, but I could tell she was humoring Ellis.

"You don't mind, do you Katrina?" Ellis grinned at me. "Angel has the most inviting body. I wanted to be closer to it."

"Go ahead," I said magnanimously as I leaned against the wall, letting it support me as I slid to a sitting position. "Do what you have to." I wanted to see how far Angel would take it, wanted to know what I'd be in store for in the future. At the moment, she seemed to be letting Ellis call the shots.

Deleen got up to open another bottle of champagne, and I saw a frown on her painted lips.

"What are you up to, Ellis?" she asked, her buzz obviously worn off. Deleen's demeanor surprised me, considering how she'd flirted with me when we'd met.

"Just goin' for a ride," Ellis slurred, leaving no doubts that Angel was to be her horse.

Deleen clicked her tongue against the roof of her mouth, and then sat down on the nearest sofa, forcing Arianna and Sara to move aside. They protested for a second before resuming their positions: Sara had undone Arianna's leather jeans and was very quietly sucking on the strap-on dildo that Arianna wore in a harness. The darkness of the room had concealed their activity, but they didn't seem to mind being revealed. Arianna's moans and Sara's kitten-like suckling noises testified to that.

"What is it with you, Ellis?" Deleen's voice was very softly menacing. "It's been three hours since you last came, is that too long for you?"

Ellis looked at Deleen through clouded eyes. "I'm just entertaining our guests, Del," she said.

"Uh-uh, baby, I'm not going to play that game." Deleen slid her hand through her silvery hair, apparently trying to calm herself down. Deleen's hair is completely gray and has been since her teens. She wears it combed off her forehead, and it falls like an old lion's mane straight down her back. "Get your little ass over here."

Ellis stood up quickly, a worried look replacing the lecherous one she'd worn only a second earlier.

"Now," Deleen ordered, when she saw Ellis hesitate.

Angel watched the whole scene with her features set. She appeared emotionless, a statue, but I could tell she was getting turned on. I was already able to read her expressions, the slight wrinkle in her brow or tightening of her jaw. I settled against her and she put an arm around me, gently turning my face to kiss my lips.

Ellis cautiously walked the rest of the way over to Deleen, as if condemned. As soon as Ellis was in reaching distance, Deleen grabbed hold of her waist and threw Ellis over her lap. Ellis struggled, realizing suddenly what her Mistress meant to do, but Deleen held her firmly, scissoring one leg over Ellis's two squirming ones to keep her in place. Deleen lifted Ellis's dress by the hem, pulling it up to reveal a lavender lace G-string and matching garter belt.

"Katrina, would you mind bringing me my motorcycle gloves?" Deleen asked me, her voice unreadable except for the power in it, the command. "They're on the table in the entryway."

I looked at Angel to see if I should, but all she said was, "Go ahead, Kit-Kat. It's Del's party."

When I stood up, Deleen added, "Oh, and get me some lube, too, won't you? It's in the bathroom cabinet—the one in the hall." My heart racing, I left the room, gathered the tube of gel and the leather gloves, and walked back to Deleen, who still held the upended Ellis over her knees.

"Thanks, sweetheart," Deleen said as I handed her the items. I turned to sit down next to my Mistress again, feeling weak and confused. Angel pulled me to her, positioning me between her legs so that I could feel the wetness that pulsed through her jeans.

Deleen slipped Ellis's G-string down her thighs, but left the garter and hose in place.

"Better calm down, Ellis." her voice was hypnotic, and I realized suddenly that everyone in the room had turned to see what was going on. Sara and Arianna, after struggling into semi-upright positions, were watching intently. Liz and Beauty, who'd been up to something on their own plush sofa, were now mellowly regarding Ellis, Beauty softly explaining to Liz how Ellis and Del's relationship worked. I heard Beauty say, "Don't worry, Lizzie, it's just how it is."

Deleen had her worn leather gloves on, and she squeezed a generous supply of the jelly onto one finger and then spread Ellis's asscheeks with the other hand. Ellis continued to fight, but her slight frame was no match for Deleen's more powerful build.

"I said, 'Calm down,' Ellis."

Although Deleen hadn't raised her voice, there was a note of danger in it, one that made me sure that if I were in Ellis's position, I would be still. Ellis must have sensed it, too, for she was suddenly quiet, yet I could tell her muscles were tensed to escape if Deleen would give her the chance.

"Ellis wants to come," Deleen said, addressing the rest of us as a group for the first time. "She has an insatiable appetite." As she spoke, she worked the lube around and into Ellis's asshole. When she slipped a gloved finger inside her naughty lover, Ellis started to protest again. Deleen put her lips close to Ellis's ear, but we all heard her hiss, "Once more, baby, and I'll get the studded gloves."

Now Deleen had two fingers inside her, and moved them in and out with increasing speed. She used her thumb on Ellis's clitoris, and Ellis moaned, an obvious sound of pleasure that set off titters from Liz and Sara.

"Like that, don't you?" my Mistress whispered to me, and I nodded, leaning against her, feeling the hard synthetic cock that she was packing beneath the soft denim. Angel put both arms around me, protectively, as we continued to watch Deleen's progress with Ellis. Del was making her come slowly—bringing Ellis close to climax, then teasing her down. When she'd forced three fingers into Ellis's asshole, Ellis started to move against her

Mistress, fucking Deleen's gloved hand, working her body on it, but Del would have none of that.

"Ellis, don't," she said, a warning in her voice. It was obvious that Deleen did not want her lover to take any form of control, and I could tell that it took every ounce of Ellis's strength for her to follow this command.

"I'll make you come in my own sweet time," Deleen promised, before turning her attention to me. "Katrina? Ellis was…" she cleared her throat before saying, "*riding* your property. Would you like to be the one to punish her?" She paused to look at me before continuing, "Because as soon as she comes, she's going to need to be disciplined."

The blood drained from my cheeks, and I turned immediately to Angel for help, but my Mistress shook her head, leaving the decision up to me, *testing* me, I thought. Flashes of conversations with Melanie replayed themselves in my head. "Leather," she'd said, "Bondage and dominance. Sex games. Wild, wild parties."

"I couldn't," I whispered.

"Another time," Deleen said, letting me off with a reassuring smile. Then, in a completely different voice, a darker voice: "Did you hear me, Ellis? You'd better try to slow it down, because I'm going to spank your little bottom as soon as you come."

Ellis started crying, and I knew it was because she was close to orgasm. And that, humiliating though it might be to come in front of everyone, being spanked would be worse. Deleen continued finger-fucking her asshole and stroking her clit. I noticed how gently she stroked Ellis there, and understood that Beauty was right, that despite what Deleen had said, this was a game, with Ellis a willing player.

And then, with everyone's attention focused on her, Ellis flushed, closed her eyes tightly and let her body finally respond to Deleen's attention. She arched her back, tense with concentration, and came in a series of powerful shivers, electricity running through her body.

The roomed seemed lit by her energy, a shower of metallic sparks, alien green and copper, vibrating in the air. She was truly stripped, as if Deleen had peeled her layer by layer, leaving a nude and shimmering soul for us to see.

How awesome it must feel to be that free.

CLOTHES MAKE
THE MAN

Emilie Paris

Dress yourself up for me," Cameron said on Monday night.
"You know what I like, Charlotte."

I did of course. After nearly a year together, I know exactly
what turns on my man.

I have high-class tastes. That's the way I like to put it. My
boyfriend says I bask in the lap of luxury. But when he says
that, all thoughts of diamonds and expensive footwear disap-
pear from my mind. Because even if I do like to doll myself up
like some Parisian runway model, the lap Cameron's referring
to is his own.

I looked at the clothes in my closet, the fur-trimmed
cardigan, the red-soled heels, and all I could see was me over
Cameron's lap, my panty-clad ass in the air, my stockinged feet
kicking.

"I'm waiting," Cameron said in a tone of voice that let me
know he wouldn't wait for very much longer. He was sitting
behind me on the edge of the bed. I could feel his eyes on me.
At the moment, I only had on a pair of scarlet knickers and a

matching satin bra. If I wasn't careful, he'd start before I was ready. And satin doesn't offer much protection when a spanking's on the menu.

The clothes blurred in front of my eyes. I keep my closet in color-coded order, from midnight on the left through all the rainbow colors, ending with pristine white on the right. But nothing called out to me. Nothing screamed *spanking*.

"Charlotte..." his tone was growing more menacing by the second.

Frantic, I stuck my hand into the closet and reached for the first thing my fingers landed on. I had to laugh as I pulled out the hanger. I'd chosen a navy-blue suit, formfitting, but cut in a man's style. I turned around and held the outfit in front of me. Cameron's lips curled in a half smile.

"Wasn't exactly what I was thinking."

"I know."

When he has spanking on the brain, he generally likes to see me in something more schoolgirl kicky. A little plaid skirt or a navy-blue jumper. High-heeled Mary Janes and white kneesocks.

"But we could make that work," Cameron continued.

He left the room while I got dressed, giving me privacy. I worked as fast as I could. Nearly in a trance, I began to set the stage. I lit rows of candles on the windowsill and on the edge of the dresser. I dragged the heavy-backed chair to the center of the room, my fingers on the leather, my heart starting to pound. I wanted to be over Cameron's lap already, wanted to be experiencing the scene in which I was so deeply entrenched. But anticipation is an important part of our games. Absence doesn't necessarily make the heart grow fonder, but waiting definitely makes my pussy pulse.

Then I got dressed. Crisp white shirt. The navy suit. A red tie. Black Oxford-style shoes. I caught a glimpse of myself in the mirror over our dresser, and then (at the very last minute, hearing Cameron's steps out in the hallway), I had an idea.

"Wait..." I called out.

His footsteps halted. I could imagine him standing outside the door.

"I'll tell you when I'm ready."

I could feel him there, interest piqued, cock hard. I went to my dresser and pulled out a toy, fixed the rest of the scene, then opened the door.

"Bad girl," he said softly, "making me wait."

"Bad boy," I responded, just as soft, watching as Cameron tilted his head at me. I saw confusion in his deep-blue eyes, and I acted immediately. Before he could grab me, before he could say a word, I sat down in the leather chair. "Bend over, baby," I said, patting my thighs. "Time for your spanking."

"Charlotte..."

"Don't make me ask twice."

How many times had he spoken to me like that? How many ways had I found myself positioned for his firm hand, or his leather belt, or his paddle? Why had I never thought to respond in kind? What had the suit brought out in me?

Of course, Cameron didn't have to obey. He could have told me to get my ass out of the chair. He could have refused to take even one step forward. But he didn't. Instead, he walked toward me and bent himself over my lap.

I grinned to myself. I couldn't believe the rush of power that flared through me. Without hesitation, I slapped my hand against his ass. I knew I hadn't hurt him. My palm met the resistance of his blue jeans, and I know from many past experiences that a hand spanking through denim doesn't do much harm. But I wanted to see how far he'd let me go.

I smacked him again, and then I said, "Stand up and take down those jeans."

When he stood, I saw the look in his eyes, a look I recognized from so many times seeing the same expression in the mirror. He was loving this. He was needing it.

Cameron pulled down his jeans and bent back over my lap. He even raised his hips, begging with his body for me to continue.

I smacked my hand against his boxers, and I could feel how hard his cock was. I gave him five strokes like this before pulling the waistband of those striped boxers down to his thighs. Now, I took a moment to admire his naked ass. God, he has a beautiful body. I thought of how many times he's admired my curves from the same position of power. Then I let my hand land on his bare skin. The rush of pleasure was amazing. My palm meeting his naked ass sent an electrifying jolt through my whole body. Why had we never done this before? Why had we never even tried?

I spanked him over and over, delighting in the handprint-shaped marks I was leaving on his previously pale skin. Cameron took the spanking like a pro. He didn't squirm. He didn't beg. He didn't make any sound at all. But I could feel his cock against my thigh, and I knew he was turned on. Maybe he was as surprised as I was by this new facet of our relationship. Maybe he was stunned into silence.

I wanted to help him make noise.

Deftly, I reached behind the chair and gripped the paddle from the floor. The one I'd hidden right before he walked in the door. I didn't tell him to steel himself. I didn't warn him what was coming. I simply slapped that glossy weapon against his ass and waited for his response.

The tremor that ran through him was immediate and intense. But he didn't tell me to stop and he didn't try to get up. That gave me all the information I craved. I spanked him again and again. Each time I let the paddle land on his naked ass, I imagined what the pain was like for me, when I was in a similar submissive position. My pussy grew wetter with every blow, and I could tell that Cameron was growing even harder. His cock was a solid pole against my leg.

"Such a bad boy," I murmured. "Getting hard from a spanking. Clearly, it's been far too long since your last punishment."

Who knew I could talk like that? That there were words like those in my head, words that came easily to my tongue? I'd never even fantasized about a scenario like this one, and yet disciplining Cameron felt surprisingly natural.

I heated his ass good and proper for him, and when I was right on the verge of coming from the thrill alone, I pushed him off my lap. Cameron stared up at me, waiting. He looked like a puppy dog, his golden hair messy, his cheeks flushed. Sure, I understood what he wanted. I'd taken the front seat. He expected me to drive us to the finish line.

Quickly, I kicked off my shoes, then unzipped my slacks and pulled them off along with my knickers. I positioned myself on the edge of the bed, my thighs spread wide.

"Eat me," I told him, and he crawled forward immediately, kicking off his jeans and boxers, so that he was now half-naked, wearing only his white T-shirt. Pressing his face to the split of my body, licking my clit in delicious, dreamy circles.

Oh god that felt good. I leaned back on my arms and pushed my pussy right into his handsome face. I locked my legs around him, holding him as close as I possibly could. And then I let myself come. Bucking hard against his lips and tongue. Taking every last bit of pleasure from the ministrations of his mouth.

I couldn't remember ever coming so quickly, but spanking him had brought me right up to the brink.

When I was done, I looked down at Cameron. His lips shone with my juices, and his eyes had that hungry glow in them. He wanted his own release. I wasn't ready to let him get there yet.

"On the bed," I told him, as I slipped my slacks back on, naked now underneath them. Cameron looked horrified. I think he believed I was going to let him fuck me. But we weren't there yet. We weren't even close.

While he spread himself out on the bed, I pulled his leather belt from the loops of his discarded jeans.

"Wrong way," I told him. He was faceup on the bed. I wanted him facedown.

Meekly, humbly, my sweet boy rolled over. I could only imagine how the mattress felt against a cock so hard.

"We'll start with ten," I said, and Cameron groaned. The noise twisted something deep inside of me. I was getting to like this new partnership. The new me.

Easily, I doubled up the leather and slapped the belt against Cameron's ass. His cheeks were already rosy from the paddle. Now, I wanted to see the welts bloom. Cameron kept himself entirely still, but that wasn't enough.

"I didn't think I'd have to say," I began, "that I expect you to count."

"One," he said.

"Good try. We're going to call the first one a practice blow." I struck him again.

This time, when he said, "One," I said, "Now, ask me for another."

There was silence from the bed. He didn't want to ask. But from the way his hips were shifting on the mattress, I could tell he craved more pain.

"Ask me, Cameron, or I'll put a ball gag in your mouth, and then *I'll* determine exactly how many strokes you'll take. Let me warn you that what you think *you* can take and what *I* think you can take may be wildly differing numbers."

"May I please have another?" he murmured.

"Louder."

"May I please have another?"

I hit him again.

"Two," he said, and then, without being prompted this time, "May I please have another?"

"Mistress."

Silence.

"Ball gag," I threatened.

"May I please have another, Mistress?"

I hit him a third time. This was fun. I could do it all night. Together, we made our way up to ten, and then I saw Cameron's body relax. He thought we were done. He thought he'd made it to the end.

"Did I tell you to stop asking?"

"But..."

"Did I tell you to stop asking?"

"You said..."

God, he was slower than I'd thought.

"Did I tell you to stop asking?"

A deep sigh, then, "May I have another, Mistress?"

I hit him fiercely. He didn't hesitate to say, "Eleven. May I please have another, Mistress?"

We went to twenty. So that his ass was crisscrossed with plum-colored lines from the belt. I don't think I'd ever seen something so beautiful before. I'd created those lines. I'd done this to him. I'd given him something he needed.

I made sure the last stroke hurt. He cried out, for the first time, and then I knew he was done.

"Roll over."

Grateful, with tears in his eyes, Cameron rolled over on the bed. His cock was hard, and my pussy was so wet.

Quickly, I stripped off my clothes once more—all of them— the suit jacket, white shirt, slacks. I was me once more when I climbed onto the bed, and Cameron seemed to know that. He gripped my hips and pulled me down onto him, and then he let me ride him. I fucked him as hard as I could, swiveling my body, getting his cock so deep inside of me, then pushing up with my thighs before sliding down once more.

At least, I was almost me. A remnant of the Mistress side remained.

"Next time," I said, "I'm going to get a strap-on. Next time, I'm going to be the one who fucks you."

"Oh Jesus."

"You'd like that, wouldn't you, Cam? You'd like me to split apart your asscheeks, pour on some lube and fuck the daylights out of you."

"God, yes."

Cameron didn't seem to even feel the pain from his recent

whipping. He drove up inside me with such fierce force, and when he came, I came with him, reaching down to touch my clit as the shivering pleasure flickered through us both.

Afterward, Cameron pulled out of me, and then held me in his arms. He seemed to want to know that I was his girlfriend once more. That I'd shed my skin. That we were equals. Partners. He stroked my hair from my face, kissed my lips, kissed my palms and my wrists.

"How'd you know?" he asked softly.

"I didn't."

"Then what made you do that?"

"I don't know."

His mouth to my ear, his voice a whisper: "Will you do that again?"

"Whenever you need," I told him. "Whenever you want."

"But how will you know?"

I smiled at him and looked down at the crumpled suit on the floor. "You just leave my suit on the bed," I said. "I'll do the rest. Because you know what they say? Clothes make the man..."

KILLING THE MARABOU SLIPPERS

Molly Laster

They looked like any other innocent pair of bedroom slippers. But maybe they weren't quite so innocent. Maybe they knew what they were doing all along. You've seen the type—smug in their open-toedness. Willful in their daring high-heeled glory. Decadently trimmed with a bit of tender white marabou fluff on the front, just to get your attention.

I'd never owned shoes like these before. Sure, I'd seen versions of them in lingerie catalogs, insolently positioned with toe toward the camera, daring the casual peruser to purchase them. And I'd even drooled over such fantasy footwear when worn by my favorite forties screen stars. But those women had the clothes to go with the shoes—angel-sleeved nightgowns with three-foot trains, tight satin slips with plunging necklines. Such sexy slippers weren't meant for someone like me—a girl who owns plain white bra and panty sets, who wears gray sweats to bed, whose one experience with a pair of black fishnets was a comedic disaster. What purpose could a pair of wayward shoes like these possibly have?

Still, when I caught sight of the immoral mules at a panty sale in San Francisco, I bought them. Even though they were a size eight and I'm a size six. Even though I found the very sight of them fairly wicked. Even though my own bedroom slippers at home were made of plaid flannel and had been chewed on repeatedly by my golden retriever puppy.

I simply thought Lucas would like them.

He did.

"I'm gonna fuck those shoes," he said when I pulled them from the silver Mylar bag. "Sweetheart, those shoes are history."

I'd never seen him react like that to anything. My tall, handsome, green-eyed husband has a healthy libido. I definitely get my share of bedroom romping time. But as far as kinkiness goes, he has always appeared positively fetish free. No requests for handcuffs. No need for teddies or "special" outfits to get him in the mood. No urgent trips to the grocery store at midnight for whipped cream, chocolate sauce and maraschino cherries.

"Put them on," Lucas hissed. "Now."

I kicked off my patent leather penny-loafers, pulled off my black stockings, and slid into the marabou mules. The white bit of fluff on the toes made the shoes look like some sort of pastry, a fantasy confection created just for feet. My red toenails peeked through the opening. *Dirty*, I thought. *Indecent.*

Lucas got on the floor and kissed my exposed toes, stroked the soft feathery tips of the shoes, then stood and quickly shed his outfit.

"They're bad," he said excitedly, positioning himself over my feet as if preparing to do push-ups. He's ex-military and has excellent formation for this activity—his body becomes stiff and board-like. The sleek muscles in his back shift becomingly under his tan skin. In this position, his straining cock went directly between the two mules.

"Oh, man," he whispered. "So bad they're good."

He went up and down over my shoes, digging his cock between them, dragging it over the marabou trim, sighing with delight when the feathers got between his legs. I could only imagine how those pale white feathers tickled his most sensitive organ.

"They're so soft," he murmured.

I'd been staring down at him, at his fine ass—clenching with each depraved push-up—at his strong back, the muscles rippling. Now, I looked straight ahead, into the full-length mirror across the room, taking in the total effect of our afternoon of debauchery.

I was fully dressed: long black skirt, black mock turtleneck, my dark hair in a refined ponytail, small spectacles in place. If you ended the reflection at my shins, you might have placed me for exactly what I am, an editor at a tech company. Below my shins, however, was Lucas, doing ungodly push-ups over my brand-new shoes. My slim ankles were bare, feet sliding slightly in the too-big marabou-trimmed mules. If you disregarded the shoes, and imagined Lucas moving in stop-frame animation, he might have been culled from a series of Muybridge pictures. But with the shoes in place, and with Lucas's body moving rigidly up and down, this picture looked more like something from a fantastic pornographic movie.

I stared at our images and felt myself growing more and more aroused. My plain white panties were suddenly too containing. My skirt and sweater needed to come off. Arousal rushed through me in a shuddering wave. But I kept my peace—this wasn't my fantasy, wasn't my moment. It was Lucas's. All his.

He began speaking louder, first lauding the shoes, "Sweet, so sweet." Then criticizing the slippers as he slammed between them, "Oh, you're bad...bad."

I stayed as still as possible, watching in awe as Lucas, approaching his limit, arched up and sat back on his heels, his hand working his cock in double-time. Small bits of pure white feathers were stuck to the sticky tip of his swollen penis. More feather fluffs floated in the air around us.

"Give me one of the shoes," he demanded, and I kicked off

the right slipper. One hand still wrapped around his cock, he used the other to lift the discarded shoe and began rubbing the tip of it between his legs, moaning and sighing, his words no longer legible, no longer necessary. Then, suddenly, as if inspiration had hit him, he reached behind his body with the shoe, poking the heel of it between the cheeks of his ass, impaling himself with the slipper while he dragged the tip of his cock against the shoe I still wore.

I watched closely as his breathing caught, as he leaned back farther still and then came, ejaculating on the slipper before him, coating those naughty feathers with semen, matting the feathers into a sticky mess. Showing them once and for all who was boss.

When he had relaxed enough to speak, he looked up at me, a sheepish expression on his face. "Told you those shoes were history," he said, red cheeked. Embarrassed. "Told you, baby, didn't I?"

I just nodded, thinking: The death of an innocent pair of marabou slippers. What'd the shoes ever do to Lucas? Nothing but exist.

NOBODY'S BUSINESS

C. Thompson

I gotta admit it. I have this thing for ass-fucking. Am I a pervert? Maybe. But I don't care. If it works for me and my lover, then it's nobody else's business, right? Don't ask, don't tell—you know what I'm saying? The truth is, I appreciate every part of the equation, from checking out a pair of well-packed jeans, to revealing the naked haunches of a new lover, to slip-sliding my tool inside that tightest of entryways. I collect experiences, returning to my favorites over and over again in my mind. These images are better than fantasies, because they're real.

The summer after graduating college, I had an "ass fling" with a beautiful girl. From the first time I saw her, I knew we were going to fuck, and do it the way I like—hard and raw, skin connecting with skin. Charlene was twenty-four, built slender but with corded muscles. Her golden hair fell forward over a sun-kissed face. Light played tricks in her eyes, turning them gray one instant and pure silver the next. She shined, no question about it. She had an innocent quality that drew people to her.

And she had an ass that made me dizzy.

Whenever she wore her tight, faded jeans, I would lose myself in instant daydreams starring her tied down to my bed and me wielding my mammoth hard-on. I wanted to fuck her, but I also wanted to watch her being fucked, to see her face grow flushed, her eyes shut tight with the confusion a pleasure that decadent would bring. I had visions of slipping off her well-worn jeans, of oiling up her asshole with my spit and ravaging her from behind.

Charlene worked in an office building that houses the record company that produces my band. She served coffee and sweets in the downstairs café. You might not put us together naturally. I'm all Hollywood rock 'n' roll. Tall, tattooed and thin, with dark hair and shadowy eyes. I wear a standard uniform of black jeans and black T-shirts every day of the year, and I pull my long hair off my face into a ponytail unless I'm playing. Then I let it loose and wild, to whip around me as I move. And while Charlene's skin is bronzed from healthy weekends spent outdoors, I'm as pale as they come from long days spent in cave-like clubs rehearsing and performing. Yet we fit together, fit like pieces in a fantasy puzzle, my cock buried to the hilt in her perfect ass, shame coloring her cheeks an electric rose.

Every single time I went into the café, I sent her silent messages with my eyes. I'd buy a nectarine from the basket on the counter, and while she rang it up, I'd think about squeezing the ripe fruit in my hands until it dripped sticky sap on her body. My eyes flickered with images of lubing her asshole with the flesh from a melon, of pulling down my jeans and fucking her. Just fucking her.

Of course, I've been fucked this way, myself. I'm not one to dish out what I can't take. My introduction to the world of anal delights is clear in my memory. Not only do I possess a mental movie of that night, I remember the soundtrack, the words spoken, as well. My college girlfriend liked to talk while we fucked. Whenever we messed around, Veronica kept up a running monologue, telling me what she was going to do a split second ahead of time. She liked me because I'm the strong, silent type. I let her ramble, got into the melody of it, grooved on the sound of her voice.

On the night of my first ass-fucking, she asked for permission first. "Really?" I said. "You'd like that?" Yeah, I knew she was edgier than most of the coeds I knew, but this managed to surprise even me.

She was alive with nervous energy, moving too quickly around the room, gathering her toys, her implements, promising me that I'd love every minute. Curiosity piqued, I let her bend me over the green comforter on her bed, and I waited as she got her strap-on cock wet with lube. Then she pressed her lips to my ear and hissed, "Kelly, I'm gonna take your back door."

Honestly, I wasn't sure how to feel about this. But deep down, I wanted to know what it would be like. And Veronica understood this. She wrapped her arms around me and slid the head of her cock between my asscheeks. As she pressed forward slowly, she said, "Relax, baby, let me in." I took a deep breath, feeling the bulging head of her cock pushing forward, and I clenched. I couldn't help it. My entire body tensed so tightly I felt as if my muscles were on lockdown.

Veronica knew exactly what to do. She wrapped one fist around my cock and pumped up and down. Then she started in with what she did best: talking. Her voice was soothing. "This turns you on so much, Kelly, just the thought of it. Look at how hard your cock is. Now you've gotta open up for me."

My body would not obey. For a moment, Veronica didn't move. The head of her plastic cock and the first inch of the shaft were between my asscheeks, but she remained entirely still. Then, slowly, she began to rub back and forth, not pushing toward my entrance, but sort of tickling me with her toy. I liked that feeling, and I sighed and then moaned. At my response, she picked up the pace, pushing more of the shaft between my cheeks, still working my cock with her magic hand.

She said, "You're rock hard, Kelly. You don't know what

you want. Your brain might think it's wrong, but your body's screaming for it to happen." To prove her point, she took one of my own hands and put it between my legs, and I took over for her, working myself fiercely, feeling my climax rise. As I played, I stopped being concerned with what it all meant and started concentrating on coming.

Veronica said, "It's good being filled, right, Kelly..." and then her voice trailed off. I wasn't used to a time when my girlfriend didn't talk. She always had to tell me how good she felt or how sweet I tasted. Now, she was speechless, her faux cock pushing toward my asshole again. Then she said real quiet, "*You* talk, Kelly. Tell me how it feels. Please—" Her voice was hoarse.

I took a deep breath, then started. "It hurts good." As I spoke, my body relaxed and let her in. "Does that make sense?"

"Sure it does, baby. Sure it does. Keep talking." Carefully, she pushed forward. The muscles of my ass squeezed her, giving her a welcoming embrace. "What are you thinking, Kelly?" she asked next. "Paint a picture for me."

I closed my eyes. I wasn't sure at first *what* I was feeling. But then, in my head, I suddenly saw the act in reverse. I started describing my fantasy to Veronica. "That's my cock you're riding," I told her through gritted teeth, "I'm fucking you." I dug my body back into hers, ramming her cock all the way into me. "It feels good, doesn't it, Veronica? Being fucked like this..."

Her body was frozen.

I was doing all the work, bouncing on her cock, keeping her inside me, connecting me to her so that it was difficult to tell where one of us ended and the other began. "Can you feel me inside you?" I asked her. "Can you feel my cock in your ass?"

It was an illuminating moment for me, seeing this different view, and I came from the image, slowing my rocking motion on her pole, shooting all over the bed. She followed quickly, shuddering as she climaxed, then staying joined to me for a long time. Even after she'd pulled out, we held each other, our bodies entwined on the sofa, neither one of us saying a word.

That was my introduction to the beauty of back-door romping, and it was the beginning of a new era in sexual variations for me. With this new era came new power. I started to look for girlfriends who would like what I liked. I would get a sense about them, a feel for the type of energy they gave off. It got so I could go into a club and spot the chicklet I would take home.

And then I saw Charlene. She wasn't an easy mark because she didn't know she wanted what I had to give. But once I decided on her, I turned my attention toward the pursuit. I visited the café more often than usual, on days when I didn't even have a meeting with my producer. I sat at a table with a book, and I surreptitiously stared at the blonde-haired angel behind the counter.

It took about a week before she smiled back at me, almost a month before we were meeting behind the café on her breaks, pressing each other up against the stucco wall of our building.

I worked slowly. I didn't want to scare her off. I have a pretty good sense for people, and I got the feeling that she'd never been taken the way I wanted to take her, that she'd never been pinned down on a bed and fucked from behind. I wanted to seduce her, to plant the idea in her head and make it her fantasy. And then make her fantasy come true.

During our midday meetings, I stroked her pussy through her ripped-up jeans. I French-kissed her, leaning my body against hers, devouring her mouth, drinking in her scent. I made her come inside of her jeans, the crotch all drippy wet with nectar. I made her look into my eyes and say, "What're you doing to me, Kelly?" her lips curving into an embarrassed grin, "You're driving me crazy, you know it?"

I planned on driving her crazier still.

"I want you here," I said, reaching my hands around to cup her sweet asscheeks in her jeans. "I want to fuck you there—"

She tilted her head up to look at me, but she didn't speak.

"You want that, too, don't you, baby?

And she nodded. It was all the encouragement I needed.

When I first took her ass, it happened on top of a desk in my producer's office. He gave me the key, and then disappeared, as I'd requested. As planned, Charlene met me after she got off of work. I locked the door and stripped off my jeans. Charlene stared as I slid my boxers off, then sat down on the edge of the desk. I took her hand and put it around my cock. I let her feel it and then I put my hands on the back of her neck and pushed down so that she bent close to my tool.

She parted her lips and took the head of my cock into her mouth as I ran my fingers through her hair. "That's it," I whispered, "that's right, get it nice and wet for me. You know where it's going."

I wanted her to feel the way *I* had my first time. I wanted this to be an eye-opening experience. I let her suckle me, get the head of the cock and then the shaft lubricated with her spit. Then I pushed her back and ran my fingers up and down my cock, stroking it, rough-handling it. Charlene leaned back, watching me. She had her hands on the buckle of her belt, but she hesitated. I knew what she needed, and I gave it to her.

"Take your pants down, Charlie," I said. "You don't have to take them all the way off, just take them down to your knees."

She'd never moved so quickly before.

"Now, bend over my desk." I stood and watched as she bent over, gripping the side of the wood with both hands. She trembled, and then ducked her head. She wouldn't meet my eyes. I moved behind her, rested my cock against her naked ass, and brought my arms around her.

"Feel that?" I asked softly, "Feel it pressing against you?"

She nodded.

"I'm going to put the whole thing inside you," I said, never raising my tone. "It's gonna slide right inside your tight, virgin asshole and it's gonna feel so good it will seem unreal."

She shuddered again, then looked over her shoulder at me. I was glad we were here, in a neutral zone. If we'd been at my place, I would have wanted to tie her down. But this was better, watching her hold herself as still as she could. This was much more my speed.

"It's okay, Charlie," I told her. "We'll go nice and slow."

She seemed to relax when I said that, so I took it as the opportune time to get out my lube, slick up my rod, and slide it between her dimpled asscheeks. She sucked in her breath, then let it out in a rush. I didn't enter her, just pressed against her asshole, rocking back and forth to let her get used to the feeling. I dropped one hand in front of her and began to play with her dripping pussy, getting her nice and wet there.

When I felt the first contractions of her cunt, I drove the head of my rod into her ass. She jumped at the intrusion, then settled herself, her arms gone rigid and her knuckles white. I said, "You do it, Charlie. You work yourself back on me, taking it in at your own pace." I didn't stop tugging at her clit, but I let her decide how she wanted to play.

I could tell that she didn't think she could do it. My fucking her was one thing, but her fucking herself with my cock was something else entirely. But finally, and slowly, she pushed back on me. She took a bit more of the shaft inside, adjusted to it, and pushed again. She moaned and pressed back more, getting daring, taking it in to the hilt and then rocking on it. Then she said, "Now *you*. I can handle it now, you do it."

Music to my ears. I gripped into her shoulders and started what I do best, fucking her rhythmically. Not too hard or too fast, but hard and fast enough. I talked softly to her while my hips slid forward until our bodies were pressed together. I said, "That's it, that's the girl, you touch yourself," and I felt the muscles in her right arm jerk to life as she began stroking her clit.

I learned from the way she moved, and I began working to the beat she needed, matching her thrust for stroke. Her fingers went in and out of her cunt and my cock went in and out of her rear door. I never let the head slip out, but the shaft did the trick, stimulating places she'd never known about, building in both speed and intensity when I could tell she was about to come.

She climaxed before she knew what was happening. Lost in a double world, her hand bringing her the normal pleasure that she was well used to, my cock fulfilling her darkest, unspoken dreams.

I held her, still inside her, and then slowly pulled out. She was flustered, couldn't figure out what to do next. When she turned around, I put my hand under her chin and made her lift her gaze to mine. I said, "Don't be embarrassed, Charlie. I wanted to do that from the moment I met you."

That made her grin, and confess to me something I would never have guessed. She said, "I've wanted that, too, Kelly, I wanted that, too."

Everyone has a plan. Everyone has an agenda. I was so busy with mine that I never stopped to consider the fact that she might have one of her own.

ON FIRE

Sarah Clark

'm in love with a firefighter. She works at the station across the
street from my apartment building, and I sit on my fire escape
and watch her wash the truck. She's well built, showing off her
biceps in a white tank top, wearing faded jeans that hug her
hips and reveal her taut physique. Her muscles are alive beneath
her skin, seeming to dance whenever she moves. Sometimes,
when she's finished, she stands beneath the spray of the hose
after rinsing the truck. I can barely watch that, the revelation
of a perfect body in those drenched clothes. The dream turned
reality as her jeans get tighter on her thighs and ass. My firefighter has an ass that is what an ass lies awake at night and
dreams about being.

When I first took my apartment, the landlady warned me
about the location. She said, "You'll hear sirens all the time.
Night and day. Will that bother you?" The window was open,
and I went to it and looked out.

The previous tenants had left the window box filled with pale
pink baby roses. I drank in their heady fragrance as I looked

at the station below. My first vision of my firefighter is petal-scented. I saw the bright red truck. I saw the magnolia tree in blossom on the corner. And I saw her. Five or six other firefighters moved around the gleaming truck, but I couldn't tell you what they looked like. They were merely bit players, while she was the star of my fantasies.

My firefighter has golden skin and blue eyes. Her black hair is straight and glossy. She usually keeps it short, but now it's getting a little bit long in the front. She has to push it out of her eyes sometimes. I imagine doing the job for her, running my fingers through that midnight hair, staring into her sky-blue eyes before bringing my mouth to hers. She has full lips— lips to be licked, to be bitten at the tail end of a long, steamy French kiss.

"Will the sirens be a problem?" the landlady asked again, moving closer to me and speaking slightly louder as if I were hard of hearing.

I shook my head no, then explained that I'm an insomniac. I work nights at a twenty-four-hour café, serving coffee and breakfast to truckers at 2:00 a.m. I drink enough java myself that I stay up half the day, only crashing for a few hours in the middle of the afternoon.

Mornings, I reserve for watching her. I slip out of my starched pink uniform with the white piping, change into cutoffs and a T-shirt, slick back my short blonde hair and then wait for her to appear outside. Wait for her to look up and see me. She's not there every day, but I sit and wait anyway, rolling movies in my mind from previous visions of her, images that I now own.

I've choreographed what it would be like to meet her. In some versions, I call out, offering her a cool glass of lemonade, bringing it downstairs and across the street. Often, in these fantasies, I'm naked beneath my short white robe, and I let the neck of the robe slip open as I hand her the glass. She takes the lemonade from me, then fishes out an ice cube and runs it, sticky and sweet, along my collarbone, down the flat line between my ribs. The cube grows smaller as it makes its way along the shallow of my belly.

I have a tattoo of a butterfly below the indent of my waist. I know that she would trace the ice along the outline of my butterfly's wings, that my tattoo would shimmer under the wet coating and seem to come to life.

We've had a long, hot summer, and I easily visualize the ice cube melting on its way to meet my pussy, trailing translucent lemon-scented water down my body. I can picture my firefighter on her knees on the blazing hot cement, parting my nether lips and thrusting the chip of ice deep inside me, then sealing her mouth to my pussy and sucking the drops of moisture as they drip free.

I find myself with one hand on the seam of my frayed denim shorts as I watch her. Almost unaware of my own actions, I place my palm against the split of my body, cupping myself and rocking back and forth on this fulcrum. Wanting *more*, as I watch her muscles shift and glide with the effort of her work. Wanting her to lift me up on that engine, bind me to one of the ladders, hose me down with a spray of water.

At the diner, during the 4:00 a.m. slump when I have only two or three customers in my section, I find myself thinking about her. I wonder where she goes when she's not at the station. I've caught glimpses. I saw her biking along the beach early one Sunday morning when I was walking home from work. I'd stopped on the walkway to look at the houses below, the millionaire homes that face the water. They have hidden gardens behind tall fences, but you can see inside when you're on the cliffs.

My firefighter was biking along the path, her head down, dark hair falling over tanned forehead, legs pumping piston-fast as she rode. I wished I had my bike to follow her, wished I was down below with her, rather than observing, as always, from above.

I fantasized about standing at the side of the bike path, of her looking up and seeing me, stopping, getting off her bike. I could picture her taking my hand and walking with me in the sand, toward the sea. Neither of us caring about the lacy edge of foam licking up at our feet. Walking farther into the water, drenching our clothes, meeting and melting in an embrace as the silver waves washed in around us.

My fantasies easily changed, like dreams, and in the water our clothes were suddenly gone. She moved forward, pressing into me, her lips on the hollow of my throat, her kisses burning hot, setting me ablaze while the cool waves lapped at our skin. I knew the taste of her lips, salty from the ocean breeze, sweet because they're hers. I knew the feel of her body as it pressed against me. I knew that when she gripped my arms and stared into my green eyes she'd feel complete. Wanted.

After months, I learn her name. One of the other firefighters calls out to her, "Hey, Kendra…" And now, I have something further to use in my fantasies, a new ingredient to stir things up.

I whisper her name as my fingers find their secret place between my legs and make those magic, mystic circles. My head back on my pillows, my slender hips arched forward toward a dream lover, I say her name aloud, "Kendra, please…," feeling her hands on me, stroking my body, starting a bonfire within me by keeping me on edge. She doesn't give me what I want, not at first. She teases me, holding her body well above mine, taunting me with her lips instead, giving me long, luscious kisses. My mouth is open, hungry. I feel her breath, feel her lips on mine. She props herself up, using those fine muscles in her arms, not letting skin touch skin.

It's hot outside. It's hotter in my bed.

"Please, Kendra…" My voice is louder now, but I don't care. It's midmorning, the rest of my neighbors have gone to work. I'm ready for sleep, and this is one of the ways I know to bring it. Climaxing and sliding into a dream world, in which Kendra is featured as my one true love. But I can't come, regardless of my knowledgeable fingers, of my chanting her name. I stand, wrap my silk robe around my body and make my way to the fire escape.

She's below, washing the truck with three other firefighters.

Her hair is off her face, her body is hard and lean in faded jeans and a tank. Her buddy pokes her and she suddenly looks up at me. I feel the heat of her eyes on mine. I run my fingers through my platinum hair. I start to flush. She calls out, "Where were you? Usually you're waiting for us…"

My cheeks are crimson. She's seen me. She knows. I practically stutter, starting to say something, but having no idea what. Mid-thought, I change my mind. "Would you like some lemonade?"

She grins at me. It drives me wild, changes her face from one of mastery and art, the lines and bones of her features shifting into a vision of tomboyish charm. Her buddy nudges her again, nodding, eyes wide, saying, "Go on…go on…" Can't hear her, but I get the meaning. Kendra sets down the soapy sponge, wipes her hands on her thighs, waits for a break in traffic, and crosses the street. She looks up at me. I forget what I'm supposed to do, until she says, "Are you going to buzz me in?"

I nod, rush inside, hit the buzzer, then open the door and stand on the landing. She takes the stairs two at a time. She must, because she's in front of me in seconds. Then, shyly, she stands there and looks down at me. For the first time, she is above; she is in charge. I wait. She waits.

I say, "My name's Elena."

"Kendra."

"I know."

She smiles. We continue to stand in the hallway. I feel hot, too hot. My face is flaming, my heart beating too fast. She says, "You mentioned lemonade…," and I nod and lead her into my apartment. I walk into the kitchen, my bare feet padding on the white-and-black tile floor. She strides past me to the living room and lowers the blinds on the window. "Don't need my friends keeping an eye on me."

I blush harder as I bring her a glass of lemonade. Chips of ice bob in the pale liquid. She takes the glass from my hand, sips from it, looks me over.

"I've seen you up there, on your escape," she says.

"I didn't know. You never look at me."

"I'm sly, I guess; I didn't want to stare."

She's staring now, at the opening of my robe, at the place where silk meets skin. I am so hot. I need her to cool me down. Could I say it? Could I simply describe my fantasies and let her make them real? She's a firefighter. She'd know what to do.

She says, "I've got to tell you something," then pauses as if she's not sure if she can get up the nerve.

"Please..." I say.

In a rush, "I fantasize about you all the time, Elena."

I swallow hard.

"I mean, you're so pretty, sitting up there. I've pictured you on our truck, letting me wash you with the sponge, the soapy water all over your body, rinsing you off with the soft spray, making your skin gleam in the light."

I can't take my eyes off her. She puts one hand under my chin and strokes the line of my neck with her thumb. She searches out my pulse point, the aching beat of blood through veins, and she stops talking, mesmerized by my inner rhythm.

"I've thought about you, too..."

And I tell her. I confess. About the ice, about the thrill of it on my skin, still speaking as she leads me to the bedroom, as she tilts the glass and takes a piece of ice between her lips, as she presses this frozen heaven to my cheekbones, my own lips, the hollow of my neck. Moving lower, opening my robe, carefully sliding the fabric free from my shoulders. Numbing my nipples, first one, then the other, then pinching the cold flesh as she moves the ice in a line down my belly, getting nearer, nearer.

The chip is gone before she reaches my delta of Venus. She spreads me out on the bed and brings the lemonade with her, taking another piece of ice between her lips and tracing between my breasts, down my belly, to the fluttering wings of my butterfly tattoo. The ice is gone again, but she doesn't get another piece. She uses the tip of her tongue to trace my butterfly's vibrantly colored wings. She goes around and around with her tongue on my skin, and I'm spiraling downward with each flickering touch.

She looks up at me, up the line of my body, her mouth curving into a grin, and then she takes another sip of lemonade and sets the glass on my nightstand. I look at the glass instead of her as she moves between my legs and presses her icy mouth to the outer lips of my pussy. Then the chip of ice is suddenly thrust forward and her mouth is sealed to me, drinking me in, drinking each drop of my come as it pools inside me, and finally I look at her and into her luminous eyes.

She says, "Elena," as if she's naming me, claiming me. I moan. Can't help it. The movies in my mind are playing at fast-motion, letting me see each frame a second before she makes each fantasy come true.

"We'll go slow later. We'll go slow after…"

I nod, understanding, needing it as hot and fast as she does. I've wanted this too long.

She says, "I have to be inside you."

"Yesssss…" I say, thinking, *Oh, god, she's packing.*

And her jeans are open and her cock is out and she's above my body teasing me with the head of it before plunging inside me. I'm wet, so wet, and I take her in, grabbing her with the tight muscles of my pussy. She's up on her arms above me, filling me with steady strokes, then moving her hips in small circles that send me reeling with pleasure.

She says, "You're so beautiful. You sit and watch and make me feel…I don't know…"

"Wanted…" I say. "Complete…"

She grabs me to her, turning our bodies so that we're on our sides, and she traces my cheekbones as she rocks inside of me. Her cock is strong and powerful in me. Her fingers are flames that lick my skin. I'm on fire. I'm burning up.

We kiss as we reach that point together, her rollicking rhythm taking me there, and higher, and there and back, until I'm not thinking anymore, I'm letting those vibrations wash over me, leaning my head back on the pillow as she opens her eyes and stares into mine.

Her teeth bite into her bottom lip. Her head goes back and her dark hair falls away from her face. She says my name when she comes. She says. "Elena…"

Fantasy turned reality. Movies come to life. Kendra wraps me in her arms. We fade into sleep together to the crackling sound of the ice as it melts in the glass. Our bodies are entwined, our dreams on fire.

ONE HOT SLUT

N. T. Morley

Just getting it shaved is an epic feat. If you've never tried to shave one, I don't think you can even conceive of just how many nooks and crannies they have. If you have tried to shave a pussy, and you're not with me on the idea that this is a less-than-easy task, then you're way more coordinated than me, which probably wouldn't surprise anyone who knows me.

Once I get it shaved, though, it's pretty fucking awesome: smooth and slick and sensitive. After I finish I lean up against the wall of the shower and spread my legs and get the shower massage down there and rinse…and the warm water feels so fucking good on my pussy that I alternate between that and my fingers for about ten minutes, just kind of touching myself. Not wanking—well, not exactly, though it definitely starts to feel good. My clit feels moderately more sensitive, definitely, but FUCK! It's really the rest of me that feels totally new and intense and incredible. When I touch my outer lips it's like they've never been touched before. I want your fucking tongue down there. I want you to fucking lick me till I go crazy. I want you to lick me till I come.

Which I might do any second, I realize, if I keep rubbing myself like this.

But that's just the beginning, really, because my shaved puss is not the first thing you're going to see when you come through the door. In fact, it might be quite a long while before you *do* see it, up close and personal at least, because I've already decided that as soon as you're in the door I'm going to get your pants open and suck your cock, which is why the bright red lipstick sits on the sink half opened and glistening; I was experimenting earlier. It's a deep ruby-red color, the kind a girl wears when she has absolutely no reason to wear it except to make her lips look good gliding up and down a cock, which is why I got kind of wet earlier and decided to shave my puss.

And it's shaved, and I like it. It's shaved smooth along with the rest of my body: my slim legs, my dainty pits, everything except the hair on my head—but that, too, is altered. I spent three hours in the salon earlier today. Gone is the straight dark librarian hair I've sported since high school; I'd already decided to cut it short, so I figured why not one last fling with it, and if peroxide fries it, *c'est la vie*. It didn't get fried; it actually turned out pretty good, the color of pale straw and with about three times the volume it had before. I stand nude in the bathroom and curl and spray and fluff and tease my new platinum blonde mane until it's the revenge of the '80s super-starlet. *Oh my fucking god,* I think, as I look at myself in the mirror. Naked, without makeup, I already look like one hot slut, baby, a seriously hot fucking slut for you. I look like a whore, my hair cascading everywhere and just begging to be grabbed, grabbed hard, and pulled, and my face— *Okay, no more thinking about that,* I tell myself, taking a deep breath; if I get too worked up I'm never going to bother getting dressed, and when you get here you'll find me naked on the bed—which I'm sure would be fine, but not at all what I have planned.

What I have planned involves a mesh black garter belt and fishnet stockings. What I have planned involves me wearing a tight, tiny little see-through thong that I wriggle my snatch into and settle onto my hips with the string tugging deep in my ass...but not wearing it, understand, for very long. What I have planned involves six-inch fuck-me heels that I can barely walk on, a push-up bra that turns A-cups into B-cups—look! Cleavage!—and a cheap little black choker I got at Beadland that if I play my cards right you'll get the message is supposed to look like a dog collar. What I want tonight is for you to rip off this tiny black dress, fucking *destroy* it with your hands if you want, baby, or just yank it up and use me.

What I have planned involves a great big mop of blonde hair in a teased-out fuck-me 'do that's about as classy as a truck stop blow job. What I want, tonight, is me black-eyed with eyeliner and thick-lashed with mascara, my lips pouty and bright red gliding up and down on your cock, my ass tucked high up into the air and just begging you to fuck it. You heard me. Listen to me very carefully, honey: you can put it anywhere. Because what I want doesn't just feature me with cocksucking lips, with a shaved pussy, with tits finally big enough, or kinda looking that way, for you to slide your cock between. I did intimate things with that shower massager, baby. The hot water got me nice and clean, and now I need you to make me dirty again—all over.

Tonight I'm your whore, bought and paid for and you don't even need to leave a tip. Tonight I'm your tarted-up fucking bimbo, and I want you to use me.

I should say before you get here that none of this was my idea. It started...well, I don't want to go into too much detail, because I'm honestly not mad or anything. Just kind of hurt.

It started one of those nights you worked extra-late. You know, one of the ones—it's hard to keep them separate, isn't it?—when you called me at nine to tell me you'd be home late. You've been doing that a lot, baby, and I think I've been a good sport about it. But this was a Thursday, baby; our four-year anniversary. I hope the mailman liked his new watch.

I called Jerri and Amy and they had just gotten back from a movie. They came over and we opened off a bottle of wine—yes, that's where the Paso Robles merlot went. And the Sangiovese. And the last bottle of table red.

I know you were saving that Sangiovese in particular, which is probably why I drank it.

I was kind of broken up about all the extra hours you've been working. I got majorly drunk and told them everything. By the end of it I was crying, baby, I was crying pretty hard. Don't hold it against Jerri and Amy that by the time we made it to the table wine, they thought you were a pretty big asshole. But before that was gone, they'd hatched a plan to make you putty in my hands, and it involved an expensive bleach job and some delicate work with a disposable razor. Jerri's not as innocent as she looks. In fact, she was the one lobbying for the conclusion that you're screwing around on me. Amy said she doubted it, but maybe, and I was sure you're not. There's no way you could, baby, we've shared too much; you just couldn't do that to me. You just couldn't.

It's not just that you've been working late. It's that you haven't been that interested lately. I mean, it's been over a year since you started something. I know because I keep a diary. It's been forever since you grabbed me, forever and a day since you grabbed me and fucked me, forever and forever since you grabbed me by the hair, turned me around, bent me over and spanked me and then fucked me silly. I can't even remember the last time you fucked me without being asked.

Don't get me wrong, baby, I'm not looking for attention, really. You know what I'm like; you've always known what I'm like. I don't need flowers; I don't need candy; I don't need soft romantic music and scented candles and the lights down low. I don't even need a kiss, baby. Half the time, I don't even want one. Any time you want, baby, you know—you have to know, I swear you have to know—that you're totally entitled to just grab me and do me. Don't wonder if I'm in the mood. Don't worry about making me come. Don't worry whether I'm turned on before you enter me. Don't worry about whether I'm enjoying myself. I'm telling you, don't even worry about whether you're hurting me. Hurt me, baby, fucking hurt me if it gets you going. And I'm not kidding, darling: You...can...put...it...anywhere.

One good thing about this house on Brennan Terrace, it's got a great bedroom. When we moved here from our loft downtown, on your insistence because we were going to start a family, I was reluctant because it isolated me from all my friends, from Amy and Jerri and all the others. But I liked the house because I liked the bedroom. I liked the sliding door onto the patio right from the boudoir; it felt dirty, luxurious, decadent. I thought it was a sexy bedroom; I couldn't wait to get a nice big four-poster bed in there and have you fuck me cross-eyed in it. I can't say you ever have done that, exactly...things got pretty lukewarm right about the time that we moved. But I'm still optimistic; this bedroom is going to see some action yet.

That's why I've gotten the bedroom all ready, turning it into our own little whorehouse/pleasure palace. Brand new sheets, eight-hundred thread count Egyptian cotton, bright red—scarlet like the letter that belongs on my puss. There are candles every-where—a whole box of thirty votives, scented in musk and sandalwood, and thirty new holders. On the dresser sits a silken cloth under which rest four silicone cocks of steadily increasing size, the largest one big enough to make my eyes water just looking at it—I hope you'll put that somewhere interesting, baby, I get wet just thinking about it. There's a vibrator and a black-and-silver pair of nipple clamps, with a shiny silver chain. There's more lube on the nightstand, and a box of rubber gloves and a half-dozen condoms sitting on top of a big wooden paddle in case you miss the way I'm planning to wiggle my butt against you asking for it. I've got porn playing on the twenty-four-inch bedroom TV—dirty stuff, a four-hour DVD of nasty hair-pulling anal threesomes and gangbangs, women being fucked and spanked and double-penetrated, come on their faces, come in their hair, come all over their tits. Dirty, filthy stuff, a DVD it made me kind of wet to buy in that disgusting little sleaze shop downtown by the train station. The volume's all the way down for now, but I'll be happy to turn it up when we get started. If you want, baby. If you'd like that. If that would turn you on.

I'm not playing music because soft music would be cheesy, not at all what I want—and loud, pumping, earth-pounding ass-whacking hard-core would drown out your words when you talk dirty to me as you're fucking me hard from behind. Which I very much want you to do, baby—every dirty fucking word you've ever called a girl, do it to me tonight, baby. Slut. Whore. Bitch. Yeah, baby, even that one. Say it while you fuck me. Because I deserve it, I guess, I deserve it because this isn't the first time.

No, don't get me wrong, it's the first time for a lot of this. It's the first time for the shaving, and the slutty hair, and the candles and all that. But it's not the first time I've dressed up like a slut. It's not the first time I've wanted a man to grab me and fuck me and call me names. It's not even the first time I've wanted it... there. It's not the first time I've told a man that he could put it anywhere.

I know, baby. I know I said I'd never done it. I hadn't. I hadn't done plenty of things before the affair happened. It was maybe three months ago. And I could claim it was a mistake—I could claim that if I'd done it just once. Maybe even if it had happened twice. But no...I fucked this guy seven times, baby, seven times and a couple of blow jobs in between. Plus the hand job at the office party and about ten instances of serious phone sex.

If you read my diary it'll give you every detail of what he did to me and—Oh. My. God. It was fucking amazing. You can read it if you want, baby, you can read in my diary about how good I got fucked. I'll let you. If you want. But I won't tell you who he is, even if you ask, even if you demand to know. I won't tell you, because you might go after him; you might want to hurt him or something, and I wouldn't want that. Actually, it would be kind of hot, but it wouldn't be fair. It's not his fault he fucked me so good. It's not him you should hate, baby, it's me. It's me you should want to hurt. It's me you should be calling a whore, even if I like it a little too much.

I can't say I'm proud of it, baby; I'm not proud of cheating on you. The guilt's been consuming me. But I didn't know what else to do. He was there, he was hot, and he wanted me. He wanted me bad enough to do things to me I'd never been able to ask for with you.

I think it was a good thing for us, baby, I think I learned about myself. I think it'll be a net positive, if you can forgive me. If we can get past it. In the long term.

That's why I'm dressing up for you. I feel like a slut, and I want to be a slut—for you. I'm going to give you everything you ever wanted, and I'll never cheat on you again. I promise, baby. From now on I'm *your* slut, your little slutty whore. I'll do anything, anywhere, any filthy thing your mind can dream up.

When I'm all tarted up like this I can't figure out where to sit. I finally perch on the kitchen stool, because if I sit on the couch the dress instantly climbs up my thighs until it is far from decent. I've got the windows open and the curtains closed, fans going so it's nice and chilly; my nipples should be hard, and besides if it gets even a little warm in here I'm going to start sweating before I'm supposed to. I'm seriously hoping our creepy land-lord Bill doesn't pull one of his midnight garbage-rummaging trips looking for recycling, because what he'll find is more empty disposable enema bottles than any midsized city has use for in a decade, and if he spots me dressed up like this he's going to have very little question who's the culprit.

It's six o'clock, time for you to be home. When you don't show I get nervous; I change my thong, which is wet and feels clammy, and I fix my makeup and work on my hair a little. At six-thirty I pour myself a glass of wine. At seven I pour another, telling myself there's no reason to be pissed. You've simply forgotten. You've simply forgotten what I said this morning: "Be home on time. I've got a surprise for you." You've forgotten, and that's far from a hanging offense. I kick off my high heels, pour another glass of wine, and try to relax.

I'm on glass number four when the phone rings; I pick it up already knowing.

"Hi, baby," you say quickly, almost blurting it. "I'm sorry, baby, I have to stay late again. Tom has this problem with the Madrid project..."

Do you even remember? Even now, do you remember that I said I had a surprise for you? Have you forgotten my words entirely, or do you just not care?

Either way, I'd forgive you, baby. I'd forgive you, because you work hard, you provide for me, you're a good husband. Either way, I'd let it slide...if it wasn't for the laugh.

It's off in the distance—a feminine giggle, and the first start of a sentence. Coming out of the bathroom, probably, showering clean after she fucked you silly. Coming out of the bathroom and giggling to you how she's going to fuck you silly all over again.

But don't get me wrong, baby, it's you who tips me off. Because it could be a female coworker, stuck late at the office, coming by your desk and giggling for any reason. Any reason at all.

But if that was the explanation, you wouldn't cover the phone and make a hissing sound. And I wouldn't hear, distantly, a cruel hot whisper that sounds like "Sorry."

"Baby? Are you mad?" You ask me the question with guilt in your voice. I answer with a casual laugh.

"No, baby, of course not. You've got to work. It's no problem." I take a deep breath, because I've got to fight back the tears, but by the time I let the breath out I'm not feeling like crying anymore.

I say it before I know I'm saying it: "I'm going to go ahead and go out, then," I tell you. Now that the words are out, I can't stop—I just talk. "Amy and Jerri are catching a movie. I don't think it's over until after midnight. Maybe I'll even crash at Jerri's place, is that okay with you, baby? It's just such a long drive back from downtown that late." My voice has gotten terrifyingly even, the hint of cruelty in it doubtless undetectable to anyone except me, the slut of Brennan Terrace. I can feel the energy humming in my body, the swirling sensations of wine, the empty ache in my pussy that begs to be filled, the clean tight feel in my ass that says tonight I'll do anything—*anything*—and come home soiled and savaged, and never light candles for you again.

You sound distracted, baby. "No problem," you say absently. You even make a little sighing noise, covering it and pretending it's a yawn. Is she sucking your dick, asshole? Is she fucking down on her knees with her lips working up and down on your cock, the way I was going to be? Probably.

"See you tomorrow, then," you say.

"Goodnight, baby," I tell you.

You hang up with a sharp intake of breath—yeah, she's sucking your cock, or doing something equally nasty to you. Something I would have done, if you'd bothered to come home on time one fucking night.

Unsteady and slightly drunk, I pad into the bedroom in my fishnet-stockinged feet. I go around the room blowing out candles. In the slanted light from the hallway, I retrieve the condoms and lube, and put them in my purse. On second thought, I go back in and get the nipple clamps.

I leave everything else intact, just in case you were wondering. Not that you'll care, baby, not that you'll care. But then I'm not sure I care, either; I'm not the kind of girl who does care, anymore. I'm one hot slut, baby, I've made myself one hot slut for you, and you're not here to see it. I'm the slut of Brennan Terrace, baby—and you can fuck yourself.

QUIET, QUIET

Lucia Dixon

Shhh," he said. "Quiet. Quiet—"

"I can't."

"What'd I say?"

"I can't—"

It was his mother's bed. Let's start with that. Sure, we've made love in many bizarre places before, from the boardroom at his office to the leather table at the salon where I get biweekly massages. But this was his mother's bed, and it was in her bedroom, and she wasn't that far away. For my mental comfort, she would have had to be in Guam, or at the very least out at her country club. In reality, she was downstairs on her patio drinking mimosas with her friends, the tinkling sound of her laughter rising up through the open window.

Joshua said, "Just close your eyes, and block out everything else."

How could I? Not only was his mother within hearing range, but her two hundred guests, invited to a sumptuous garden party, were drunkenly milling around the mansion, exploring. And now her youngest son wanted to take me in the middle of the afternoon, in her bedroom, on her expensive white satin sheets.

"Someone will hear us," I hissed.

"Not unless you scream," Joshua assured me. He's never one for false words of comfort. "Now, be quiet and close your eyes, baby, and keep them closed." This time, noting his tone of voice, I obeyed. "Hands over your head," he told me next. I did that, too, and felt the familiar bite of cold metal on my skin as he slid a set of handcuffs over my wrists. He kissed me, and with my lips still parted, he slipped his tie into my mouth and fastened it behind my head. "That should help ease your worries."

I was done for, and I knew it. Gagging me meant that he thought I wouldn't be able to remain quiet on my own.

"Aren't you the slightest bit turned on, Rebecca?" he asked, sounding coy since I obviously couldn't respond. "Aren't you a little bit excited?" The weight on the bed shifted as he stood up. I guessed that he was undressing, and I tensed, listening, first for his mother, and then him unbuckling his belt and the soft hiss as he pulled the leather through the loops. What had I gotten myself into?

"Not answering, Becca?" he asked, teasing. "Then I'll have to find out for myself." He lifted my floral silk party dress, slid my lacy panties aside and felt the wetness between my legs.

He sighed. "I know my baby, don't I? Now roll over."

This was easier said than done, but I maneuvered myself on the pillows and thickly feathered duvet until I was facedown, my wrists slightly twisted in the handcuff chains.

"You might want to put your face in the pillow, sweetheart, 'cause this is going to hurt."

I made some sort of desperate, mewling sound against the gag, and he responded as if he understood, as if he could decode the worried sound of my words, blurred even as they were against the silken gag.

"It has to hurt, Becca. You know that, baby. It *always* has to hurt."

Lowering my head, I reminded myself that I could have avoided the whole mess. Joshua always gives me choices. He'd told me not to wear panties, I'd ignored him and this was the punishment to fit the crime. If I'd followed his instructions in the first place, he would undoubtedly have chosen a less frightening place to make love, somewhere out in the gargantuan backyard, hidden by a miniature palm tree or lost among the honeysuckle vines. Now, not only were we in his mother's boudoir, he was going to exact his punishment on me with his belt.

"Ten," he said. "Ten here. We'll take care of the rest later."

I wasn't worried about that. In the privacy of our apartment, I can withstand almost anything. Joshua knows this, and because of this fact he rarely lets me get away with being disciplined at home. I didn't have much time to contemplate the future, however, because he was off, striking the first blow with the belt on my naked ass and then lining up the second and third before the initial sparks of pain had even properly registered.

As I drew in a gasp, he climbed onto the bed and plunged inside me. His cock sought out the wetness he'd already found with his probing fingers, and it told him everything he needed to know. That despite my protests and attempts to talk him out of the humiliating games he plays with me, I live for them as much as he does.

He struck the fourth and fifth blows while he was fucking me. Pulling back to catch the lowest, roundest part of my ass, and then driving his cock between my thighs, so that the pain was lost against the pleasure of the ride.

"Told you how to dress today, baby. Should have listened to me."

But then I wouldn't be getting this. The feel of his throbbing cock inside me, perfectly balanced with the pain from the belt.

"When I'm done," he said, coming close to me now that he was whispering, his breath hot against my skin. "When I'm done thrashing you, I'm going to fuck your ass."

My lips started forming begging words and I pulled at the chains on my wrists, as if that could possibly help me. The metal made music against the brass railing of the headboard.

"Quiet, baby," he said, "you're the one making all the noise, and I thought you didn't want to be caught."

I tried to obey, hoping that if I were really good for the remainder of the session he might ease up, forget the rest until later. How could he fuck my ass now? When I had to go down and have dinner with his mother and a few hundred of her closest friends. When he knew it would make me cry.

He blocked my worries by continuing with the discipline, pulling my long hair so that I arched my back, and then slapping my ass in an almost friendly way with the belt. Heating me up with it. I felt the wetness in my cunt spread out to my thighs, and he took advantage of the slippery juices, diving back in me, driving back in me and then placing the head of his cock on my asshole.

I tensed, and he sensed it, not entering me but moving away, standing by the bed to finish the job. The belt licked at my skin, and I could picture the blows in my head, the neatness of them, overlapping lines that would be purplish later if I looked at them in the mirror.

He gave me more than ten. He always does. Naming the reasons. How I didn't hold still, didn't behave correctly, didn't accept my punishment like a well-chastised girl should. I never get it right. This is why he loves me.

And then, because he'd told me he would, he climbed back onto the bed and took me, sliding his cock between the cheeks of my ass and then pushing forward, making me grit my teeth, making me grip the cold metal of the headboard, wrap my fingers around the curlicues of brass, trying to gain some sense of stability when everything in my world was swirling around in weightlessness.

Joshua found a rhythm that went dark and velvety in my head, taking me to faraway places with his cock, with the heat that was still in my skin, with the shame that colored my face and made me shut my eyes even more tightly.

He whispered things while he fucked me, told me how pretty I looked captured to the bed. Captured so simply and purely to his mother's bed. The whole fantasy was mixed up, messed up, twisted and dirty, and it made me come, as he must have known it would. Made me come in a series of rapid bucking movements that almost drove him out of me. He held on, though; he's a fighter, and he kept on going until it was his turn, until he gripped my arms, bit my shoulder hard through the silky fabric of my dress and hissed, "Dirty girl. Such a dirty girl. Coming in my mother's bed."

Joshua cradled me afterward, brushed my hair out of my eyes, slid the cuffs off and rubbed the skin on my wrists. He kissed my blushing cheeks and my forehead and the tip of my nose and then whispered to me of how long he'd planned it, how much thought had gone into this tryst. How I couldn't have avoided it if I'd wanted to.

I never can. This is why I love him.

ROGER'S FAULT

Eric Williams

It was Roger's fault that we were late.

"What a fucking day," he said, looking over at the piles of spreadsheets on my desk. "Let's go grab a beer."

I looked at my watch and shook my head.

"*One* beer," he insisted, and when I told him that I couldn't—when I said that you were at home waiting—he asked, "What are you, man? Pussy-whipped?"

So, Christ, Elena. What was I going to do? One beer turned into two, turned into an hour and a half of playing darts at that dive down near the pier. By the time I realized how long we'd been playing, well, it was too fucking late to call and explain, anyway.

"We'll buy her something nice to make her feel better," Roger said, pushing me out the door to the parking lot. I shrugged uselessly. What could that possibly be? Flowers? Candy? No way to buy back nearly two hours of lost time.

"Trust me," Roger said, "I know the perfect gift."

Then we were back in his shiny black pickup, cruising along

the main drag before cresting downtown. I had my hand on my cell phone, trying to think up some excuse that didn't sound too lame, but he said, "It won't help to call now. We'll just show up with our gift and smooth things over."

Roger acted as if he really knew what he was talking about, and it sounded good, the way he said it. But when he pulled into the parking lot of the sex toy store, I honestly thought he'd lost his mind.

"Come on," I smiled, shaking my head, "I'm not going into a vibrator store with you." Roger didn't even answer. It was obvious that he'd leave me in the truck if I didn't follow, so I kicked open the door and trailed after him. "You're crazy," I said, but he ignored my words, making me hurry to catch up, tripping down the steps and into the wonderful world of sex toys.

What a sight we made. Two guys in expensive work suits, perusing the aisles of marabou-trimmed nighties, edible panties, inflatable dolls, vibrators, paddles, lubricant. Roger acted casual about the whole thing, as if he shopped in stores like that every day. And then there was me, late as hell already, not knowing what the fuck we were doing there.

"Trust me," Roger said again, this time hefting a huge, ribbed purple dildo and poking around in a basket for a suitable leather harness, one that would fit your slim hips without looking foolish. He wanted to find a quality-made harness with a delicate buckle. Not too large.

"You've got to be kidding," I said.

"Elena will love it. You'll see."

"You're not buying my girlfriend a dildo."

"You're right," he agreed, and I thought I saw sanity again in my buddy's eyes. "I'm not buying it. *You* are."

"There's no way."

"Chet," he said, "you can't go home empty-handed. She's going to be upset as a wildcat that you're this late as it is."

"So, what?" I asked him, incredulous. "So I'm going to tell her to strap this thing on and fuck her aggression out on me?"

"Something like that."

And then suddenly, I understood. I'd been set up.

"She told you?" I asked, my voice cracking. I couldn't help but back away from him, standing against what I thought was a wall, but what turned out to be a display of realistic rubber ladies, ready for a man to insert his cock in their mouths, asses and pussies. Vinyl skin reached out to touch me, and I took a step forward, quickly, then whispered again. "She told you." This time, I wasn't asking.

"No problem with having a fantasy," Roger grinned now. He looked incredibly handsome with that knowing half smile, his short dark hair, and a start of evening shadow on his strong jaw. "Especially when everyone gets off."

After that, he didn't say anything else. Simply grabbed the items he was looking for, snagged an extra-large bottle of lube from the display by the counter and paid for his purchases. I have to admit, I had no idea what to do. First, there was the fact of my immediate erection, already making itself known against my leg. I felt as if I were back in college, getting hard whenever the wind blew—or, more honestly, whenever the little cheerleaders made their way onto the field for afternoon practice. Those tiny pleated skirts flipping up each time they cheered. What filthy mind created outfits like that?

And then there was the fact that my best buddy in the world knew that I wanted my girlfriend to ass-fuck me—and not only me, but to fuck him, as well. It had taken a lot of vodka before I'd confessed that particular kinky fantasy. Never thought the words would make their way to his ears.

Yes, Elena, I should have known, way back when we were sharing secrets. I ought to have guessed that you'd do something like this. Always ready to push the barriers in life, which is why I love you. But thinking back, I realize that's why your blue eyes gleamed so brightly when I whispered the dirty words that made up my most private daydream. In your head, you were already playing this out: Roger and me, on our king-sized bed, and you, the queen of the night, going back and forth between us. Dipping into us. Taking us.

But still, I didn't think it would ever happen.

"Come on, Chet," Roger said, throwing one arm over my shoulder and herding me back to his truck as if he were leading a drunken man to shelter. "Elena's waiting."

Ten minutes later, we were back at our house, Roger leaning hard on the doorbell before I could get my key out, and you, opening the door in your sleek leather pants, tight white tank top, high-heeled boots. You looked so fierce, I could have come on the spot.

"Boys," you said as a greeting. Just that word. Your eyes told me that I should have known better. That I was too slow to figure things out. Before I could respond in my own defense, we were walking after you like delinquents heading toward the principal's office. Roger was the ringleader, taking my hand and pulling me down the hall to the bedroom, showing you the present he'd bought and actually undressing you and helping you put it on.

Fuck, Elena, the way you looked stripped down with that harness. Your pale skin, long dark hair, midnight eyes alert and shining. I wanted—well, you know damn well what I wanted. But I'll spell it out anyway. I wanted to go on my knees and get your cock all nice and wet with my mouth, to suck on it until the plastic dripped with my saliva and then watch as you fucked my best friend. I wanted to help glide the synthetic prick between the cheeks of his well-muscled ass, to watch you pump him hard, stay sealed into him, then pump in and out again. I couldn't wait to stand against the wall, one hand on my own pulsing cock, jerking, pulling, coming in a shower on the floor. Not caring what kind of mess I made, because, shit, I was beyond caring about anything like that.

That's not what happened, of course. We were in the wrong, coming back late like that. Me, especially, since I had a will of my own. I could have insisted we go back to the house on time. Could have at least called. No, you wouldn't reward me by taking him first, letting me get off easy as the observer. That wasn't your plan.

"Naughty boy," you said. "Roger, help me bend him over."

At your words, there was a tightening in the pit of my stomach, like a fist around my belly. A cold metal taste filled my mouth, and it was suddenly difficult for me to swallow. Roger's seemingly experienced hands unbuckled my belt, pulled off my shoes, slipped my pants off and took down my black satin boxers. Leaving those around my knees, he bent me over the bed, his exploring fingers trailing along the crack of my ass and making me moan involuntarily. Calloused fingertips just brushing my hole. Never felt anything that dirty, that decadent.

He was the one to help you. The assistant. Pouring the oil in a gilded river between my asscheeks, rubbing it in, his fingertips casually slipping inside of me. Probing and touching in such a personal manner that I could have cried. I wanted him to finger-fuck me, to use two, three, four fingers. I knew what it would be like to have his whole fucking fist inside of me. And, Elena, did I ever want that. Roger, behind me, getting the full motion of his arm into it. But then his strong hands spread me open as you guided the head of that mammoth, obscene purple cock into my asshole. And I wanted that even more.

Jesus fucking Christ, Elena. How did you know? I mean, I told you, of course, that night at the beach, draining the bottle between us as we stared up at the stars and out at the silver-lipped ocean. Your pussy so wet and slippery as you confessed your secret, five-star fantasy of fucking a guy. And me, harder than steel as I answered that it was what I wanted, as well.

But how did you know how to do it? How to talk like that? Sweet thing like you. Fucking me like a professional and talking like a trucker.

"Such a bad boy, needing to be ass-fucked," you told me, your voice a husky sounding purr. "That's what you need, right, Chet? You need my cock deep in your hole."

That's what I needed, all right, and it was what you gave me. That dildo reaming my asshole, with Roger there, spreading my cheeks wide until it hurt. The right kind of hurt. Pain at being pulled, stretched open. Embarrassment flooding through me and making the precome drip freely from my cock. I could feel the sweat on me, droplets beading on my forehead as I gripped the pillow and held on. Never been fucked before, never taken, and here my best friend was watching. Helping.

As fantasies go, you never know what will happen when they come true. I turned to look in the mirror on the closet doors as Roger moved behind you, saw that your bare ass was plenty available since you were wearing only that harness. He wasn't rough with you the way you were with me. He knew how to do it, how you like it. On his knees behind you, parting your luscious cheeks and tickling your velvety hole with his tongue. Playing peekaboo games back there, driving the tip of it into your asshole and licking you inside out. Making you moan and tilt your head back, your hair falling away from your face, your cheeks flushed.

Then he was the one to pour oil all over his cock, to rub it in and part your heart-shaped cheeks and take you. I saw a glimpse of his pole before it disappeared into your ass, and the length of it made me suck in my breath. What it must have done to you. Impaling you, possessing you as he took you on a ride.

The three of us fucked in a rhythm together like some deranged beast. You in my asshole and him in yours. Joined and sticky, reduced to animals who simply couldn't get enough. I didn't want to watch, but I had to, as the three of us came, bucking hard in a pileup on the bed. Groaning, because it was so good. Better than good. It was sublime. Unreal.

But, in my defense, I have to say again that it was all Roger's fault.

Next Friday night, we'll be there on time, Elena. I promise.

SPRING CLEANING

Samantha Mallery

've always liked it," Eleanor told me. "I mean, always."

We were seated in the kitchen, sharing a glass of red wine. When Eleanor passed the glass to me, her fingers brushed mine, shocking me with a tiny electric spark. Even though we've been together nearly six years, just the touch of her skin can give me a thrill.

"I don't know," I said. "It doesn't really sound like much of a turn-on to me." I took a sip of the wine and handed it back to her. I enjoy drinking from the same glass she does, lining my lips up with her crimson kiss imprints.

"Imagine," she started, "you tied down to the bed. Me with a feather duster in my hand, running the pretty pink feathers all over your naked body. You wouldn't be able to stand it."

"That's what I'm afraid of," I told her, honestly. "Not being able to stand it."

Eleanor smiled. "No, this would be in a good way. You'd be squirming, pushing against the bindings, *trying* to beg me to let you go, but laughing too hard to get the words out. I'd tickle you until you came close to wetting the bed."

My eyes must have widened when she said that, because she sensed I was about to agree. "Come on, Jackie," she continued, leaning over the Formica kitchen table and grazing my lips with hers in a quick kiss. "You're always up for something interesting."

I thought about it. Interesting, yes. But interesting conjures up images of making love beneath the pier, of necking passionately while riding the Ferris wheel, of doing it on a train. Tickling didn't fit the concept.

My lover sat back in her chair and regarded me with a look I could not immediately read. Her dark-brown eyes seemed thoughtful. She worried her full bottom lip with her teeth, the way she does when she's figuring something out. After a moment she said, "On my next cleaning night, I'll introduce you to the concept. If you don't like it, we can stop. I mean, if you *really* don't like being tickled. But somehow, I think you will."

Eleanor and I take turns planning cleaning nights. The goal is to try and make cleaning our apartment a bit more exciting. It takes the drudgery out of everything from polishing silverware to washing windows. We have come up with sexual uses for even the most mundane household cleaning items, and because we take turns planning, we're always trying to surprise each other. But there's no surprise to the way the evenings end: with our breathing rapid and our bodies shiny with sweat and come. *And* our apartment not much more organized than it was before. Scrubbing the shower and waxing the kitchen floor have both become exciting and hotly anticipated events in our lives because of cleaning nights.

Now, I found myself filled with trepidation at the thought of our next weekend's tickling fest, and wondering how it might be tied in with a cleaning scenario. Would she polish me with a felt rag? Would she tickle me with the scrub brush? Eleanor is a creative woman; I knew she would surprise me.

I am always turned on, whether I'm in charge of one of these nights or she is, but this time the fluttering in my stomach was made of something new. Fear? How could I be afraid of being tickled? That just didn't make sense.

On Friday night, I got dressed for our date. I stood for a long time in front of the mirror regarding my reflection. I am five foot six, and I have straight blonde hair that barely reaches my shoulders. I wasn't sure of the appropriate attire to wear while being tickled. When we have spanking nights (which usually come when we're cleaning the kitchen because of the plentiful wooden spoon paddles), I know to put on a pair of my sweet, lace-edged panties. When we're doing laundry, we'll undoubtedly wind up making love on the washer, and I wear nothing but a terry-cloth towel, for padding. But tickling? I ended up in a marabou-trimmed nightgown and robe, with marabou fluff on my high-heeled slippers. The outfit itself practically tickled me when I went to answer the door.

Eleanor nodded her immediate approval. She stood on our patio, a tissue-wrapped bouquet in her lovely hands. I let her in, feeling shy, as I always do when she's in charge. It's fun taking turns this way. It gives us both the opportunity to play different roles. When Eleanor is in charge, her very appearance seems to change. She has light honey-colored hair and freckled skin. Her eyes are a deep brown, and they seem to glow when she's in charge. They have a heat to them, and they flicker like the purple-gold flames in a campfire.

As Eleanor walked into the dining room, she unwrapped the bouquet and I noticed that it wasn't flowers, but feather dusters, an assortment of four different colors—turquoise, a deep rose, a much paler pink, and bright lavender. She waved them at me, teasingly brushing the tip of my nose, and then she set them on the dining room table and took off her jacket. Underneath, she was dressed all in black, including a black feather boa that she had sneakily tucked beneath her coat.

"Bedroom," she said, grinning, that one word setting the tone for the events of the evening. I tripped down the hall in my heels and then stood next to the bed, waiting for her next instruction.

She was right behind me, hadn't even entered the room before saying, "Now, strip." I mentally chided myself for agonizing over my attire—it was so quickly removed and tossed on the chair by the bed. Before I could ask her what to do next, she had come forward and wrapped her feather boa around my wrists. She pushed me down to a sitting position and then back so that I was sprawled on the bed. I watched as she set the feather dusters down on the pillow, then moved to position me exactly how she wanted—my legs spread apart, my bound wrists over my head, the edge of the boa caught neatly on the hook in the wall. The "handcuff hook," we call it.

"You ready?" she asked, binding my ankles to the posters of my bed with silky scarves. "Ready to be tickled until you come?"

I wanted to shake my head, but I didn't. Instead, I said, "You know I'm game, Eleanor," and then I waited for her to begin. She didn't rush into it. She never does. She always makes me wait, because she knows anticipation has a definite effect on me. The waiting makes my pussy get into the groove, makes me start to grow wet and ready even before the action begins. This time was no different. In fact, I think I got wetter because I really didn't know what to expect. Anticipation mixed with confusion.

Eleanor said, "You don't have to look so afraid. I'm not going to hurt you."

I nodded. "I know, but...," and that was all I got to say. She came forward, one feather duster in each hand, and began running the toys up and down my rib cage. I started to jerk on the boa, but Eleanor shook her head. "Careful," she said, "I don't want you to rip that." More bad news for me. How could I squirm if I had to be careful? I sent her pleading, puppy-dog looks with my eyes, but she took no pity on me. Instead, she continued with the fancy dusters, running them lightly under my armpits, then down my arms, then using one on my legs and another on my tummy. She was like an octopus, an eight-legged

creature. Whenever one area of my body started to tickle too
badly, she was instantly somewhere else.

"Such a good girl," she cooed, now standing by the bed and
walking to the foot of it. I knew where she was going. I didn't
think I'd be able to stand it.

"Oh god," I said as she started to run the dusters up and
down my bare feet. "Eleanor, I can't..." My words dissolved
into helpless laughter.

"Yes, you can," she said, continuing her tickling journey.
She ran the feathers over the soles of my feet and then brushed
them along the tips of my painted toenails. I couldn't heed her
warning anymore. I yanked on the bindings holding my wrists
to the wall. The boa snagged and bits of glossy black feathers
fluttered down on top of me. But my wrists stayed bound. I
bucked on the bed, raising my hips as high as I could, slamming
down to the mattress each time. She'd tied my ankles tight. I was
going nowhere.

My laughter rang out in the room. My body started to hurt
from how hard I was giggling.

"Shhh," Eleanor admonished. Slowly, I began to give in,
to let myself become overwhelmed with the tickling, taunting
sensation. And giving in somehow made it bearable, although
my body still shook with silent laughter. But then, that too
began to subside, as Eleanor made her way catlike onto the bed,
moving between my legs and positioning herself right before my
open cunt.

"Here?" she asked.

I took a deep, shuddering breath. I realized that I wanted
to feel the feathers there. More than anything I'd ever craved
before. I was dying to know what those tickling colored bits of
fluff would feel like against my swollen clit.

"Please," I finally managed.

She whisked the duster over my pussy once, then slid it back
again. I moaned. She took a duster in each hand and whisked
back and forth, so lightly that her touch was maddening. I raised

up for more pressure, but couldn't get it. She continued dusting me, lightly, gently, until my moans turned to hoarse begging sounds and the moisture in my cunt made the feathers wet.

"Come on," I begged, "I need…"

"I know what you need." Eleanor smiled at me, turning one of the dusters around to show me the smooth wooden handle. Oh, yes. That's exactly what I needed. With the same slow movements, Eleanor spread my pussy lips open and lightly tapped the edge of the handle against my throbbing clit. I wasn't laughing anymore. This was no longer funny. I gritted my teeth and mentally willed her to stop her teasing games. I needed fulfillment. I needed release.

Watching me carefully, my lover slid the handle inside my pussy. My cunt instantly gripped on to it, squeezing as Eleanor rocked it in and out. She knows the way to do it. Oh, yes, my lover girl knows everything about what I like and how I like it. I closed my eyes, sighing gratefully, and then was rewarded as Eleanor used her free hand to tickle my clit with the turquoise duster.

The combination of the two sensations was unbelievable. My cunt contracted on the handle of one duster as those lovely, bright blue-green feathers tickled me to perfection. I floated in the bed, my head back, my hips rising up and down to the rhythm Eleanor set.

In mere moments, she had dusted me right into an electrifying orgasm. And I had shredded her feather boa by stretching it with my wrists. Eleanor looked up my body, meeting my eyes with hers.

"I've never had so much fun…" She grinned. "You know, dusting."

Next weekend is my turn. And we're going to be working on the floor in the kitchen. Until then I'm going to be wracking my brain, trying to find interesting uses for our mop.

THUNDER AND LIGHTNING

Sommer Marsden

It's the first flash that wakes me. White-blue light tattooed on the inside of my eyelids. I'm roused before the first rolling boom is heard. It rattles the windows, and I open my eyes.

2:00 a.m. The night is as black as sin until that lightning flares again, reminding me of the sodium-vapor shine of a road flare.

Next to me, Jase snores on.

I climb slowly out of bed, part of me completely paranoid that my movement—my acknowledgment of the storm—will make it fade. That it will flee me and my awareness. It's silly really, but storms do strange things to me and when they are short or fleeting I'm left disappointed. Often frustrated.

Storms make me feel alive. And wild. They inspire something in me that others find in running or bungee jumping or playing music. My heart beats faster, my awareness expands, my body feels electric as if I'm being juiced by nature herself.

And I get horny.

I stand by the window, one hand planted to the cooling

glass. It's been hot—beyond hot—for weeks now and this is what happens. A cool front forms and slams into the muggy-thick Baltimore night and boom! Literally. The windows rattle once again with a rolling groan of the storm. The lightning forks looking like the spear of some dark god. I press my hand more firmly to the glass square and wait.

My skin tingles, my cunt thumps, my heart ratchets up to flutter and dance. I watch the rain beat the window and the trees. Jase turns in his sleep, snorts once, finds a comfortable spot. And I watch him—his handsome face, prickly with stubble, is painted by the brief and glaring flashes of light.

I drop to my knees and crawl across the carpet, dragging my knees through splashes of light and dark dots painted there by the ambient light from the windows. Every inch closer I get to our bed, the more I want him. The more I want to be with him as the storm rages on. I crawl up over the end of the bed, imagining myself some mythical storm goddess or maybe a panther—something sexy, something fierce. But when I dip my head beneath the blanket and continue my travels, it makes me laugh, this make-believe of mine.

"Whatchadoin?" It all comes out in one word and Jase's hand finds my head beneath the blanket. Then: "Hey."

"Hey," I whisper against his skin. I drag a kiss along the top of his thigh and then over his pubic bone.

"What's this?" Then he goes still as I drag my teeth lower. His cock has stood up to greet me. He might have a muzzy-headed sleep confusion but his body does not. It's simply on board no matter what's causing this interlude.

"Me. Getting off during a storm."

With that the thunder booms loud enough to make me jump. I feel his large, warm hands steady me by pressing against my shoulders. I take that as a sign to slip the top of his cock into my mouth. To suck. To draw on that sweet, soft place on him that makes me crazy. I drag the satiny flesh along my lower lip and then suck again.

"Are you sure it's you getting off?"

I'm still under the blanket and he hasn't drawn it back to look at me, but his hand smoothes along my hair in a comforting motion. I suck him deeper, dragging my lips slowly down the length of his shaft until I feel his cockhead brush the back of my throat. I gag just a little, but I like it. So I do it again.

Jase groans, laughs once as I see the blanket grow lighter with a flash of lightning. He tosses the covers back and eyes me in the gloom. There's just enough light and my eyes are adjusted just enough that I can see him. Mostly.

"If you keep doing that, Harley, I'm a dead man. I'll never get to fuck you. You're sort of—" His words break off when I push myself all the way down, my lips brushing his pubic hair, his cock stuffing my throat.

"Shh, just a bit more," I plead, gripping him and working my fist up and down his length. His hips arch up to meet me and I suck again, harder this time, hollowing my cheeks with the effort.

"Harl—"

"Shh," I say again and then I move up over him, walking forward on my knees. He finds the hem of my small sleep shirt and pushes it up. He gets up on his elbows and his mouth dips to kiss my navel, my hip bones. Before I see it coming, he tips me off balance and onto my back. He pins me, kissing me once, licking my lips that have just been on his cock.

"Spread your legs," he says.

I obey. It doesn't take much more than simple words from him for me to listen. Outside the thunder rages on, the lightning streaks the sky. His mouth is on me, hot and sweet, in a flat second. The flashes of nature's rage light the side of his face, accent golden hairs and some silver. Show me the side of his rugged face lit in stark relief. He looks, in that perfect moment, like a hero in a panel of a comic book. All black and white and shades of gray and blue.

His fingers trace the pout of my outer lips, nudge between

them, drag relentless and soft over my swollen clit. I clutch at him and he bats my hands away, chuckling. "Stay there, Harley. Stay still."

His mouth latches on to me and the heat is searing. The feel of his mouth drawing on me causes the thunder to rattle my bones, the lightning to illuminate my soul. I feel magical and with a simple, slow flick of his tongue he gets me off. Fast and hard. I'm that primed.

"Easy date tonight, girl. Is it the late hour or the storm?"

I push him back even as he's kissing me and have a moment of gratitude that we went to bed with the curtains wide and the blinds up. The storm is a backlight to me straddling him, pushing my wet swollen pussy to his belly and grinding until he grabs my wrists roughly and says, "Enough teasing."

I laugh and lift up to take him, torturing us both further by running my slippery sex up and back along his shaft with my moving hips. Finally, when my breath is a wild thing lodged in my throat, I push the tip of his cock to my split and ease down. Slowly. Slow enough that I want to scream and one glance at him says Jase's gritting his teeth in frustration.

He grabs my hips and yanks, plunging me down, filling me up, taking my control and making it his.

There is a silence then. Us and the storm. Everything is still. Everything is in limbo. Then a startling crack splits the silence and we're moving together. It's a dance. It's symbiotic. I try to pin his arms as I lean over to kiss him, grinding my hips as pleasure floods my pelvis. He lets me hold him still long enough to get close, to nearly come for the second time, before he grabs my wrists and reverses the hold. His big arms push my fists down by my undulating hips, holding me there. Keeping me immobile.

I drag my body up and down, up and down, feeling the slip and slide of my clit as I do it. I'm wet, I'm beyond wet actually, like my yard, like my house—I am drenched and Jase notices.

"Super slippery, babe," he says, finding me with his thumb,

even in the murky light. He's released one of my hands to do it. I steady myself on that trembling arm as he begins short, swift revolutions of his thumb on my clitoris.

"Jas—"

"I know."

"I'm going to—"

I'm trembling and quaking and as the blue-white electric light of the storm flares, he presses gently and slides his thumb against me once more and I come. Biting my lips, shaking my head, my eyes swimming with tears as I let go for the second time. Taken down and swept under from the pleasure I always get being with him. Sharing with him.

"Shh." He cups his hand over my mouth, trapping my sounds. He thrusts his hips up good and hard, filling me with wild jabs and every time he does, he hits slick tender places that sing with bliss.

I come again with a cry that is swallowed by a boom of thunder. And it's only after that third orgasm—"three's the charm" is what Jase says—that he grabs my hips and holds me steady, thrusting up with a power that makes his belly muscles ripple and his face tense.

When he comes I throw myself forward, kissing him even as he continues to shake. I lick all the good noises of his release off his lips and fall to the side, letting him wrap his arms around me.

"Sorry," I say, touching the sweat slick on his stomach.

"For what?" We watch the nature-made night-light and the air conditioner cuts on to blow away the heat we've just generated.

"For waking you up. You know what they do to me. Thunderboomers." That's our name for the storms that shake the windows and "stir up the woman." Another saying of Jase's.

"You or the storm would have woken me eventually," he says, kissing my hand, my hair and then my forehead. "I much prefer it was you."

I grin in the dark and watch another alien fork of greenish light split the navy-blue sky. The rain is slowing down. It's getting ready to pass. "God, I love storm season," I blurt.

"Me too, Harl. Me too."

UNDERWATER

Emilie Paris

M y days are long and lazy. I hang out at the beach with the skate rats and the surfers, baking beneath the rays, not caring where the next rent check is coming from. The young sun gods all live together, crashed out in a big house by the ocean, thirteen or fourteen guys sharing one phone, mattresses on the floors and in the hallways. Their house needs a paint job, but they don't care. The front steps are battered, broken, but they sit on them anyway, kicking their bare feet up on the wall and watching the sunset. The surf stars don't seem to have visible means of support, but somehow they always manage to scrounge up the rent money by the end of the month. It appears, like magic, finding its way into the envelope they hand over to their bemused landlord.

I don't worry about rent either, but I don't have to. I've got a high-paying job, one that works me to a near-breaking point for months on end and then releases me for much-needed regrouping. If you live in Los Angeles, you know people like me. Movie people. We power-work night and day on a film, then

relax until the phone rings again. But unlike the faces on the
screen, I'm not well known. I've never been linked in the tabloids
to any celebrity. When I have free time, I can hide among the
riffraff without being recognized. That's how it is when you're
behind the camera. Only those truly in the know can pick me
out of a crowd.

So, in days after a movie is finished, I pull my favorite faded
jeans from the closet, snag a tank top left by a long-gone lover,
slip on my shades and hit the shimmering sidewalk at Venice
Beach. I buy a soft-serve vanilla ice-cream cone and lick it as I
make my way to the ramp where the rats are jumping. When I
get close, I find a shady spot beneath a palm tree, and sit down
to watch the boys do their tricks. From my favorite location, I
can keep track of both the skateboarders on their ramps and the
surfers as they dive and dance among the waves. It thrills me,
watching the kings of the beach kick ass on their respective slats,
the skaters going upside down over nothing but concrete, the
surfers slicing through the waves.

Other girls gather around, too, summertime chicks clad in
brightly colored string bikinis or sheer, halter-style dresses. They
ooh and *ahh* at each fabulous trick, at each display of testos-
terone. These girls bring iced sodas and snacks and rub suntan
lotion on the broad-shouldered backs of the weary beach boys.
I never get quite that involved. If I want to make an impression,
I leave the picnic stuff at home.

When I see someone I want, I take off my sunglasses and
wait.

I'm not as young as most of the gang. I'm twenty-eight,
which is ancient by Hollywood standards, but I have a thin,
tight-muscled body, and I can pass for a coed when I need to.
My strawberry-blonde hair is long in front, with bangs I peek
out from under. I scrape it off my face and into a sleek ponytail when I'm working, but "off" times, I wear it hanging free,
down to my sharp shoulder blades in back and to the tips of my
eyelashes in front. In the summer, my hair gets lighter, bleaches

out in streaks to give me that true California girl look. I don't cultivate the image, but it serves the purpose when I want it to.

I have blue eyes, blue like the sky without any smog, clear and intense. When I take off my sunglasses, my eyes are what guys notice first. That is, if they haven't seen me smile. My smile is a grabber. I have small, animal teeth. Guys see me grin and instantly have visions of my teeth sinking into their naked skin. I know how to leave just the right marks, not too deep. Little reminders of a wild night, a whirlwind romance in the shadows of a sand dune. My love bites are souvenirs, and I think my partners are always sad when the last remnants of my incisors fade away.

Some of my friends would be shocked by my tastes. I simply don't look the part of the dominatrix. I'm slight, but I'm tough. My lovers have always submitted to my needs. There's never been a question about it. I call to them, the ones that like to bow down. I don't seek them out; they come to me.

But *I* come to the boys of summer. I am drawn to the way they flip up in the air. Pulled in by the tricks they do. Captivated by their gravity-defying moves. I align myself with that free-flying attitude. These heavenly contenders don't care about pain. If they fall down, they get back the fuck up again, and do it over. And *over*. They have scars on their slim bodies from accidents past. They have tattoos, like colorful birthmarks, wrapped around their arms, legs, decorating their skin like splashes of paint on tautly stretched canvases.

I appreciate them, and they know it. I'm different from the bikini babes. I have a power that they sense. I can make them blush simply by watching them play, and my presence somehow brings out their best. They land all their moves when I'm nearby, watching. They shine when I'm around.

I don't take the daredevils the way I take other men. I have sex with them, sure, but I don't conquer them. I let their moves steal over us both. I let them turn my bed into a playground, a jungle gym, and take over from there. Or I find myself in their beds, playing by their rules, which is infinitely easy because they have none.

That's how I know about the mattresses in the hallways. It's how I know about the single phone and the shared bathroom. I have found myself in an arched-back position on more than one of those mattresses, watching my reflection in a window at the end of the long, narrow hallway. No sheet beneath me, just the blue-and-white-striped ticking of an old bedroll. None of the niceties you'd find in the apartments of the movie folks I work with. No bedside table displaying a fashionable artsy lamp. No signed and framed artwork over the leather sofa in the living room.

I don't like those things, don't need them.

What I need is some nineteen-year-old, golden-skinned boy behind me, a twisted, faded friendship band around his wrist and nothing else on his perfect body. In the window-mirror, I see that his eyes are closed, but I watch. We do it doggie-style, with me on all fours and him on his knees in back of me. He holds on to my hips, impales me, moves to a beat he can hear in his head. I try to hear that same beat. I rock my body forward and back. I like the way his rough hands feel on my skin, like the way his tanned body looks against my pale figure. I can see that in the window, but I can't see the color of his eyes, because they're closed. And I can't hear the music that he hears, because he's young and in the groove of summertime and skate-rat dreams. And to him, I'm this little blonde chick he met on the beach that he wanted to go upside down with.

But I'm a grownup, a voice says in my head, and I can't lose myself in the moves anymore. I am present while he fucks me. My mind doesn't take off on a fantasy trip. I feel his fingers digging into my skin. I hear his breath coming in a rush. I know that he's trying to keep himself from shooting too soon when he moves back, when he turns me on the mattress so I'm on my side, and he's in me from behind, spooning this time. Those calloused fingertips find my clit and rub, getting me up to his speed, helping me to forget myself and learn the rhythm of his choosing. His fingers are knowledgeable. They sense when to dart into my pussy and get wet and slippery with my liquid sex. They know to rub over my clit, over and over, then around and around. I am in love with the touch of his fingers. I lean back against his chest and shut my eyes.

In my mind, I can picture our bodies together. I see us like a painting, his dark burnished skin to my pale body, his short, scruffy goatee framing an impish smile, his light eyes an oasis shimmering in the heat. We could be a graffiti painting on the outside of one of the warehouses near the beach, a sprawling vision by some barrio artist, combining colors and lights and shadows.

He moves me again, whispering something, his mouth pressed against my ear, saying, "How do you like it, baby? How do you like it?"

I roll onto my back and look at him, memorizing the lines of his face. I smile at him when he opens his eyes, green-gray eyes that seem glazed as he stares back at me. He asks it again, "How do you like it?" Then, "How do you need it?" Stressing that one word. *Need.*

I can't tell him, so I say, "Just like this," as he climbs on top of me, starts doing push-ups over my body, the muscles in his fine arms bulging. He teases me with the head of his cock between my lightly furred pussy lips, pulling out, all the way out so that I'm stretching, straining to reach him, and then giving me a shy sort of naughty grin and slipping the tip back in again. I squeeze him with my muscles, try to drain him with my power. He's good, though. He makes the most of the ride, whatever the ride may be, whether he's skimming the surf on a neon-painted boogie board, doing those death-defying moves on a skate ramp with no safety net or going upside down with me on his mattress.

He says, "Talk to me, baby...tell me what you like."

Could I tell him that I like *him*? That I like his spirit, and that I see it when he rides his board. I don't think so. I would sound phony. I would sound old, trying to capture a bit of his youth and make it my own. But it is what I like. His strong body against mine. The way his hair smells of wind and sea spray and his skin actually tastes of summertime, of heat.

He croons, "Tell me, baby, talk to me."

I shake my head, still trying to pull him inside me, to keep him inside me, my pussy making a juicy, kissing sound each time he rocks in and out. I turn it around. I say, "I like it like this. Just like this. But tell me. You tell me what you like."

He's got his answer ready. He was waiting the whole time. Still working me, without missing a beat, he says, "It sends me when a girl says my name as she's coming."

Then he bends and starts to kiss the underside of my jawline, the hollow of my neck. He tickles me with the pointy tip of his tongue and I almost laugh. He takes hold of my wrists and pins them over my head and then moves down my body to kiss my small breasts, licking and sucking with his ravenous mouth. His cock is pressed up against my leg, slick and wet from the juices of my sex, but I can tell he's not going to enter me again until I ask what needs to be asked.

I strain to see if he'll hold me down, and he does. Then, awful as it may sound, I confess, "I don't know your name."

He says, "My name's on my body. It's like a treasure hunt... see if you can find it." Then he lets go of my wrists and stands up, leaning against the wall, regarding me with a look of total satisfaction.

He's like a statue. Still, absolutely still, his cock straining out and away from him. His eyes, half-closed, let me know he has all the time we need. I look up the line of his body, seeing the different tattoos, the different marks and scars. I sit on my heels, begin tracing the designs with my tongue. He turns, slowly, his face to the wall now, and I see the black-inked word on his lower back: Eden. I start to say it, but he turns around again quickly, shaking his head at me, coming back down on the mattress, moving us so that I am over him, riding him, my body split at the middle, my legs pumping, keeping him deep inside me. I move without thinking, without planning. I am on him, sliding up and down his cock with graceful ease, not doing it because he wants it or I want it, but doing it because it's right.

"When you come," he says, his voice hoarse, letting me know how it's going to be. "Say it when you come."

I ride him hard. I don't let his cock slip out of me again, but I pound myself on it, fucking him now. This is how I'm used to doing it, holding my partner down with my will alone, my body easy and light. But he's different. He's not in it to be overpowered. He's in it to watch my face change when I come. He's in it for the experience, for that heart-stopping feeling of reaching your peak and looking down from the sky above. Making love to him lets me see the world as he does, see what it would be like to ride the waves, to feel the board beneath my feet and duck through a tunnel of blue-green sun-drenched water.

He trails his fingers over my cheekbones. He presses his thumb against my bottom lip. I lick it, draw it into my mouth, suck on his thumb while I fuck him. He sighs. His body shifts beneath me, my still-pumping legs, my sweat-slicked thighs. He grabs hold of my waist and moves me so that we are on our sides, facing each other, staring into each other's eyes.

And then I move my head, look over his shoulder and see his roommates in the other room. There the whole time. I freeze for one moment, stop moving against Eden. I'm startled by their presence, but they smile at me, grinning to show how easygoing they are. Their bodies are tanned and strong. The five of them drink lemonade and inhale clove cigarettes, blowing wispy breaths of fragrant smoke toward the ceiling.

I don't smile when I see them, but I feel elated. The group gazes at us as if we're a movie put on for their sole pleasure. They view us in the same manner they watch other athletes at the beach, genuinely impressed with the show. Letting someone else entertain them. I come from seeing them there, from the audience, from the youth of the boys around me. It brings me down for a moment, holds me under for just long enough to get off.

Eden feels those vibrations around his cock, and he starts to move his hands on my body, up my slender waist toward my breasts, stroking me all over, coming with me and playing me to make it last. I have seen him carry his skateboard with that same amount of gentleness, or roughness, or some combination of the two that shows how much he appreciates it. I come and collapse against him, the warmth of our bodies complementary, the warmth in the room and in the glowing eyes of our audience a small fire of purity.

I'm underwater. His touch brings me back to the surface.

I'm not sure how much I like being up above, able to breathe free again, to see the crescent moon through the window, to see the hazy smoke clouds the skate rats exhale with each breath. I'd rather be under, held down, his body on mine, topsy-turvy in a slick and sweaty sixty-nine, his warm cock in my mouth, my pussy throbbing under his tongue. The sweet, sweat-salt taste of his skin a mixture of hard work and a bath in the sea after a long day's ramping. I know the feel of him pressing into me, pushing me back down under the waves. I trail my fingers along the tribal design of a blue-inked tattoo that is a part of him, the ink like blood in the veins pounding under his skin.

I say, "I forgot...," but he just looks at me. I tilt my head back, arch my body on the mattress, wanting his tongue down there, between my legs, and he nods as he turns his body so that his face is between my thighs and his cock, wet and dripping from my sex, is poised just over my lips. Knowing that others are watching makes me shiver inside. I open my mouth and he slides inside. I suck on him, drink from him, roll my tongue around his straining rod, so well-oiled with my own wetness. I'm gone again, deep under his body, deep underwater, pressed down into the mattress, loving him with my mouth while he plays in-and-out games with his tongue in my pussy.

I've had many different lovers taking me over the edge, but my mind never truly goes on hold unless I'm with one of the boys of summer. Someone like Eden, with the scars he wears like badges of honor, with the tattoos saved hard for and paid for in cash. He'll never grow up. Maybe that's what I like most about him. He'll get older, but his heart will always be alert and alive, doing backflips off a homemade ramp without any fear of the ground rushing up from below.

I hear the waves outside, crashing against the sand. He hears the ocean, too, and uses the rhythm of the surf in the way he kisses me, finding my clit between his lips and sucking on it to that beat. Hard and then soft, lapping for a moment and then suckling again. He knows how to do it. He knows just how to give the most pleasure, taking me upward until I have a view of the very top, before sliding me back down again. I break and crest. I ride the peaks and valleys. I forget who I am, what I do, what language I speak. I know only one thing, his name, and I say it over and over, his cock still in my mouth, the word slurred.

I say, "Eden," just as he asked me to, just as he told me to. I say, "E-den," dragging out his name, making it last. I'm underwater when I reach it. I hold my breath, hear my heart pounding in my ears. I feel faint, dizzy, spreading my legs wide apart, my head tossed back, my hips thrusting forward. I shake with the climax, letting out my air, finally, taking a deep, shuddering breath in, finding the surface and breaking free.

MISS ME

Mary Jo Vaughn

They're deadly—those dirty martinis. They're mean, they are. They'll blow you away.

I'm not a lightweight. Don't even let that thought enter your head. I can do tequila body shots all night long. But the dirty martinis are different. They sneak the fuck up on you when you're not looking, when you're not thinking much except, "Mmmm...that was good. I'll have another."

I was in that sort of a state when Mira found me. I was leaning up against the cool wood bar, my face flushed, my hair pulled high off my neck and captured there with a sterling silver clip. I had on a black turtleneck that I'd just freed from storage and it smelled a bit like the sachet I'd tucked into the box: faded roses and baby powder. A comfort smell.

Mira glided up behind me. I didn't notice her until I saw her reflection in the blue-tinted mirror behind the bar. She said, "Buy you the next?"

I didn't turn toward her, simply steeled myself and met her eyes in the mirror. She looked clear and crisp, her short white-blonde hair slicked back, her eyes razor sharp, even in the dim light of the bar.

"You bet," I said, nodding, feeling her hand snake down the back of my loose jeans. She was checking to see if I had on panties. I didn't.

The bartender replaced my dead drink with a new one, and Mira turned sideways and watched me down it. When I'd finished, she grabbed my hand and led me down the dark hallway to the ladies' room.

"You smell like sex," she said, under her breath, as she pulled me along.

"Roses and baby powder," I corrected her, taking a whiff of my sweater.

She pulled me after her into the ladies' room and locked the door behind us.

"And sex," she said again, pulling the turtleneck over my head, propping me up against the sink while she pulled my jeans down, leaving them on me.

The sink was cold against my naked ass, but her hands were warm as they spread my cunt lips, and her mouth was hot as she pressed it against me. I liked the feel of the metal ball that rides her tongue as she tickled my clit with it. Warm mouth and cool silver combined can start a fire within me. Mira knows that well.

I held on to the edge of the sink, kicked off my shoes and waited for her to pull my jeans all the way off. Then, balancing most of my weight on the sink, I wrapped my slender legs around her, capturing her to me, capturing her face to my cunt. If she wanted to play, we'd play my way, half-drunk though I was.

I loved the feeling of that silver ball rolling back and forth over my clit and then icing my insides as she used her tongue like a cock and probed me deeper. Mira knows what to do. Yes, she does.

There are two mirrors in the ladies' room, and I stared in the one across the way to watch my face as I came. I moved again so I was standing, and I placed my hands on the back of

Mira's shaved neck and jammed her hard against me, rolling her with the vibrations that swelled inside me and cascaded over. I bounced back and forth, slamming my ass against the rim of the sink and then forward, into her face, and she punished me for the intensity of my movements by digging that silver ball right into my clit, spiraling me into a violent world of pain and pleasure and pain and pleasure...and pain.

"Hurts so good," she grinned at me when she stood up, wiping her mouth on the back of her hand, "doesn't it?"

"It always does when you ride the helm," I agreed, staring into her clear eyes and waiting.

"I miss you," she said next, working hard to get that hurt look to her face that doesn't belong on it. Mira doesn't feel any real emotions, so far as I can tell. And after dating her for four years and recently being the one to instigate the breakup, I should know.

"Miss me," I said as I left her alone in the bathroom. I poked my head in for one last dig, "But thanks for the climax. It was great."

WAR MOVIES

Elle McCaul

Connor invites me to a party at his house. I dress for it, in black fishnets and a short silk skirt, thinking tonight will finally be the night. This is date number four and I'm desperate to fuck him. We have that type of white-hot connection that makes me tremble whenever he touches my hand. After our last date, I couldn't fall asleep without first stroking myself, imagining it was him teasing me as I brought myself to climax.

To my dismay, the party turns out to be him and his two male roommates watching war movies all night. I'm overdressed and underwhelmed. That is, until I notice that Connor's focused on me instead of the movie.

"Why'd you ask me here?" I whisper to him. "I mean, here with your roommates."

"I just wanted you to come over. The 'party' was an excuse."

I tilt my head and look at him, startled. "You don't need an excuse," I say softly, surprised that he can't sense how much he turns me on. "I would have come over for any reason at all. For no reason, in fact." Suddenly, he seems to get it, because his eyes light up and he slips one hand in mine. As in the past, the touch of his fingers sends waves of heat through me, and I blink meaningfully at him, then look over at the stairs. This is the only hint he needs.

We leave the boys in the den and go up to his bedroom. He's got a water bed with zebra-striped sheets and he grabs me around the waist and tosses me onto it. The bed rocks beneath me and I giggle at the ride, but I have to stop laughing as he begins to undress. I've waited for this moment for over a month, and I'm more excited than I've ever been about a guy.

There is something about Connor that defies logical expectations. He's handsome, but he doesn't know it. He's a banker, but he's got a water bed. And now I see, as he pulls off his faded jeans and unbuttons his white shirt, that he has several tattoos, a lick of barbed wire curling around his upper bicep, and a forties-style pinup girl on his hip. His body is muscular in all the right places, and I practically lick my lips when he's down to his flannel boxers, but then I realize I'm still dressed. I'm losing this game.

Quickly, I pull my stretchy black top over my head, kick off my short skirt and slide out of my fishnets. Then Connor takes over, undoing my bra and pulling off my matching panties. His hands are warm and sturdy, and he could make me come in an instant if he brought his fingertips between my legs. Just touched me there. A quick circle, a firm stroke. But he doesn't. We're going to make this last. I can tell it's going to be a night to remember.

"You look good on my bed," he says, staring at me before making his move. "Your black hair and pale skin against my sheets."

"Just like this?" I ask, stretching my arms over my head and holding the pose. I choose a position that matches the girl on his hip, and he gets it and smiles.

"As pretty as a picture."

"A moving picture," I remind him, arching my hips and beckoning with my body.

"You've been in the movies?" he wants to know, bringing his mouth, finally, *finally*, to my neck and kissing me. I can't answer right away. He has found my weakness, my all-time favorite place, and he licks and kisses in a line down my throat to my breasts. But he stops before reaching my nipples, pausing to say, "Keep talking," and I instantly understand that he wants a conversation while we fuck. He wants to play dirty.

"It was on a first date," I say.

"Bad girl."

"You have no idea." The look he gives me makes me even more excited and I grip his waist with my legs as he lifts me up. "I can be the baddest," I say, and he shakes his head as if he doesn't believe me. Reaching forward, I brush his light-brown hair out of his eyes, and then I stare at him, daring him to break the connection.

"He had a camera and a tripod—" I tell him. "And a fantasy script that he wanted to act out."

"You were the damsel in distress and he was the hero, coming to rescue you."

"Coming," I repeat, smiling. "That part's right."

Connor grins back at me, and then resumes his kissing games, licking my lower lip, biting it so that I can't speak. His hands wander over my body and he helps me to slide onto his cock. It's the best feeling I can ever remember. The first taste of his hard rod in my dripping pussy. I forget what I was saying until he whispers, "So you had this undeniable urge to star on the silver screen?"

"No," I tell him, surprised at how normal I sound. "Not the silver screen. The TV screen." Connor is making my body hum with pleasure, and the way he moves me up and down lets me know that this ride is going to last.

"You filmed and then watched?" he asks.

"We filmed and then fucked," I tell him, "with the two of us on the TV in the background. Every once in a while, I'd look up and see myself being taken doggie-style, or sucking his cock, and it would make me excited all over again."

He shakes his head as if he can't believe I would do something like that. Not someone as sweet and innocent as I am. But looks can be deceiving, and I can tell he's reevaluating his opinion of me and that I am getting bonus points by the second. I can also tell that he wants to ask me more questions, but it's my turn to quiz him now, and so I say, "And you? Your kinkiest time ever?"

Connor doesn't even hesitate. "She blindfolded me," he says. I don't know who "she" was, and for once I don't care. I'm not jealous of the ghost lovers in Connor's past. But I am curious.

"Did you like it?" I ask.

"At first. She tied a black silk scarf over my eyes and made me promise not to peek. Then she staged a sort of quiz show, rubbing these different objects over my—" he hesitates before saying "cock," which I think is sort of cute since I'm bouncing on it.

"Then what?" I ask, breathing hard.

"I had to guess what the item was before she tried another one."

"What did she rub on you?"

"A stuffed animal. A wooden coaster. A CD." He runs his fingers up and down my ribs, almost absentmindedly. His sturdy hands move up, finding my nipples, and he lightly pinches them between thumb and forefinger, making them hard in an instant. I'm learning quickly that Connor is one of those casual lovemakers who is very, very good. I can barely remember what I'm supposed to say next, but he reminds me.

"Have you ever done anything like that?"

I shake my head and my long hair brushes my shoulders. Never. "What happened?" I'm panting. "What did she do next?"

"She rubbed something cold and hard against me."

He's rubbing something warm and hard between my legs. The talking part of this game is getting more difficult. "And it was?" I finally manage to murmur. My voice no longer sounds like me. It's a hungry whispering sound, an animal, a porn star.

"I couldn't guess."

"So she kept rubbing?"

He sighs and nods.

"And you didn't have any idea?" I'm thinking, cold and hard. A metal spoon. A cucumber. A Popsicle.

"I knew," he says, pushing up with his hips so that I buck forward. I grip his shoulders to keep myself steady and start to work my body more seriously against his. The feel of his cock, slicked up with my juices, is making it difficult for me to stay focused. But I'm a competitive type of girl. I hate to lose at anything. So I force myself to continue.

"You didn't want to guess?"

"I knew what it was," he continues, "I just didn't want to believe it. I couldn't make myself say the word."

I slide back and forth on him. Oh, man, is he good. I could keep riding and riding, except that now he's working his hand down my flat belly, finding the right spot between my legs to flick with his fingertips. His fingers make tiny circles that miss my clit on purpose. I shift my hips to make a connection, but he continues to play his teasing tricks. Circles that come within a breath of where I need them and then flicker off course. Just out of reach. He's driving me crazy, which is definitely the point. Still, I'm almost there.

"What was it?" I whisper, about to reach the top.

"A knife," he says. "She was running the flat side of it up and down my cock. Not playing with the blade, but letting me feel that cool, smooth surface. When I finally had the guts to say it aloud, she put the knife down, climbed on top of me and fucked the living daylights out of me."

The image makes him seem both vulnerable and strong, powerless and powerful, and this is what makes me come. I don't know why, but it does.

"And after?" I ask him softly. He's still inside me, and I can tell by the look in his eyes that he's almost reached his peak. His cock throbs within my pussy, going deeper still, deeper than I thought possible. Another stroke, another plunge, and he'll be there.

"We broke up," he says through clenched teeth. "I mean, if she could do something like that on a whim, how could I ever trust her?"

He's bigger than me, so strong, and he grips me around the waist and pulls me even harder onto him, sealing our bodies together and groaning as he reaches that place, that fantasy place, and lets loose.

Downstairs, in the den, I can hear rockets going off.

FARM FRESH

Dante Davidson

JUICY.
PLUMP.
LUSCIOUS.
MOUTH-WATERING.
DELICIOUS—

I was rock hard by the time I got to the farm. The words appeared on old-fashioned signs, hand-painted in a startlingly bright red on small squares of yellow cardboard. The signs stood in a lopsided line by the side of the road, and their faux-innocent words had gotten to me. Again. Gotten to me as they did nearly every day on my commute home from work. I knew it didn't make much sense. Why was I aroused by a series of adjectives used to describe fruit? It's not as if I'm the type of geek who uses a thesaurus to turn himself on, and clearly whoever had created these signs had possessed a good friend in *Roget's*.

But there it was—sense or no sense, I possessed yet another raging erection that made it difficult to continue driving, coupled with an undeniable desire to pull over and try the new crop of strawberries. Maybe that's all I needed. More fruit in my diet. Never seem to make that five-a-day goal. Perhaps an apple a day, or a strawberry or two, might deflect my ever-growing libido.

And maybe the girl would be there. Maybe the girl had something to do with it. She was a stunning blonde with a goddess body and a long wave of blonde hair, and she stood at the ready behind the counter at the fruit stand. At least, usually, she stood there. Occasionally, I'd catch her walking out to the fields, and I'd note the way her hips moved under her faded jeans. Sometimes, she even seemed to notice me back, watching until I turned the corner and lost sight of her in my rearview mirror.

Why hadn't I stopped before now? I don't know. Desire to be home and end my day for real would win out over potential embarrassment as I shared my erection with a brand-new friend. Now, in the late spring sunlight, I felt as if the time had finally come.

It took me a few minutes to get myself under control before I exited the car and walked to the produce stand. Instantly, I realized all that deep breathing and thinking about baseball had been a waste. Here I was, hard all over again. Not because of any signs. Or because I have a hard-on for fresh produce. But because of her. Fact is, I could have used every one of those words to describe her.

Ripe.

Juicy.

Ready.

Sweet.

She smiled when I approached, and then she raised a hand to me, as if we were old friends. I gave her what must have been my most baffled expression. Was she beckoning me to do her? That's what I was hoping, because it was clear in my mind how we'd make it work. Shove the berry baskets aside, pluck her up onto the counter, and ravish that sweet, ripe body of hers.

"Taste?" she asked, and my vision went blurry. Taste? Yeah,

I wanted a taste. I wanted to start at her lips, which were bare of any cosmetic, but full and plump and pink. Then I wanted to move along the hollow of her throat, to drink in deep of her peaches-and-cream complexion. She was wearing a little white apron over a blue-and-white-checked shirt. She had on faded jeans and tiny hoop earrings, and every time she moved, she made me want her even more. The way she pushed her wheat-gold hair out of her eyes. The way she seemed to possess a berry-hued blush in the apples of her cheeks. She was a meal—a meal at a five-star restaurant. And she was out here on the farm.

I wanted to devour her.

"Taste," she repeated, no longer asking a question. I saw now that she was offering samples, and I stepped forward and put out my hand. "You're from the city," she said, and when my eyebrows went up in a query, I saw her motioning to my sports car out in the dirt lot.

"Yeah," I said, embarrassed.

"You don't get quality like this from the supermarket," she assured me. "For the best taste, you need to come out to the farm."

"Let me judge," I said, teasing her. Of course, I was prepared to assure her that anything she put in my mouth was heavenly, but I wanted to hear her keep talking. She had a slice of peach ready and waiting, and she handed it over quickly. I took a bite, felt the juices swell in my mouth and thought about what it would feel like to peel down her jeans and lick the split of her body.

"Sweet?" she asked.

I nodded.

"Then try this—"

Next was a berry, the ripest, roundest, most perfect straw-berry I'd ever seen. I greedily reached for it, but now the girl was teasing me. She held the berry out of reach, and said, "What will you give me if I'm right?"

"Right?"

"About this being better than any berries you've had in the city."

"What do you want?" I asked.

"Ride in your car."

I smiled. She was no hick. Yes, this was a farm, but it was a farm on the road between two major cities. The girl had seen plenty of fancy cars before, and probably driven in several. Maybe her family even owned one. With her good looks, all the guys in a twenty-mile radius must have been hounding her for years. But I played along. She wanted to be country mouse, I'd be her city mouse without batting an eye.

"You got it," I told her.

"Have to play fair," she said. "You have to tell me for real if this is the sweetest fruit you've ever had."

Then she pushed it forward, and I put the whole strawberry in my mouth and bit down. Trust me when I saw that this was by far the most delicious piece of fruit that I'd ever tasted. Trust me again when I say that she could tell by my expression I was hungry for far more than her fruit stand could provide.

"You win," I said softly.

"I think we both will," she told me, untying her apron and coming out from behind the counter.

"Can you just leave?"

"I can do whatever I want," she said, and I could hear the sound of a rebel in her voice. I liked that tone a lot. "Just give me a minute." I nodded, and then watched her hurry to the house behind the stand, and I prepared myself for being chased by some hillbilly with a shotgun. But no, a pretty girl—sister? Mother?—came out with her and took over her spot at the stand, and then my blonde goddess rushed her way over to me.

"Where to?" I asked, ushering her to the car.

"I've seen the way you drive," she said, and I realized she'd caught sight of me slowing down to gaze at her. That I wasn't so top secret after all. "Why don't you let me take you for a spin?"

Without a thought, I handed her the keys, and within

moments, she'd motored us along a back road to an empty spot
overlooking a flower-filled meadow. It would have been a lovely
place to picnic, or to set up an easel to paint, or to—

"Taste?" she said, in the exact same way she'd offered me
that first bite of peach, and now I looked to see that she'd split
her jeans and was staring at me with a hungry, yearning expression that had to have matched my own. Matched, and perhaps
surpassed.

I didn't answer this question with words. I answered it with
my tongue, pressed to the split of her panties, where I could
already make out the scent of the first juices of her arousal. For
the first time, I realized how much like juices a woman's liquid
was. I breathed in deep and thought of fragrant ripe fruits,
thought of the berries and peach that I'd consumed earlier.

Crazy, but there was something again so fresh about her.
So untouched and unmanufactured. My mind took me on a
memory trip of the perfumed city girls I tend to go for. The tall
lean ones with minty-clean breath and carefully blown-out hair.
The ones who won't go out in the rain in case they get "the
frizzies." And then I looked up at this girl, and I said, "Let's get
out," knowing somehow that she would roll in the dirt with me
if I asked. That she would get all sloppy and messy and wet and
everything would be fine.

More than fine.

She moved faster than I did, coming around to my side of
the car and grabbing my hand. She brought me after her to the
center of the field, where a tree stood, gnarled by winds and
time. Beneath it, she turned around, so that I could see her
before she began to undress. Now, she moved slowly. Letting me
see. Letting me appreciate the show. Her checked shirt popping
open button by button. Her jeans sliding down her lean thighs.
Then her white bra and panties, a simple matched set, carelessly
strewn on the ground. I was behind her, still dressed in my suit
and unprepared for what it would feel like when she came naked
into my arms.

Sure, my fantasies had gotten me to this point. But reality can blow you away. Think about it: picturing a ripe strawberry will make your mouth water. Biting into one is an entirely different experience. And I was ready to bite into her. To bring my mouth to the rise of her shoulders and nip at her. To move in a line down her flat belly until I was kneeling on the dirt, pressing my open, hungry mouth now to the naked skin of her sex.

So this is what I did. Everything that her signs had made me want to do. She was juicy. And sweet. And ripe. She was succulent and mouthwatering, and—

"Delicious," I murmured, and she gripped me as I ate her. I pressed my tongue up inside of her pussy, drove it deep in there to get the sweetest tasting juices I'd ever savored. She moaned softly as I brought her ever closer to climax, and her noises simply urged me on. The intensity of the moment filled my head. How pure it seemed to be fucking outdoors. How smooth her skin was under my fingertips. Part of me couldn't believe this was real, and part of me knew not to analyze anymore, but to give in, and to drink in, and to dine.

The taste of her was pure sweetness. The sensation of her cunt against my tongue was as unbelievable as was her next statement. "I want to come on you."

Oh god, I thought. *I want that, too.*

"I want to milk your cock," she murmured.

I ripped out of my clothes, tossing down my jacket for some sort of cushion against the dirt, and then waiting only long enough to see in her eyes what she wanted. I sucked in my breath as I lay down on the dirt and let her get between my legs. She was a vixen, her lips parting around my cock and drawing me in, giving me a slow, long lick and a short, firm suck. She worked me up and down, using her fingertips to stroke my balls, cradling them in the palm of her hand as she continued to play those naughty games with her mouth. When she'd gotten me as ripe as she wanted, she climbed astride, her body opening up and taking me deep within her. I knew she wanted to control the ride. I don't know how. I just knew. Maybe from the way she'd handled my sports car. Or maybe from the sparkling light in her eyes. I didn't care who was in the driver's seat this time. All that mattered was the way her pussy squeezed and released, the way her hips bucked up and down, the weight of her like a warmth on me I'd never felt before.

She leaned forward, her hands on my shoulders, and she rocked her pelvis against me, back and forth, and I could tell from the look on her face each time her clit made contact with my body. It was like an electric flicker passed through her eyes, making them a brighter blue, momentarily rivaling the sky before they settled back to their normal, deep color.

I thought of what she said, the word she'd used—"milk"— and that's what it felt like. Her pussy squeezed me so perfectly, over and over, until I knew just one more moment and I would come. I put my hands around her waist, moving her slightly faster, and she understood, and I saw her concentrating as I said, "I'm going to—"

She said, "Yes—" her breath a rush.

"Now," I said.

"Yes!"

And we reached it, with me bucking her off the ground, raising her up in the air as I came, and her finding her space a moment after, so that her cunt held me tight as I crested back down. Back down to a level that was still higher than any previous plateau.

The sky was that periwinkle blue of twilight as she came into my arms, her hair spreading over my naked chest, her pert body still sealed to my own. She looked directly into my eyes, and again I saw a glint of a rebel—or maybe a full-fledged rebel— gazing at me. And I saw those words again in my head. Ripe. Succulent. Juicy. All of them. All of them were her.

"See what I mean?" she said afterward, her lovely blonde hair falling forward over her face. I reached out to brush away those corn-husk soft tendrils, and I raised my eyebrows, waiting for her to continue. "The fresher the better. Can't get quality like that in a sterile city environment, can you?"

Now, I understood, and I shook my head. "You're right," I agreed, smiling. "The only way to go is farm fresh."

X-RATED CONVERSATIONS

Becky Chapel

Baby, you ready?"

So ready. I've been waiting for this call, dressed in my pale-green silk negligee, my hair rustling in lustrous curls past my shoulders, my skin still warm and buffed from a day on the beach. I've been in bed with a fashion magazine open before me—not reading, not even looking at the pictures of silky, feline women—just turning the pages and waiting.

"Stefanie-girl…," Giselle continues, "take your panties down, take them down to your ankles and bend over on the bed."

I do it without thinking, ignoring the voice in my head that taunts me, *She's not here, not really, you can just pretend.* That's a lie. I do it because she *is* here, throwing me forward on the bed and bending on her knees to eat me from behind—thrusting her pink tongue between my porcelain thighs and drinking from the split of my body. She *is* here with me, commanding me to spread my legs wider, to bend over farther, and I do it, hands clutching the phone, breathing ragged, heartbeat exploding in my ears.

"Turn over," she orders, and I'm with her, her hands gripping my waist, lifting me off the bed with each forward drive of her hips, each thrust impaling me with her strap-on cock. "That's the girl," she says, her voice urgent, "Oh, how beautiful you are." Her fingers trail along my belly, up to my breasts, cupping them, teasing my nipples, brushing the tips. She anchors me with her weight, her body on top of mine, and she leans forward to kiss me, slow and long, her skin warm on my own, her lips smooth and dry. We're so close together that I feel her heartbeat link with my own. It's like music, the way we move, the rhythm of the dance. It's like fire, the glow in her eyes, the heat of her skin.

It's like she's here with me.

"C'mon, Stefanie, kiss me, darling."

My head tilts against the cool satin of my pillow, my lips part, as if I am kissing a demon lover, an incubus. My body rocks beneath the phantom, invisible, unreal, and then the currents work through me.

I can picture her in my mind, her pale curls, like an angel's, her eyes shut tight, the blonde lashes against her tanned skin. Her mouth is tense, canine teeth biting into her bottom lip, the urgency creasing her sculptured face. She arches her head back as she moans aloud—the image of ecstasy. I bask in the sublime look that crosses her face as she reaches the climax. I own that look.

"Darling," Giselle sighs, her breathing gone dark and heavy. "That was amazing."

"Yes..."

"Call me tomorrow...," she whispers, no talk of her day—of mine—of the work that separates us.

"Yes," I say, with another sigh, filled with satisfaction. "Yes, Giselle. Tomorrow," and I roll over and set the phone quietly into place on the bedside table. Cutting the cord.

For that is the bane of a long-distance lover, the knowing that three weeks have passed since I saw her last, and three more will come and go before I see her again.

Tomorrow and tomorrow, and tomorrow. And now it's two

weeks until I see her, two weeks until I climb on the plane and fly from sunny California to wintry New York City. We are having a December like no other, eighty-six degrees, too hot to wear jeans, too hot to wear anything but gauzy, summer-print dresses that skim my hips and thighs and flit and flirt when I walk.

Too hot to make love? Never.

"The kitchen," I say when it's my turn to call. "On the countertop."

"The cool tile," she says back, and I know she's with me. "You can watch your reflection in the windows behind me."

I can see it, my green eyes glimmering in the light from the city, while all the lights in the apartment are out. I can feel her arms, the muscles in them, the shift and slide of the muscles beneath her skin. She is holding me tight, and my legs are wrapped firmly around her waist. I've got the cock on this time, and I drive it in and out and hard, *hard*, my fingers digging into her arms, my teeth on the ridge of her shoulder, biting to stifle the scream. I work her without a break, like a machine, like a wonderful fucking machine, our parts well oiled, interlocking, caught in a groove with one destination in sight.

She lifts her hands to the back of my head, cradling me, losing her fingers in the gold foil of my hair. Her kiss is like water, sliding, cool. Her kiss is like the ocean, like I've brought the ocean with me. Her full cat-mouth on mine is like a dream that makes me sorry to wake up.

Her kiss is like she's with me.

And, in a way, she is.

"Watch us," Giselle says, "Watch the way we move." I peer at our reflection, the black-and-white tile floor beneath her bare feet, the white marble counter beneath my ass—the reflection of our bodies moving, working, shimmering in the mirror-window.

"You're perfect," I tell her, "Just like that. Keep it going, now. Just like that."

In and out and HARD. Can you feel it? Hard, like a piston, well oiled, moving up and down, sliding in and out. Too good.

Too right. I can taste it, oh god, I can taste it, my hips sliding
on the counter, my body working against hers, my hips snapping against hers, too good, too right..."Ohhhh!" It's a shriek,
louder than I expected, louder than I planned, "Ohhh, my
sweet...," and she echoes it back to me, calling out my name,
"Stefanie!" as we come together, three thousand miles apart, as
we come together and explode.

"Tomorrow," I tell her.

"Tomorrow," she promises.

And tomorrow, and tomorrow, and tomorrow.

It's a week until I see her, and my suitcase is already on the
floor, silk skirts and velvet dresses, high heels, jeans and leather
boots. My jacket is back from the cleaners, hanging in plastic
from the hook on my door. My lingerie is new, packed in its
little compartment, ribbons and lace and fancy things to make
her moan. My hair is longer, I think, and it looks different than
before, the bangs hanging low over my forehead, the rest a
tousled mane that falls past my shoulder blades. I inspect myself
as I hope she will—as I know she will—turning in front of the
full-length mirror, admiring the lines in my calves, the tone of
my thighs, the sleek curves of my waist and breasts.

I imagine her hands on me, her fingers exploring, parting,
dipping. I imagine myself through her eyes, and I feel a longing
steal over me that is impossible to shake. I lie down on the bed,
holding the phone to my chest, wanting to call—but it's too
early—wanting her voice to wrap me up and carry me to her.

I press the buttons slowly, the glowing green buttons that
mock me somehow, and she answers immediately.

"I want," I start, "Giselle, I want..."

"Slower, this time," she says, her voice a lesson in control.
"Slower, girl, don't rush it."

"Slower," I breathe back to her, "Okay, all right." Steady
now, my fingers probing, steady now, through the soft curtain of
my panties. But I can't. "On the floor," I order, my voice strong,
my passion winning. "On the floor, Giselle."

And I hear the laugh in her voice, the surprise in her voice, as she says. "Yes, all right. The living room floor."

"I'm on top."

She knows it.

"I'm on top and I'm holding you down."

Oh, yes. She knows it. My hands flat against her shoulders, pinning her to the plush carpet, my knees spread wide at her hips, my body in charge, my will in charge. Faster, I need it faster, and I'm controlling the speed, I'm running this machine.

She arches her fine hips to help me, to give me some leverage. Her hands find my waist and she keeps me steady, keeps that steady, raging beat. Her synthetic cock is a part of me, the hard, throbbing rod a part of my body. I never release it entirely. I hold it within me and ride it, squeezing it, the contractions running through my body into her, *tight and hard*, release, *tight and hard*, release; her breathing sounds like sobbing to me, her face is flushed with the effort of it, the effort to hold back. She can't, though, because I'm in charge and I don't want her to hold back.

I work her harder, watching her face change. Her curls are matted, her cheeks are covered in a thin sheen of sweat. She's biting her bottom lip as she always does before she comes, and she's moaning, repeating, like a mantra, over and over, "Yes, baby, yes, baby, yes..."

I feel it happen inside me, the change inside me, and her fingers dig deeper into my waist, needing to capture me, to hold me to her. I go forward against her, onto her chest, never stopping the pounding rhythm of my hips, faster than ever, faster than anything. She lifts me forward with her hips and we're slamming into each other, slamming like two trains meeting, the crash reverberating through both of our bodies. The crash and then the aftermath of the sparks and fires that shoot through us, every nerve ending tingling, every fiber burning.

She closes her eyes and wraps me in her arms. She holds me to her beating heart and wraps me in her arms. Her voice caresses me, her fingertips soothe me. And it's as if she's here, with me, and not three thousand miles away.

"Tomorrow," she says, the catch still in her voice.

"Tomorrow," I sigh.

And tomorrow, and tomorrow, and tomorrow.

The plane lands at 6:05. I'm the first one up, the first pushy passenger to the door, and the flight attendant gives me a little "schoolteacher" frown, as if I should be made to sit down until everyone else has left. But we're grownups here, aren't we? And she can only glower at me while I slide past her with my carry-on suitcase and fly up the enclosed hallway to the gate.

She's right at the front of the greeters. And she has a placard that says STEFANIE in bold black pen and I LOVE YOU beneath it in red. She's wearing a long navy trench coat still dusted with snow, and she's holding a bouquet of white roses. I'm in her arms before they're fully open to me, snuggling against her chest and bear-hugging her.

"Luggage?" she asks.

"This is it...I didn't want to wait."

She grins and takes my hand, leading me to the car park, kissing me while we walk. "Missed you," she sighs, stopping us again and staring into my face. "Missed you so much, Stefanie-girl."

My eyes are wide open, seeing her, and yet I can't really see her. I need to touch her, need the feel of her skin beneath my hands. And I grab her arm and pull her forward. "Giselle," I say, "I want..."

She drives too fast to get me home. She takes all the short-cuts, weaving in and out of traffic, and she drives much too fast. But not fast enough. I snake my hand into her lap while we cruise, I stroke her strap-on firmly through her slacks, longing making my fingers work harder than they should, pressing the molded dildo back against her body—but she sighs and in my mind the bulge there grows.

I lean against her, unbuckling and unzipping and revealing,

lean down to take her in my mouth, to take this rigid cock into my mouth and bathe it in sweet, velvety warmth. Her juices have dampened the cock and it tastes of summer, even in this wintery city, she tastes of sinning and heat, like summer, and her cock seems to grow even larger in my throat as I stroke it with my tongue, work it between my lips—though I know this is only an illusion. It seems as if she grows and presses against the back of my throat, and her hand presses against the back of my head, twining her fingers in my hair.

Then she quickly pulls me back and says, "Wait, Stefanie. Wait this time. Go slower this time."

She wants to savor it, and I shiver, regaining my control, and move back in my seat. I stare at her as we drive, memorizing her features, matching them with the image of her in my head. Her golden curls are longer, too, a bit shaggy to the top of her jacket collar. Her eyes are the dark blue of a winter sky at dusk, the clear blue of the water outside my Malibu tower.

I want to devour her, want to dine on her, but I lean back in my seat, set my hand on her thigh, and close my eyes. My heart races, and I mentally try to slow it down. My heart races, and I listen to it beat in my ears. *Slow down*, I whisper, *Slow down*.

We're there: in the garage, in the elevator, in the hallway, in her apartment. We're there: in the living room, in the kitchen, down the hallway, to her bedroom. We're there: stripping— *too quickly, slow it down*—stripping off layers of clothing, watching each other but not helping each other—*off, off, off*—I lose buttons in the process, tearing through my traveling suit, she swears at her shoes, at the knot in the laces of her leather oxfords, and then yanks them off without untying.

On the bed, in her arms, fast, I need her fast. I need her now and hard and fast.

"Shh, baby, slow." Giselle says it, I hear it, but I can't do it.

"I need," I tell her, "I *need*."

And she needs it too, we'll go slow later, we'll go slow after. She turns me on my side and plunges forward, driving inside me, bucking inside me, her eyes open and staring down at me, blue eyes as clear as a midnight sky. Her lips are parted, her teeth clenched, her jaw tight. There's a sheen of sweat on her forehead and the rise of her cheekbones. Her curls are matted, her smell is all around me, her body is all around me. I lose myself in the feeling of her fingers on my breasts, of her warm open mouth on my neck, of her skin against mine. I arch forward, capturing her to me, meeting her lips with my own, drinking in her kisses, drinking in her love.

Our hips snap together, and I open up and take her inside me, draining her with my muscles. She is everywhere at once, pulling out and going down between my legs to taste me there, licking me, lapping at my flood of juices. She turns and I am suckling from her, drinking her as I did in the car, lapping all of my juices away. I work steadier—"keep that rhythm"—then quickly she is up and positioning me on the bed and she is in me from behind, working me, and I arch and rock her back. And when I feel it, feel the tremors build inside her, the shudders that work through the muscles of her thighs, I pull away and order her, with just a flick of my hair, with just a look in my eyes, "On the bed—on your back."

And I'm on her, on top of her, riding, driving, taking her so deep inside me and making that connection happen. Our hearts connecting, our blood rushing at the same beat, at that same crazy beat. Her eyes lock on mine, her hands are in my hair, on my waist, cupping my breasts. Her mouth says, "Kiss me," and I do. Her eyes say, "Love me," and I do. And I do: Love her, kiss her, work her, devour her, *savor* her. Until there is nothing left. Until those waves of power roll over us both and there is nothing left.

In her arms, her smell around me, in her arms with my hair over her shoulders and over my breasts, she says, softly, joking with me, teasing me, "Tomorrow…"

And I smile, and I kiss her gently, and I say, "Tonight."

SURRENDER

Sophia Valenti

I cross the threshold of his office, standing before his desk while he silently shuffles papers and pretends not to notice me. But I know he's aware of my presence. I can tell by his unnatural posture—slightly stiff and without an ounce of relaxation. That pleases me a tiny bit, but the sight does nothing to quell the beautiful apprehension and delicious fear that's welling up inside me.

I'm here because of what he can give me—because of what I need. He's the only man who's been able to truly satisfy all of those dark cravings swirling inside me. I see him a few times a year, when he's in town on business. A simple text tells me the date and time, and I let myself into his spacious penthouse apartment, dressed as he expects: in a sheer white blouse and short plaid skirt—no panties.

The window behind him is filled with a stunning view, the bright lights of the skyline punctuating the velvety blackness of the sky. The city is humming with the rhythmic pulsations of the night, and that energy is pumping through my veins.

He looks up, his face expressionless but his eyes glowing with erotic hunger.

"Yes?" he asks, feigning ignorance and making my cheeks heat with embarrassment. This is our routine, but no matter how many times we play, the words don't come to me any easier. I swallow nervously, trying to find my voice.

"I'm here for my appointment, Sir," I manage to utter.

"Appointment? For what?" He tries to stay in character, but his lips curl up in a subtle smile. My pussy grows damper with each passing second.

"For my punishment." The words fall from my lips as a whisper. On most visits, that hushed confession wouldn't be enough. The fact that he didn't make me repeat myself lets me know how eager he is for this scene to begin. And how much he wants to hurt me.

He glances at his desk calendar and nods. "Oh, yes—it's right here: *Midnight: Bend a naughty girl over your desk and spank her bare ass until she's learned her lesson.*"

He stands, and my heart leaps into my throat. In seconds, he's pushed me forward. I grasp the far edge of the desk, feeling my breasts crush beneath me as he flips up my skirt. Cool air wafts over my naked cunt, and I blush even more deeply, knowing how wet I am.

I gaze up at the window, the city lights seeming to dim as his reflection captures my attention. I arch my back, offering myself to him even as I hold my breath in anticipation of that first spark of pain. Grabbing my hair, he holds my body taut. His free hand connects and pain flares through me, reminding me that this is the one place—the one moment—where I feel whole. My world is reduced to this room, where my Master obliterates all of my thoughts and truths. I am no more than his plaything to punish and please.

The pain loses its sharpness, but its fiery heat consumes me. I lose count of how many times his hand lands. The numbers don't matter. What does matter is my surrender. He knows the exact moment it happens. He feels the stubbornness leave me, my sense of self scattering on the wind of my sighs.

His cock fills me in an instant, and I'm so grateful I nearly cry. Burying my face in my folded arms, I let him take me as hard and fast as he needs, because each thrust of his hips, each slap of his balls against my clit, takes me higher and higher.

He groans as his shaft pulses inside me, and my cunt clutches him in rhythmic spasms as pleasure flows through me. I will myself to hold on to this perfect feeling until we meet again.

TO LOLA,
WITH LOVE

Alison Tyler

'm not exactly sure how to admit this—it sounds funny to say, and looks funnier on paper—but my girlfriend is having an affair with my vagina. She'll readily admit to it. She's even written love letters to it. Yes, indeed, Jo, my normally sane, very lovely, dyke-sweetheart has taken pen in hand and written to my cunt.

At first, she simply cooed to it, sliding one deft pointer between my nether lips, then lifting that finger to her mouth to drink the juice from the tip, whispering softly, "Oooh, pretty thing, pretty pussy. Oooh, what darling kitty lips you have. I'm gonna lick 'em. Yesss, I am. I'm gonna drink all that sticky sap from deep inside. Oh, yes, darlin', oh yes."

She employed the exact same voice that some slightly deranged people use when talking to babies or small animals. That singsong, nonsense tone. That wuvvy-duvvy cartoonish croon. That nausea-inspiring simper that suggests the very early stages of puppy love.

But this love has lasted.

And so has the love affair Jo has held with my vagina.

Now, she's not totally off the deep end. I mean, she hasn't proposed marriage to it or anything. But she brings it presents.

"Won't you look pretty in these satin panties?" she crows. "Oh, yes, oh yes, so pretty..."

Excuse me?

"Mama Jo got them special. See the lace, pretty lace..."

Okay, she's talking to my cunt, I thought, at first. *I can handle this. I can get a grip.* Except, she was talking to it as if it had the brain of, say, cement. So, I came to a decision: if my cunt was going to have a love affair behind my back—no, that's impossible—*in front of* my back, then it had better get treated with some respect. I wanted intelligent conversation, not baby-doll cooing. And I told her so.

"None of your business, really," is what Jo had to say.

"Excuse me?"

"It's none of your business what Lola and I do, or how we talk."

"Lola?"

"Yes, that's her name."

"*You named my cunt?*"

"No...she told me."

Too much. Too fucking much.

"My cunt *told* you her name?"

"Well," Jo said, shrugging her built shoulders at me and giving me a withering stare, "Not in so many words, but I knew."

I didn't have anything to say to that. Not at first, anyway. I told myself that perhaps I was being naive. I'd only been in one long-term relationship before Jo, and that was with a girl even shyer than me. Maybe normal couples talked to each other's pussies every day. Maybe I was overreacting. Still, waking up to Jo saying, "Good morning, Lola," was a little difficult to get used to. I mean, Lola didn't have to go to work. Lola didn't want fresh coffee. Lola was just fine sleeping late. Didn't Jo want to wish *me* a good morning? I was, after all, the one who ironed her work clothes. Who ran out for bagels and the Sunday paper. Lola couldn't do *any* of that.

Finally, I decided to discuss the situation with my best friend. Katy wasn't the least bit sympathetic. She said I should be happy, that I should be pleased with all the attention I was getting. The love letters written on the bathroom mirror. The presents. She said that I should count my blessings and think of all the lonely heart dykes out there who don't have gorgeous girlfriends wanting to make love to them all the time.

"But she talks to it," I said.

"So?" Katy asked. "Don't you ever talk to yourself? Talk to your computer? People talk to their cars, even. It's not so strange." Katy paused. "What would be strange is if Lola talked back." She paused again, thoughtfully. "Now *there's* a ventriloquist act I wouldn't mind catching."

"She named it," I told her, even though that was one of things I wasn't sure I was going to reveal. There are some pieces of information people should probably keep to themselves. But I know enough of Katy's secrets that I was sure mine would be safe with her.

Katy saw no problem with this little tidbit either. "Guys name theirs all the time. Mr. Happy. Little Willie. Big Johnson. Hairy Larry."

"How would you know about what guys do?" I asked.

"I have ears," Katy said. "I hear things."

"Anyway," I told her, indignantly, "*I* didn't give it a name. She did. Lola wouldn't even have been in my top ten list."

"Lovers give each other pet names all the time," Katy said. "Remember how Grace used to call me Puddytat."

"And it drove you mad," I reminded her. "Plus," I pointed out, "Jo's not calling *me* Lola. She's calling my pussy Lola."

"Well, why don't you name her cooch? Let her see what it feels like?"

I considered it. I pictured a naked Jo standing in front of me, called up a mental image of her full-figured body, and the strip of fuzz she shaves Mohawk style, covering the lips of her pussy. The only name that came to my mind was Chuck. Don't ask me why. Maybe the shortness of her hair made me think of a pilot I once met at a bar. I could just imagine how well that nickname would go over. No, beating Jo at her own game wasn't going to work.

"Any other ideas?" I asked Katy. She was being less than helpful.

"I simply don't see what the big deal is," Katy told me. "You've got a girlfriend who loves you more than anything. Who pampers you and plays with you. Who's gone so far as to make up nicknames for your body parts. Why are you trying to make problems where there aren't any? Are you one of those women who's simply never satisfied?"

"No," I said, honestly. "I'm more than satisfied."

"Does she call you from work, make you put Lola on the phone?"

I shook my head.

"Has she asked to be alone with Lola?"

I hesitated, unsure about whether I was ready to confess the rest of it. But with her staring at me like that, waiting, practically daring me, I said in a low voice, so nobody else in the café could hear, "She asked her to dance."

This made Katy laugh out loud. "There's a vision," she said, enthralled. "Did she get down on the floor, first? Right down there on her knees in the sawdust? Did she look at Lola eye to eye? Or mouth to mouth? Or really, lips to lips?"

I shook my head.

"Come on," Katy said, "All dancing is about sex. Body parts pressed up against body parts. It's a form of publicly accepted foreplay. With you and Jo, the results were going to be the same. You'd be in bed together by the end of the evening whether you danced with her or not. What's the difference whether she asked your whole self to dance or just your cunt?"

"This wasn't the hokey pokey," I told her. "This was me and Jo, at a bar. On one of our little dates."

"Give it a break," Katy said. "Your girlfriend wanted to dance with you. There's nothing abnormal about that at all. She's a bit eccentric in the way she asked."

Which is really all I wanted to hear. Because, honestly, I was starting to like the added attention. And the dancing thing had been sort of cute. Sort of sweet in an odd, unbelievable way. It had happened after a long day at work, when we'd decided to relax and go out to Ladies' Night. You know, the bar on Fourth Street and Main. Me and Jo were sitting on those tall, wooden chairs and drinking our shots, watching as the fools tried their hand at line dancing. Can you believe they still teach that? Every Thursday from six to seven. But this one night, when the class was over, Jo walked to the jukebox and started slipping in the quarters. And all of a sudden, "The Girl from Ipanema"—our song—poured out of the speakers and there was Jo, standing in front of me, looking me up and down in that way of hers, as if she's adding up a long list of numbers. A list of very large numbers, nodding as if she approves of the total sum.

"Wanna dance—" she asked softly. Before I could give her an answer, which would have been yes, of course, she finished the question, "Wanna dance, Lola?"

"Lola?" I said, surprised.

"Can't I dance with her?" Jo pouted, acting hurt, as if I were depriving her of a great delight by saying no.

"H-How...?" I stammered. Did she want me to get undressed for her at the bar? Slip off my clothes and let her dance with Lola? Jo has asked me to do much odder things than that in our three years together. She's taken my panties away from me during a long car ride, had me spread my legs up on the dashboard and let her watch while I've pleasured myself. At her insistence, we joined the mile high club. The mile low club on the Chunnel when we took a vacation from London to Paris. We've even joined the yard wide club in the back of my VW bug. What was she asking for now?

"Just trust me," Jo said, "And let me lead." So, against my

better judgment, I let her. Felt those strong arms come around me, groove me over to the dance floor, position me right and then move with me. Back and forth. Gyrating. My little body was tight against her larger, more substantial form. And in the heat of it, the dimness of the bar, the sound of the music around us, everything started to make sense.

I swear. With Lola pressed up like that against Jo, the rest of my body simply melted away. I started to realize that there was something about the swing and the sway of it. I started to get into this whole ménage à trois thing. This ménage à trois for the mind. I could tell Jo was pleased with my behavior. And I could tell that Lola was feeling pretty enthusiastic, as well.

Maybe Katy was right. What girl wouldn't be happy? Dancing. Presents. Drinks all night at her favorite bar.

And that, I thought, was that.

At least, until Valentine's Day, when the flowers arrived. She'd sent them with a pastel note that read in gently sloping cursive: *To Lola, with love.* For some reason, this pushed me over the edge. Dancing was one thing. Pretty panties were another. But flowers for Lola? Flowers for *her* instead of for me? Sent with love on the most romantic day of the year? I started to feel—I don't know how to say this—but I started to feel left out. But before doing anything truly stupid, I called Katy for advice.

"What is your problem?" she asked.

"She sent Lola flowers."

"Do you know what I got for Valentine's Day?" Katy asked.

Uh-oh, I thought. "What?" I asked, hopefully.

"Nothing. Not one thing. Not a card. Not candy. Not a single flower. *You* didn't even send me one of those pathetic girl cards that friends send to their loser friends who don't have Valentines. Do you think I'm the right person to be talking to?"

"Maybe not," I admitted.

"*I* didn't get flowers. And my cunt didn't get flowers." Katy sighed, then calmed down. A little. "Really, Angel. What exactly is your problem today?"

"She sent the flowers to Lola. Not me."

"How can you be green about your own pussy?" Katy asked. "It's like a topic on one of those talk shows: Women Who Are Jealous of Their Vaginas."

"Ha, ha," I said.

"Isn't this like being jealous of an inanimate object?" Katy continued, "Like those women who are jealous of baseball because their husbands are always watching the game."

"Hey..." I said, not liking the tone of her voice or, to be perfectly honest, the way she was talking about Lola, comparing her to a sport. Really.

"Or of a pet," Katy continued. "Jealous of a dog or a—"

"Pussy?" I interrupted.

"Remember what the Bible says?" Katy asked, switching subjects so fast that she lost me in the changeover.

"No," I said, wondering what in god's name the Bible had to do with any of this.

"Thou shalt not covet thy neighbor's—"

"What?" I asked, interrupting again. "Wife?"

"Something like that," Katy said. "I never paid much attention at Sunday school."

"It feels as if she's cheating on me," I finally admitted. "It feels as if she's sent flowers to another woman, this Lola woman, and that I found out by accident." I paused. "You know that I caught my ex-girlfriend in bed with someone else. You know how hard it is for me to trust people."

"So you're saying that Jo's committing adultery with your own pussy," Katy said, "Is that right? Have I got all the facts straight?"

"Yeah," I muttered. When she put it like that the whole thing sounded ridiculous.

"This is way too confusing for me," Katy said. "I think you'd better talk to Jo. Or get yourself some therapy."

If those were the two choices, I knew which one to pick. So I called Jo at work.

Jo answered right away, that familiar smile in her husky voice, "You've reached the bar..."

"Jo, why did you send my cunt flowers?"

"Hey!" she said, "You weren't supposed to open the card, it was for *her*."

"Um, what's 'she' gonna do with them?"

"Smell them. Enjoy them."

"We have to talk," I said.

"Sure, Angel. I'll be home at one."

I paced through the apartment, unable to park myself at the computer and get my work done. I'd started to feel as if sitting were a bad thing... I mean, sitting on *her*. And I suddenly felt the urge to take a bath, to shave Lola cleanly, to stand naked in front of the bouquet so she *could* enjoy them.

I ran the water in our claw-foot tub, adding raspberry-scented bubble bath and lighting a few candles. Normally, I wouldn't get so carried away, but this seemed to be a special occasion—flowers and all. As I spread on the shaving cream, I found that I touched myself more gently than normal. I slid the razor over that softest skin and admired it. When I was through, I powdered all over, then went and got the pretty panties Jo had bought and put them on.

Lola was happy. I could tell.

Jo came home on schedule, a wrapped present under one arm.

I was sitting on the couch, nude save for the panties, the flowers well within smelling-range on the coffee table.

"For Lola?" I asked, unable to keep the green-eyed monster at bay.

"Naw, cutie, for you."

I felt myself melt, reaching greedily for the gift. Inside, nestled in fluffy tissue paper, lay a silvery dildo and a black leather harness.

"Well," Jo conceded, "Not *only* for you, but for Lola, as well."

"Oh..." I sighed when I saw it, stroking the molded plastic.

I felt a tightness in my chest. I wanted that toy. And, from the response going on down in my panties, Lola wanted it, too.

"Wait in the bedroom," Jo told me. "I think the three of us can work all this out."

"Yeah," I agreed shyly, growing even damper at the thought of what was in store. "Yeah, I think so, too."

I followed her order, quickly walking through the living room and to our bedroom. I lay on the bed, staring at my reflection in the mirror on the back of our dresser. My cheeks were flushed, my dark eyes on fire. I tossed my raven mane away from my face, feeling the warmth at the back of my neck, beneath my heavy tresses. Every part of my body was growing hot. *Especially* Lola. I waited, impatiently, for Jo to join me—I mean, *us*—and while I did, I snaked one hand under the satin panties and began to stroke Lola.

She was ready, all right. Sticky juices were dripping from her hungry lips. I slid my fingers in and out, getting them wet, then spreading the warm honey all over her shaved skin.

Finally, Jo entered. She had stripped and was wearing the harness and molded synthetic cock. It stuck out, away from her body, pointing directly at me.

"You *are* jealous, aren't you?" she asked, coming toward the bed so quickly that I didn't notice the handcuffs concealed in one of her large hands.

"I..."

She captured my wrists easily, setting the chain of the cuffs neatly in the hook over our headboard. Now, without having to rush, she fastened my ankles with crimson silk loops and tied them to the posters of our bed.

"Such a jealous girl. Jealous of the attention I've bestowed on your little friend. Why is that, Angel? It doesn't really make much sense."

I couldn't explain.

"I love you, darlin'," Jo said to me, slipping into her slight, South Texas drawl. "I love you desperately. And I love her, as

well." She cupped one hand protectively over my cunt. I still had
the panties on, and I wondered how she'd get around them. Jo
had no problems, though, no worries. She simply reached for
a pair of sewing scissors on the dresser and sliced through the
filmy material.

"Oh," she sighed, once Lola was revealed, "You shaved."
Now she pressed her heart-shaped lips to my nether lips and
began to lick, lapping deliciously at the flood of juices that
glistened on my cunt, and thighs, and ass. "Yes, you did. You
shaved for Mama."

I didn't think it was polite for me to answer, not being directly
spoken to. But I was unable to keep silent.

"I…" I started.

"Yes, Angel?" Jo asked looking up at me. Her chin was glossy
with my honey, her lips wet and shiny.

"*I* shaved for you."

That made her smile. "Thank you, Angel. I know you did."

Ah, sanity. Sweet sanity. I saw it once again in my lover's
lake-green eyes.

"Lola told you that I wanted her to be clean, right?"

"I…" I started again, unsure of how to answer.

"Not in so many words, of course," Jo said, quoting from
herself, "But you knew, right?"

I nodded. Yes, I'd known.

"Good. Now lie back, sweetheart, and let Mama go to work."

I had no problem with that. I relaxed against the pillows and
closed my eyes. Jo spread Lola's lips with her fingers, and her
knowing tongue quickly began making the darting little circles
that I love best. She went round and round with the tip of her
tongue, moving away from my clit, then closer to it. I arched
my hips, sliding on the crisp white sheets, helping her. I tensed
my muscles against the ribbons of fabric that held me in place.
I moaned and sighed. I shivered as I got closer to the moment
of truth.

Then everything stopped.

I opened my eyes, startled, desperate. Jo was looking back at me, a coy smile on her lips. She sat on her heels, regarding my supine form, then she began to stroke the dildo, just watching me, not saying anything.

I swallowed hard, wanting to beg, but not sure if that would get me anywhere. When Jo has that look in her jewel-toned eyes, that *knowing* look, it means "watch out." I stared as she spit into her right palm and began oiling the cock. I stared as she slid her fingers around it, pulling on it, working it. I felt my pussy lips part, I felt the juices trickle through the swollen crack. I was dying.

"Now, listen," Jo said, her voice gone dark and low and sweet, like thick molasses pouring slowly all over my body. "And listen well, Angel..."

I nodded.

"I love you. You know I love you. I see you as a whole: your brain, your heart, your soul, your cunt—all of your parts work together to make up the you that I love. And sometimes, in some phases of our relationship, I've focused on your mind...think back, you know I'm telling the truth." I closed my eyes, considering, and then nodded. She was right. "And sometimes," she continued, and now I could hear the teasing in her voice, "I have courted your heart." I nodded again, knowing now where she was going with this. "And, Angel, there have been phases that I've gone directly for your soul. Am I speaking the truth?"

She waited until I opened my eyes again and said, "Yes, Jo, you are."

"Well, now," she said, still in that low voice, "I am having a love affair with your cunt. I adore her. I want to pamper her, to play with her, to give her everything she needs...like this..." She moved forward, placing the head of the dildo on the flat bone above my pussy. "Just like this, 'cause you need this, and I need this, and Lola needs this."

I leaned my head back against the pillow, my whole body straining. I wanted her IN. I would have agreed to anything as long as she went IN. But she didn't, she only rocked back and forth, taunting me.

"Yes," I finally managed. "Yes, I understand."

"Ah, good... I knew you would."

With that, she slid down the two inches that she was from paradise and thrust forward, deep, probing me, fucking me—or fucking *her*. And I was no longer jealous, though I did feel as if there were three of us in bed, the way Jo talked, the way she crooned in that syrupy voice, "That's it, doll, that's right," not differentiating between me and Lola, but definitely talking to us both. I could feel the honey flow, coating the molded cock, making it slick with nectar, and it no longer mattered who was speaking, who was being spoken to.

"Oh, yes," Jo sighed. "Just like that, get it nice and wet for me." Then her hand under my chin, tilting my head forward, "'Cause *you're* gonna suck it clean, right, Angel? You're gonna get it all nice and clean for me."

"Yes," I promised. "Yes, Jo, whatever you say."

"I want you to taste her," Jo said, her eyes gone dreamy, her voice still lost in that soft, commanding tone. "She's so fuckin' sweet."

"Yes, Jo, yesss."

She kept it up, that steady rhythm, the beat I needed, the beat she needed, the beat Lola needed. Kept it up...ragged, desperate, endless. I moaned and writhed, I bucked and screamed, and I got so wet that the bed was a pool of my come, my thighs dripping with liquid sex. The scent was all around us—we were swimming in it—and I breathed in deep and drank the perfume in, as if I were smelling someone else, some other lover. Everything seemed new to me, taking it from Jo's point of view. I felt newly discovered, newly found out, virginal in a way, and I basked in it, bathed in it...closed my eyes and jumped.

ABOUT THE AUTHORS

CLARICE ALEXANDER spends a lot of time in dressing rooms. She is currently working on a novel about sex and shopping, her two most favorite naughty passions.

BECKY CHAPEL writes under different names for magazines.

SARAH CLARK writes for several Los Angeles–based entertainment newspapers, doing movie and restaurant reviews and celebrity interviews. Her stories have appeared in anthologies including *Batteries Not Included*.

DANTE DAVIDSON is the coauthor of the bestselling *Bondage on a Budget* and *Secrets for Great Sex After Fifty*. His short stories have also appeared in *Bondage* (Masquerade), in the anthology *Sweet Life* (Cleis) and on the website goodvibes.com.

LUCIA DIXON lives a quiet life—at least, it would appear so on the surface. But, as evidenced in her story, you just never know what goes on behind closed doors... Her work has appeared in *Girls on the Go, Gone Is the Shame* and in the upcoming anthology *Bondage on a Budget, Volume II*.

SHANE FOWLER divides her time between Paris and L.A. Under a variety of pen names, her work has appeared in publications including the *Best Lesbian Erotica* series.

MOLLY LASTER is a writer based in Canada. She divides her time between doing the type of writing she likes (erotica) and the type of writing that pays her bills (you don't want to know). Her short stories have also appeared in *Girls on the Go* and *Gone Is the Shame*, both published by Masquerade Books.

ELLE McCAUL writes historical romance novels for several different companies. This is her first erotic short story.

SAMANTHA MALLERY lives on Hilton Head Island, where she teaches golf. Her writing has appeared in the magazines *Zed* and *Eye* and in the anthology *Batteries Not Included*.

SOMMER MARSDEN (sommermarsden.blogspot.com) is the wine-swigging, wiener-dog-owning, wannabe-runner author responsible for *Learning to Drown, Hard Lessons, Wanderlust* and *Lucky 13*. Her work has cropped up all over the web.

BEAU MORGAN is a freelance photographer and full-time professor. He has never stopped his search for the perfect model.

N. T. MORLEY is the author of such erotic novels as *The Parlor, The Castle, The Limousine, The Library, The Circle* and *The Office*, published by Masquerade Books.

ISABELLE NATHAN has written for anthologies including *Come Quickly for Girls on the Go* (Rosebud) and *A Century of*

Lesbian Erotica (Masquerade). Her work has appeared on the website goodvibes.com.

LISA PACHECO dedicates her story to all of the creative people who like to play in public.

EMILIE PARIS is a writer and editor. Her first novel, *Valentine*, (Blue Moon) is available on audiotape by Passion Press. She abridged the seventeenth-century novel, *The Carnal Prayer Mat* for Passion Press, which won a *Publishers Weekly* best audio award. Her work has recently appeared in *Bent Over His Desk* and *Filthy Housewives*.

J. RICHARDS works at a production company in Los Angeles. She is currently cowriting a screenplay about the Internet. Her work has appeared in the anthology *Batteries Not Included* (Diva) and on the website goodvibes.com.

THOMAS S. ROCHE is the editor of the *Noirotica* series, currently being published and reprinted by San Francisco's Black Books. His short stories have appeared in more than one hundred magazines and anthologies, including his solo collection *Dark Matter,* and he has written and published more than two hundred nonfiction articles.

C. THOMPSON is a musician living the Hollywood lifestyle in L.A. Look for him hanging out at sidewalk cafés —but not before noon.

SOPHIA VALENTI (sophiavalenti.blogspot.com) is the author of *Indecent Desires*, an erotic novella of spanking and submission. Her fiction has appeared in a variety of anthologies, including *Sudden Sex: 69 Sultry Short Stories*, *The Big Book of Bondage* and *Kiss My Ass*.

MARY JO VAUGHN has written stories for *Girls on the Go* (Masquerade), *Batteries Not Included* (Diva) and *Bondage on a Budget, Volume II* (Pretty Things Press). She's always anxious to try a new drink.

ERIC WILLIAMS has written for anthologies including *Sweet Life* (Cleis) and *Bondage on a Budget, Volume II* (Pretty Things Press).

ABOUT THE EDITOR

Called "a trollop with a laptop" by *East Bay Express,* "a literary siren" by Good Vibrations and "the mistress of literary erotica" by Violet Blue, **ALISON TYLER** is naughty and she knows it. Over the past two decades, Ms. Tyler has written more than twenty-five explicit novels, including *Tiffany Twisted, Melt with You* and *The ESP Affair.* Her novels and short stories have been translated into Japanese, Dutch, German, Italian, Norwegian, Spanish and Greek. When not writing sultry short stories, she edits erotic anthologies, including *Alison's Wonderland, Kiss My Ass, Skirting the Issue* and *Torn.*

Ms. Tyler is loyal to coffee (black), lipstick (red) and tequila (straight). She has tattoos, but no piercings; a wicked tongue, but a quick smile; and bittersweet memories, but no regrets. She believes it won't rain if she doesn't bring an umbrella, prefers hot and dry to cold and wet and loves to spout her favorite motto: you can sleep when you're dead. She chooses Led Zeppelin over the Beatles, the Cure over NIN and the Stones over everyone. Yet although she appreciates good rock, she has a pitiful weakness for '80s hair bands.

In all things important, she remains faithful to her partner of nearly twenty years, but she still can't choose just one perfume.